GEORGIA HILL

I used to live in London, where I worked in the theatre. Then I got the bizarre job of teaching road safety to the U.S. navy – in Marble Arch! A few years ago, I did an 'Escape to the Country'. I now live in a tiny Herefordshire village, where I scandalise the neighbours by not keeping 'country hours' and being unable to make a decent pot of plum jam. Home is a converted oast house, which I share with my two beloved spaniels, husband (also beloved) and a ghost called Zoe. I've been lucky enough to travel widely, though prefer to set my novels closer to home. Perhaps more research is needed? I've always wanted to base a book in the Caribbean! I am addicted to Belgian chocolate, Jane Austen and, most of all, Strictly Come Dancing. Keep dancing, everyone!

You can follow me on Twitter @georgiawrites.

Say it with Sequins

The Complete Series

GEORGIA HILL

Harper
impulse
we've got the love

Harper*Impulse* an imprint of
HarperCollins*Publishers* Ltd
77–85 Fulham Palace Road
Hammersmith, London W6 8JB

www.harpercollins.co.uk

A Paperback Original 2014

First published in Great Britain in ebook format by Harper*Impulse* 2014

Cover images © Shutterstock.com

Georgia Hill asserts the moral right to
be identified as the author of this work

A catalogue record for this book
is available from the British Library

ISBN: 9780008113568

This novel is entirely a work of fiction.
The names, characters and incidents portrayed in it are
the work of the author's imagination. Any resemblance to
actual persons, living or dead, events or localities is
entirely coincidental.

Automatically produced by Atomik ePublisher from Easypress

For Mum, who loved to jitterbug.

The Rumba: a dance full of passion.

"The rumba is my favourite dance; it's really sexy. It gives you a great excuse to get up close and personal with your partner!" Bob Dandry, Executive Producer and Director, Who Dares, Dances.

Step One.
"You can do this!" she said in her head.

Julia Cooper, not yet star of stage and screen, bit her lip and tried to follow her own advice – and her partner's lead. Trouble was, when you were a novice and dancing with a monosyllabic and bad-tempered hulk of a Russian, it wasn't easy to pick up the steps. Or should that be steppes? Julia giggled and muttered her mantra again, "Concentrate, you can do this!"

"What?" said the Russian hulk from somewhere above her. "What you say? No, Julia. Have told you. Like this!"

For the umpteenth time that day, Julia wondered just what she had got herself into. *Who Dares Dances* was supposed to be a fun dance competition come reality show, wasn't it? She was supposed to be having fun!

"We'd better raise a barrel load of money to make this worth it," she mumbled, as she was swung round so hard her neck ricked. She'd never worked so hard in her life. The charity, *Pennies for*

Pencils, for which the show raised money, had better be grateful.

"Julia! Have told you. Like this. Concentrate!"

"That's just what I've been telling myself, Jan." Julia looked up at her partner with a bright smile. "But it doesn't seem to be working. Can we stop now? Don't we need to get ready for the launch party?" She made a hopeful face, which was completely lost on the Russian.

"Pah! Party!" he spat. "We must work, work, work. Have much to learn. Stand up. Chin to left. More. More! Count in head."

"One, two, buckle my shoe," Julia began and it sounded facetious, even to herself. But she really was exhausted. They'd been practising since eight that morning.

"One, two, *three,* one. two, three," Jan inevitably corrected her in his harsh way and they stumbled round the room one more time.

Julia gritted her teeth and did her best to stand straight, hold her head at the right angle, keep her elbows up and remember her steps. Who would have thought learning how to waltz could be so hard!

***

The launch party was in full swing by the time Harri got there. Filming had overrun and he was late as usual. And, as usual, he hated it. He was a man who'd been brought up to be on time. Nowadays he seemed to be constantly chasing his rear and life was never less than hectic.

He loved fronting the children's TV show most of the time though. In the three years he'd presented it, he'd been all around the world, had done the most incredible death defying stunts, had met and interviewed some of the most famous people in the world. He was one lucky bloke. Fizz TV had set up *Red Pepper* as a direct rival to *Blue Peter* and it was gradually getting more and more popular. Harri had thought at one time he might have a go at getting the big job – *Blue Peter* itself - but peculiar though it

2

seemed to him, at thirty-one he was getting too old for the plum role. But still here he was, an ordinary guy, Harri Morgan from Swansea, who had struck lucky. He knew his looks had helped but he hoped it was more than that, he hoped he was thought of as someone with genuine talent. He'd certainly worked his way up the hard way, spending six years in the niche world of Welsh television learning his craft.

So why, if he was happy with his career, had he agreed to this? To Fizz TV's dance show? When the suggestion had come from his agent, he'd been mildly interested, had never watched the programme but he knew of it and knew it raised millions for charity. When he'd signed up, he thought he'd treat it as another physical challenge, just like learning to fly a jet, or bungee jumping off the San Francisco Bridge. He liked learning new physical skills and it would show his mates back home in Swansea that he could dance after all.

In his heart though, he knew he'd taken this on for another reason. His life expectancy as a children's TV presenter was running out and it was notoriously difficult to make the transition to adult TV. Producers seemed to think that if you worked with, and for, young children you had the intellect to match. Harri knew he had a lot more to offer, it was just that he didn't know what it was or how to achieve it. The invitation to do *Who Dares Dances* seemed to be the answer. He could have a go at a new challenge, and get himself noticed by a completely different audience.

So far it had been, well, interesting. He'd spent four weeks in training with Eva, his Swedish professional dance partner, and it was a lot tougher than he expected. He wasn't sure why. He could pick up the steps pretty easily, his rugby and fencing training helped with the footwork, but he just couldn't get into it somehow. Since the cocaine fiasco on another well known children's TV show a few years ago, the producers of *Red Pepper* had upped the censor code on the programme and on its presenters. They had even gone as far as forcing him to sign a 'no personal relationships' clause with any of the other dancers in *Who Dares Dances*. He'd always had to conduct any relationship with complete discretion beforehand and now he was in an even worse situation. Any whiff of scandal or smut, and he'd be summarily dismissed. He knew it had taken that infamous children's presenter years to get his career back on track and Harri didn't want to risk the same. So he felt uncomfortable mixing his kid's TV persona with the blatantly erotic things Eva expected him to do.

He grabbed a drink from a passing tray and sipped the warm white wine thoughtfully. He grimaced, it didn't do the job like a pint of Brains bitter but it would help him unwind. He didn't seem to have the time to catch his breath nowadays. Was he getting old? Was he losing the hunger for all of this? He hoped not. He didn't know what else he could do.

***

Julia spotted Harri come in from the corner of her eye. Half listening to what a fellow competitor was saying, she saw him making his way around the edge of the party. She liked the way his nose crinkled up as he tasted the wine – it *was* vile – and then she watched as he got into an animated conversation with Callum, the enormous Scottish prop forward. Talking about rugby no doubt – or trashing England. Funny how the Welsh and the Scots had those two things in common.

She giggled. The wine may taste foul but she'd hardly eaten anything all day and it was going to her head. She put her half-empty glass down on the table behind her.

"Revolting isn't it?" Fellow actress, Lavinia Smart, sidled up to her and did the same. "You can tell it's not the beeb, can't you? These new TV channels just don't seem to get things quite right. I can't wait to see what excuse they'll serve as food! But darling, tell me, how's your gorgeous man of a partner?"

Julia thought about Jan the professional dance partner she'd been assigned. If only she had had a choice! He was tall, impossibly fit, blonde and beautiful, she admitted that much. He was also a terrible bully. "He's lovely," she said finally, "but I've never worked so hard in my life. I ache in places I never knew existed!"

"Oh darling, I'm the same. Warren is a darling, an absolute hoot but can you imagine, at my age? Any minute during training, I swear it's all going to drop off – or out."

Julia laughed. Lavinia was the oldest in the group of competitors by far. She claimed to be thirty-nine but was probably closer to sixty. Julia had seen her in films dating from way back. She'd assumed the role of mother hen over them all and did things strictly her way – didn't rehearse before eleven, broke for a two-hour lunch at one and finished on the dot of four. Her dancing partner Warren, a little man from Stoke-on-Trent and as ordinary as Lavinia was exotic, despaired. He'd won the competition last year and had been hoping to do what had never been achieved before – two successive wins. Julia thought his chances this year with Lavinia were remote to say the least.

She turned to the older woman: "The competition is pretty fierce this year isn't it?"

In an automatic gesture, Lavinia captured another glass of wine off a waiter, took a sip and called him back.

He came immediately, people tended to do as Lavinia said, Julia noticed. She had that bitchy, middle class, actressy quality that was thankfully rare in the profession nowadays.

"Another one for my friend if I may," Lavinia ordered. She passed the glass to Julia. "There darling, this one must be a new bottle, same wine but at least it's so cold you can't taste it! What were you saying?"

"That the competition is tough. Who do you think is going to win?"

"Well my angel, I know who desperately *wants* to win." Lavinia smirked and nodded to where eighteen year old model and aspiring actress, Casey, was batting her enormous false eyelashes at Harri.

5

Someone had tacked up a bedraggled sprig of mistletoe as an early nod to Christmas and Casey had half an eye on it.

The poor man was trapped. He was visibly backing off from the torrent of giggles and nonsense that passed as conversation from the girl.

"Met her type before," Lavinia sniffed. "God, I think I *was* her once a long time ago. All hair and short skirts and dangerous ambition. When you're older you learn how to hide it better."

"What, stupidity?" Julia said, without thinking.

Lavinia snorted. "She's not stupid, she'll go far. No, you learn how to play the game with a little more finesse, a little more decorum." Lavinia's eyebrows rose. "Look at the length of that skirt!"

Julia laughed again, Lavinia was always good company. "I'd wear skirts like that if I had the legs."

"Keep training as we've been doing and you will, darling. Have you ever met a chubby dancer?"

Julia tried not to bridle at the inference that she was fat, she'd lost a stone and a half already. She'd been consoling herself with the thought that if this TV show didn't revive her flagging acting career, at least she'd have a fit and toned body at the end of it.

Lavinia eyed her closely. "I know why Casey's doing it," she said, as they watched the girl run her fingers up an alarmed Harri's arm, "but why did you get involved in this farce, angel? I thought you were legit theatre?"

Julia shrugged. "I am, when I can get it. In between the funding crisis and all these big name American TV stars coming over and getting the plum roles, I seem to have hit a dry spot."

"It was ever thus." Lavinia gave a theatrical sigh. "Are you hoping it'll get your face known on the box, darling?"

Julia nodded. "And it raises money for a good cause."

"Ah yes, the charity." Lavinia smiled. "Never harms one's profile to be seen doing something good for charity."

Julia was silent for a moment. Lavinia had misunderstood her but she let it go. It hadn't quite been what she'd meant. She needed some publicity, it was true, but didn't want to support the charity simply in a cynical bid to get it. She really believed in the cause.

They all forgot why they were really here sometimes. The children's charity, *Pennies for Pencils*, raised money and awareness for a range of education projects, in the UK and abroad. This was really why they were all still in the studio, after a long day's rehearsal, supposedly mingling and getting to know one another better.

Lavinia trilled goodbye, wandered off and left the younger woman alone. Julia watched the crowd. She enjoyed people watching; she loved to see how people moved, how they related to one another.

The show was only a week old, they'd done the pre-practice rehearsals and were about to film the first programme before a live studio audience.

On the eve of filming, the producers had brought everyone together tonight as an icebreaker. Lavinia was now talking to Daniel Cunningham, Casey's stunning professional dance partner and Ted, another actor, and a recent refugee from *Eastenders*. He was a nice man thought Julia and he deserved to do well. But, as everyone knew, nice didn't count for much in the acting business.

Julia watched as Casey, having given up on Harri, was flirting with Callum instead. In contrast to the younger man, he seemed to be taking Casey in his stride. One large hand was fondling her naked back. As she was wearing a criminally low halter-top, access to naked flesh was made easy. Casey never seemed to wear many clothes and Callum's hairy hand was inching its way to her barely concealed bottom. He was edging her nearer the mistletoe and she didn't look at all unhappy to be led. The girl had better watch out, thought Julia. Rumour had it that Callum was unhappily married and on the lookout. Julia had already fended off his inebriated advances earlier in the evening.

Harri looked across at Julia and caught her eye. He smiled in his friendly way and made his way over to her. "Thought I'd leave

7

them to it," he grinned.

"Um, yes, they certainly seem to be getting on well." Julia averted her eyes as Callum's hand found its target and squeezed.

She turned back to Harri. He'd been dwarfed by Callum, but away from the rugby player's bulk, she could see he was actually quite tall in his own right.

Julia had never seen *Red Pepper* but her twelve-year-old niece was crazy about it and mainly because of this man. She could see the attraction. He'd been blessed with the unthreatening good looks of the boy next door, a warm smile, and dark hair, fashionably gelled up at the front.

Looking closer though, Julia saw the broken nose of a sportsman and high cheekbones, which any actor would happily die for. He had beautifully shaped expressive eyebrows too.

On the surface he appeared to be Harri Morgan, TV presenter with a reputation for being a daredevil, a laugh a minute and game for anything. Underneath, Julia thought she sensed a reserved, rather shy man. He had something more complicated in his soul and she was intrigued.

At the moment, however, it seemed Harri's thoughts were centred on the simple things in life. "God, this wine's terrible!" He looked around him longingly. "What I wouldn't do for a pint."

"I know what you mean." She laughed up at him and was mesmerised for a second by the intensity in his warm dark eyes.

The moment was interrupted by Bob Dandry, the executive producer and director of the show, tapping his glass.

"Ladies and gentlemen. Thank you for coming and welcome to the wonderful world of *Who Dares Dances*. I know you're going to have a truly marvellous time tonight getting to know your fellow competitors but just before the food is served I'd like to say a few words."

Julia groaned and Harri leaned closer. "I know, anyone who says a few words usually means the exact opposite. Do you think we can escape? I know a good pub just over the road."

Julia giggled and shushed him and turned to listen. Bob droned on about it being a fantastic show that drew in an audience of over two million and had raised, in its six year run, nearly thirty million pounds. There was applause at this point and Bob put out his hands in a gesture of mock humility. "No, no please. We do all we can for *Pennies for Pencils*. I'm sure you'll agree it's a worthy cause." He smoothed a strand of ginger hair over his bald spot and smiled greasily.

"Not to mention that it boosts one or two careers," Harri whispered in her ear, his Welsh accent smooth and seductive. She stifled another giggle and elbowed him in the ribs.

"Ow!" He rubbed the offended part in pretend outrage and a few heads turned their way with interest. Anything was better than Bob's speech.

But then the producer said something which caught everyone's attention. "As you know, we try to keep the show fresh, to keep the audience interested and voting - and raising money of course. And we need to keep our image separate from that other little dance show on TV."

Julia caught Lavinia's eye and they grinned at one another. 'That other little dance show' was the riotously popular BBC *Strictly Come Dancing*. The elephant in the room, Lord Voldemort, never to be named in the studios of *Who Dares Dances*.

"So we're proposing," continued Bob, "that, just for one dance when we come back for the Christmas special, to put two competitors together. This means that two non dancers will dance with one another.

At the ripple of shock Bob put out his hands again placatingly. "You will be coached by your professional dancers of course and it's just a bit of fun."

Fun. There was that word again. What fun? wondered Julia. I'm having enough trouble dancing with Jan, let alone someone who doesn't know what they're doing!

Everyone else appeared to be having similar thoughts as a buzz of panicked chatter rose around the room.

"I'll let you know your partners now," Bob ploughed on, "so you can make arrangements for rehearsals. Remember it's in only seven weeks so time is of the essence!"

"Uffern dan!" Julia heard from Harri, all his boyish twinkly humour gone.

She closed her eyes and whispered a little prayer. "Please don't let my partner be Callum. Please don't let it be Callum!" She wasn't sure she could put up with his groping for the next seven weeks and there was something about his huge oafishness that was very off-putting. "I'll do most things for charity but not that."

"Sorry?" Harri leaned a little closer, to hear better over the noise in the room.

Julia blinked, she hadn't realised she'd said it out loud. "I said I didn't know this was in the contract."

"It wasn't, but there were rumours they had something up their sleeve for this year. I just hope I don't get -"

She never heard who Harri didn't want as a partner as Bob began to read out the new non professional dancing partnerships. "Lavinia, you'll be partnered with Sam."

Julia looked over to where Lavinia stood with Charlie and Carol the presenters of the show. Sam was a Liverpudlian comedian known for his coarse humour. Lavinia didn't look happy.

"Casey, you'll be partnered with Ted." Casey looked equally displeased.

"Callum, you'll be with Suni."

Julia felt a pang of sympathy for Suni, an elegant celebrity TV cook and then heaved a sigh of relief as she realised she'd been spared Callum's groping fingers. She was so busy being relieved that she missed the next few announcements.

"And finally, as I'm sure you'll have worked out by now, the last two celebrities not allocated partners are Julia and Harri." Bob beamed at them. "So they will be dancing together. That's all. Have a wonderful evening. Any questions address them to Maria, my assistant. And, don't forget – who dares dances!" With this, Bob hurried from the studio.

Coward, thought Julia. Drop the bombshell and run off. She turned to look at Harri. "Well, not too bad for us I suppose?" She looked questioningly up at him.

"I think we'll work together alright won't we? But whether we'll be able to dance mind, that's another story." He winked, his humour obviously restored.

To Julia's pleasure, he sounded relieved. She could do a lot worse than spend time with this man she thought.

"Like some food?" he asked her cheerfully. "I'm going to get some, I'm starving, been filming all day, see."

She nodded and watched him as he made his way over to the table where a buffet was being laid. He had a good pair of shoulders and a neat set of hips. And his bottom was, well quite frankly, it was gorgeous. Yes, she could do a lot worse.

Step Two.

They were all back in the studio the following day. It was show day and last minute dress rehearsals had begun at nine, except for Lavinia who showed up two hours later much to the annoyance of Warren. Julia had left the party early with Harri; they'd shared a cab home, as he lived not far from her in north London. They agreed they'd both had a long day and wanted to call it a night.

And now, thought Julia, it all starts in earnest. She looked around the studio – the same room that they had partied in last night. All remnants of the party had disappeared and there was workmanlike mood this morning. It reminded her of her days in the theatre, of dress rehearsals, of the buzzy adrenalin-filled quality of the atmosphere.

She was nervous but excited. She and Jan were going to dance a waltz and she was pleased it was a reasonably simple routine. She'd found it hard to memorise the steps and was completely reliant on Jan leading her round. He did so with barely concealed

11

Russian impatience, swearing quietly whenever she did something wrong - which was often. He scared her a little. She worked best with encouragement and praise and his arrogant bullying wasn't making for an ideal partnership.

She watched enviously as Daniel and Casey cruised round the floor in an American smooth. Daniel Cunningham was as tall and as good lookingly blonde as Jan but was much kinder and encouraging and, as a result, Casey was already dancing with impressive skill.

"They're good aren't they?" a Welsh voice whispered in her ear.

She turned and smiled at Harri. "They are. Do you think they'll win?"

He shrugged. "They might. But my money's on Scott and Suni." He nodded to where the couple were trying out some of the moves to their quickstep. "Scott's determined to win, He's incredibly competitive and Suni is …." he trailed off as he looked at them.

"So graceful," she finished for him. "Yes, she is isn't she?" Julia blew out a breath.

"Something wrong?"

"Just wondering what I'm doing here, that's all. I've discovered I've got two left feet."

Harri grinned. "Not from where I was watching. You and Jan look great together."

"Only because he's lugging me round. Still at least the long dress will cover any wrong steps! It's got so many feathers sewn onto it you can't actually see me."

"Wish I had the same sort of costume," Harri laughed. "Poor Eva's given up on me ever being able to move my hips."

"You've got a hard dance to start with, haven't you? I wouldn't fancy doing the salsa so early on in the competition." Julia made a sympathetic face.

"Yup, Eva's one hell of a taskmaster. Bullied me into submission so I agreed to do it. But if I go wrong I can at least make a bit up, it's not as technical as their dance." He gestured again to

12

Suni and Scott.

"Agreed. Jan's the same, a terrific bully." She sighed.

"I suppose that's what it takes to get to the top of their field. Total dedication and one hundred percent competitiveness." Harri regarded her thoughtfully.

"Yes, but he could be nicer about it … oh hello Jan!" she said brightly as the man in question came up to them.

"No time," he wagged a finger at them, "no time for gossip. We work. Now!" He snatched at Julia's hand and marched her to the dance floor.

Harri watched her go and raised a hand as she pulled a silly face back at him. He liked her. He'd seen her on stage last year and had liked her ever since.

She'd been brilliant. It was the first night of a Noel Coward play and she was brittle and arch and poignant, all the things that Coward demanded. He was relieved, when he met her briefly at the after show party, that she was none of those things in real life. She was actually funny and self deprecating and quite shy.

They'd chatted and then he was dragged off to another party. He left reluctantly; he'd enjoyed talking to her.

Now, as he watched her being swung smoothly round the dance floor by her Russian giant of a partner, he decided he really liked her. He had little time for a personal life and the producers of *Red Pepper* were always on the lookout for scandal so he had to be extremely circumspect. That's why he backed off whenever Casey came near, gorgeous though she was, her body clearly displayed in clothes that were too tight or slipped off revealing lots of naked flesh. He knew women like Casey were big trouble. One night and she'd be rushing to the papers with the story. His career wouldn't withstand that, Fizz TV had made it more than clear that if there were any sex or drugs stories, he'd be out. One glance at Casey and all those things were on the cards. But Julia, now she was a different woman. She was easy to get along with. Attractive too, with her mane of black hair and those flashing green eyes. He felt himself stirring. God, he *really* liked her. The irritating 'no relationships' clause niggled at the back of his mind. It was too frustrating. He'd have to be careful. No rushing into anything.

"Larry!" It was Eva, her Swedish accent could never quite master his Welsh name.

"It's Harri," he muttered under his breath and then pinned a cheery smile on his face as he turned to his professional dance partner. His coach. His nemesis.

"We will work now, I think. Come. And Larry, hold me like a man this time please."

Harri gritted his teeth and got into position. With any luck, he'd be so dire they'd be voted off in the first show. Then he wouldn't have to put up with this termagant any longer. But he didn't really mean it; already the old competitiveness, a relic from his college rugby playing days, had taken hold. He was in it to win it, he decided as he was steered round the floor by the determined arms of his partner.

"No Larry, take the lead! Hold me like you mean it!"

***

Before she knew it, Julia had completed her waltz to subdued applause from the audience and was standing in front of the judges, waiting for their comments. Her heart sank; she could see from Jan's rigid shoulders that he wasn't pleased with her performance.

Arthur, the senior judge, was first to comment. He had a reputation for being straight-talking but kind. "Well you had a good attempt, you sell the dance well but you were letting Jan do all the hard work. You need to something about raising your ribcage and your neckline is dreadful. Not a bad effort, work on those things and you'll get better."

Not *that* bad, Julia thought cautiously.

But the others were much harsher, even cruel. Her timing was out, her footwork was bad and they repeated Arthur's criticism

14

about her poor posture. Jan dropped her hand as soon as they left the main studio and went to the back room for the results. He was a silent mountain of disappointment. The scores were disappointing too – a paltry ten in total and they were in penultimate place at the bottom of the leader board, with –inexplicably - Suni and Scott taking the other last place.

"Don't worry," said Harri as he went past to get ready for his dance; he was up next. He squeezed her arm quickly and then left.

Jan stormed off in search of water, muttering Russian curses. Julia went to sit on the sofa with the others and got her breath back.

"Well, I thought it was fine," said Suni. "In fact, it looked really good from back here." She patted Julia's arm kindly.

Julia, her breathing back to normal, watched on the TV monitor as Harri entered the studio to rapturous applause; he was the show's favourite and, despite what he'd said about Suni, was tipped to win. His salsa, however, was a bit flat. According to the judges, he hadn't made a connection with his partner and there was no charisma between them. Julia wondered about their sanity, it looked perfect from where she was watching. He and Eva came backstage to wait for their results and Harri quirked an eyebrow at Julia making her laugh. He really was one gorgeous man.

"The results are in!" screamed Carol, trying to get some excitement going within the audience. "Seven, seven and an eight! That makes a total of …" she paused, obviously unable to work it out, "twenty two! Our highest score this evening. Well Harri, although the judges' comments were critical they've scored you well. How do you feel?"

Her voice whined on and she kept touching Harri, Julia noticed, on his arm, on his shoulder, on his back, quite low down on his back in fact, near that well shaped and neat behind. Obviously the man's attractions had been noted by more than her.

And then it was all over; all they had to do was wait for the public vote and the dance off. Julia had a horrible feeling she might be in it and wasn't sure how she felt. On the one hand, she

15

wouldn't have to go through the torture Jan inflicted on her for five hours a day, but it would be a shame to let go this project so soon.

They all had a short break, filled with interviews and frantically snatched gulps of water and then the dance off was announced.

To Julia's total surprise, it was between Suni and Ted. Everyone sat in the backstage room, hunched up on the cream sofas and watched the little monitor in the corner intently. Scott and Suni danced first and, to Julia's mind, brilliantly. Suni was as graceful and as elegant as ever. The judges pronounced her the winner after Ted had stumbled through his routine and they voted him off.

"Jeez, just goes to prove none of us is safe doesn't it?" Harri said in a shocked voice. He gave Julia a swift, hard hug, which sent shockwaves of desire straight through her. Then he got yanked to his feet by Eva, to return to the floor for the finale.

It was exhausting, Julia thought. Was she really going to have to do this all again next Saturday? She wasn't sure she had the mental or physical energy. She went up to Ted and his partner Alicia and muttered her condolences. As she looked over, to where Casey was congratulating herself on staying in and where Callum had found enough alcohol to begin the night's partying early, she thought the wrong people had been sent home.

Step Three.

The following Tuesday was earmarked for a quick run through of the dance she and Harri were to perform in the Christmas special. It seemed crazy to Julia that they were practising it when she hadn't even got the hang of the steps for the dance she and Jan were going to do *this* Saturday. Jan had been a nightmare the day before and, if it hadn't have been for the cameras watching their every move, Julia would have retaliated.

A smiling Harri arrived with a determined Eva in tow. "They've picked the dances out of the hat and we've got the rumba," he said with a grin. "The dance of passion!"

Oh Christ, thought Julia, it's getting worse. Now I've got to make out that I'm in love with the man. Well, she consoled herself, at least he's easy on the eye, so it might not be all that difficult. He was certainly looking good this morning; fresh and relaxed in dark jeans and a navy t-shirt. Julia gazed down at herself. Jan had called an early rehearsal and they'd already been hard at it for two hours. She was hot and sweaty and definitely did not look her best. She looked over at Eva, in all her blonde coolness, and blew out a frustrated breath. But it was no good, she realised, she would never be like her. She was a completely different body shape for a start. Where Julia was curvy, Eva was tiny, with a waist that was hardly there. And in contrast to Julia's generously sized eyes and mouth, Eva had narrow, refined features. The huge mirrors, which lined every wall in the dance studio Jan preferred to use, accentuated any comparison. They cruelly pointed out the differences between the two women.

Julia gritted her teeth and spent the time waiting for Eva and Harri to warm up by nipping out and freshening herself up as best she could. Feeling a little better, she ventured back into the studio.

Eva clapped her hands. "Now we start!"

And so they did.

Thirty minutes later and Julia was feeling distinctly uncomfortable. She liked Harri, no correction; she *really* liked him, certainly much more than Jan. She felt far more relaxed with him than with her pro-dancer partner but this was too much. Some of the moves Jan and Eva had choreographed were incredibly intimate. Far too intimate for two people who had only met a few times and were just casual friends. And it was very apparent that Harri was having similar misgivings.

"Not so!" barked Jan at Harri. "Put your hand on her breast bone and stroke like so. It is the dance of love. Make love to her!"

"I've never felt less like making love to anyone," Harri muttered to Julia. "No offence."

Julia scrunched up her eyes, she couldn't bear to look; she could feel Harri's embarrassment from here. Her t-shirt was sticking sweatily to her back where his arm was holding her and she was mortified that he had to do this.

"Bend back more, Julia! Arch over. More!" Eva demanded.

Julia tried her best but only succeeded in straining Harri's strength too far and fell to the floor.

"Are you all right?" he asked and bent over her in concern.

"Tsk!" Jan exclaimed and strode off in yet another Russian temper.

"Please tell me why we ever lowered the iron curtain and warmed up the cold front?" said Julia to Harri as he helped her to her feet. She covered her embarrassment by straightening her rucked up t-shirt and smoothing her hair.

"We finish for break now. Ten minutes only!" Eva snarled and banged out behind Jan.

Harri looked at Julia, one brow quirked in humour. "And the Swedish were always supposed to be our allies. Come on," he said as he took her arm. "I'll buy you a nice coffee from the vending machine."

"What, the one where it tastes like Bovril?"

"That's the one," he said flippantly.

"You know how to treat a woman."

"Only the best for you, cariad," he replied and Julia grinned at the unfamiliar Welsh word. "And, if you're really lucky, I might even get you a mince-pie; the canteen have just started selling them."

"Be still my beating heart!" Julia laughed and realised her heart *was* pumping fast – and it was nothing to do with the promise of a Christmassy sugar rush.

Step Four.

The week continued in much the same vein. They had one more rehearsal of their rumba together which was equally disastrous and then Jan and Eva declared that they must all concentrate on the dances for the next show.

Jan had chosen wisely again. He and Julia were to dance the

18

American smooth, which meant that Julia could safely rely on him to lead her. There was a tricky moment when she was out of hold but Jan had choreographed most of the dance so that he could control her every move. She needed it; she was still finding it incredibly difficult. She could now master the steps but when it came to adding in all the other details like her head hold or her arm shape, then it all went wrong. And then Jan dropped his bomb shell.

"We will do lift!" he declared and proceeded to show her.

"He wants to lift me up and swing me round then hold me on his shoulder!" she bleated a little desperately, to Harri as they shared a pizza after Thursday's rehearsal. "And he goes and tries to put it into the routine today. We've only got two more days to practise!"

"Seriously?" Harri raised his eyebrows in shock. "Well, don't do it unless you feel confident enough. He's a tall bloke."

"Tell me about it. He got me up there for the first time this morning and it's like being hoisted onboard a giraffe!"

"How tall is he?"

"I don't know. Six three, six four? Whatever, it feels bloody scary, I can tell you."

"Well, don't worry. He's one of the world's best dancers; He's not going to drop you." Harri smiled at her comfortingly.

"He'd better not! I'd break my neck. Are they paying us danger money for this?"

Harri laughed and took another slice of pepperoni, holding the stringy cheese up to his mouth.

Julia watched him as he ate and something warm inside her unfurled. He was nice she thought. Easy company, a great sense of humour and - nice. She relaxed a little and looked around her.

The restaurant they'd ended up in was buzzing with office workers getting early into the Christmas spirit. To their immediate left was a party of twelve, bedecked in ribbons of tinsel and paper hats and looking red-cheeked with high spirits. A soundtrack of cheesy Christmas hits played in the background. London was well and truly gearing itself up for the festive season.

"I've never been so hungry," Harri said through a mouthful, as Slade's *Merry Xmas Everybody* blasted out. "I'm eating like a horse and I've lost half a stone already!"

Julia looked at him, at his broad shoulders and well shaped arms with their subtle muscles. "You don't look as if you need to lose any."

"I don't, that's the problem. Eva's a bloody tyrant. She's got me rehearsing five or six hours at a time." He flexed an impressive bicep and grinned. "Mind, I've never been in better shape. Reckon I'm about as fit as I've ever been. What about you?"

"Well, I tried to get fitter before all this started and I certainly needed to lose some weight." Julia picked at a cheesy crust and nibbled.

"No, you didn't," Harri interrupted. "I like my women with a bit of flesh on them. Can't stand Eva's skinny bits." He shuddered visibly.

Julia preened a little; she quite liked the idea of being one of Harri's women. "No, I really needed to lose some. I wasn't getting any parts." She looked up at him to see he was watching her closely. "Mine's a cruel profession. No room for the fatties."

Harri put his hand on hers. It was slightly greasy from his pizza but she didn't mind. His dark eyes burned into hers but all he said was, "You'll do."

As compliments went, it wasn't the most effusive Julia had ever received but the warm glow inside her spread and she blushed hotly.

"So, what's next for you?" Harri picked up his tumbler of water and emptied it in one swallow.

He was a man of hearty appetites Julia thought and, watching him, the question of what he'd be like in bed pinged into her head. Blushing yet more, she tried to concentrate on her answer. "There are - erm - one or two things in the pipeline," she said carefully.

"Things that bad, eh?"

From anyone else the comment would have grated but Harri's cheerful sympathy just made her feel better. She nodded. "That bad."

"I loved you in *Still Life*."

Julia smiled. "It was a great production, a great team. But the run was cut short. No money left. And no angel stepped in."

For a minute Harri thought she was talking literally and then realised what she meant. "Oh, you mean a backer. So, have you really got nothing lined up then?"

"There's a possibility … but it's only a slight possibility so I'd like you to keep it under your hat at the moment, that I might get *Cabaret*."

Harri sat up, his eyes shone as a grin spread over his face. "Sally Bowles? At the Endcott?"

"Maybe." She saw his grin widen. He had a lovely smile, she thought, it lit up his entire face and then reached his eyes so that they almost disappeared. Such a charming man. She shook out any carnal thoughts which persisted in pre-occupying her, and got back to the more mundane subject of her career. "They saw I was going to be in this and mentioned they might audition me."

"So you've got a lot riding on *Who Dares Dances* then?"

Julia shrugged. "Yes, I suppose so." She finished her glass of wine, she shouldn't drink midweek really, it stopped her from sleeping but she really needed to unwind after the latest session with Jan.

"Another?" Harri asked and, at her nod, summoned the waitress. "A house red and I'll have a Becks please," he said when the girl came over.

"Are you, are you Harri Morgan?" The girl, a younger waitress than the one who had served their meal, gasped and pushed back her felt reindeer antlers. "Oh my God, oh my God! I can't believe it. Is it really you?"

"I was the last time I looked," Harri said cheerfully.

"Could I … would you mind, could I have your autograph?

I love *Red Pepper*. Oh I know I'm too old for it," she chattered on as Harri took note of her tinselled name badge and signed a paper napkin for her, "but my younger sister got me into it and now I *always* watch it when I'm on lates." She giggled and blushed bright red.

Julia smiled to herself, and thought the attraction of the programme probably wasn't just how to learn to use sticky backed plastic.

"There you go then," Harri handed over the serviette. "Would you like me to do one for your sister too?"

"Oh, would you? Thank you!"

Harri reached for another napkin. "What's her name?"

"Debs," the waitress squealed. "Wait 'til I tell her who's been in!" She turned to Julia: "Course, we get loads of celebs in here, it being so near the TV studios and everything but Harri's the only one whose autograph I've wanted." She did a double take and looked at Julia more closely. "Oh hell, you're, you're -"

"Julia Cooper," Julia supplied.

The waitress looked from one to the other. "You're both doing *Who Dares Dances* aren't you?"

"That's right." Harri, his voice even and controlled, handed over the other serviette. "And that would be a Becks and a glass of house red please, Abi."

The waitress took another long look at both of them and Julia wondered what was going through her mind. Then she took the hint, nodded and went off to get their drinks.

Julia giggled slightly. This sort of fame was new to her. Apart from a few hardy souls who waited at the stage door for her, she could get through ordinary life unencumbered by such encounters. She was intrigued by how Harri had handled it. "Does that happen often to you?"

Harri raised his dark eyebrows and grimaced. "Not too much when I'm not expecting it, like tonight. It's different if you're visiting somewhere, a school or a lifeboat station. Then you get yourself geared up for it."

"Do you mind?"

He frowned. "No, comes with the territory, doesn't it? It doesn't get to me unless they get a bit over the top. One night a girl sat down at the table with us. Wouldn't have minded but it was a family meal out for my mam's birthday, see." He winced. "Not the most tactful thing to do."

Julia laughed in sympathy and agreed. She lapsed into silence as Abi returned and, with infinite care, served their drinks and left. Then she asked him "So what's in this for you? *Who Dares Dances*, I mean."

Harri glanced at her over the rim of his bottle, took a long gulp, considered her question and finally answered. "What do children's TV presenters do when they're too old to jump out of helicopters and make pencil pots out of loo rolls?"

Julia giggled again. "I don't know."

"God, they end up presenting naff ghost hunting shows or sail around the Med on their yacht or disappear onto a digital radio station."

"And none of that is for you?"

Harri shook his head. "No," he said. "I know what I don't want but I'm thirty two next year, I'm getting a bit past it for kids' TV. So what do I do next?"

Julia shrugged.

"Exactly. What I'm hoping for is that I'll get some kind of offer come in, something to broaden my career, something exciting. And," at this he grinned again, "at least I'll have the satisfaction of learning a brand new skill and raising some money at the same time."

"Ah yes, the money, somehow we all forget that don't we." Julia grinned back at him and raised her glass. "To the charity *Pennies for Pencils*, then. May it prosper from our bumps, humiliations and bruises!"

Harri laughed out loud and clinked his beer bottle against her glass. "To *Pennies for Pencils!*"

Their quick meal over, they left the Christmas revellers to it and wandered out into the icy night. It had become chilly over the last few days and now the air sparkled with their frosty breath. Julia hugged herself; she loved this time of year. There was something truly magical about it, despite the cheap tinsel and clichéd pop songs.

Harri raised his hand and, almost immediately, a taxi did a neat U-turn and drew up at the kerb. He looked down at Julia, the flashing Christmas lights from the restaurant turning his face alternatively red then white. It made reading his expression difficult.

"Goodnight then, Julia, cariad." He seemed awkward suddenly.

"Night night, Harri." She reached up and kissed his slightly stubbly and very warm cheek. As she did so, he moved and his mouth came to within a whisper of touching hers. But, too soon, it was gone. A cold space replaced the fuzzy feeling Julia had enjoyed all evening.

"See you tomorrow then, Harri," she called, disappointed that he hadn't kissed her properly. She got into the cab and looked back for him but he'd already disappeared into the neon coloured night.

Step Five.

Julia allowed herself to be led to her mark to receive the verdict from the judges. She could tell yet again that Jan wasn't pleased, his smile was forced and the arm he held around her was like banded steel – so tense was he with anger.

It was the third show. Julia had scraped through - somehow - without ending up in the dance off but her points had been consistently low. That she was still in the competition was as big a mystery to her as it patently was to the judges. But, for some reason, the public kept ringing in and still wanted her there, fighting her corner and staying in to dance another day.

As if in slow motion she saw Kevin, the most outspoken of the judges, open his mouth. Oh God, she thought, here comes another stream of abuse. Over the weeks, Kevin had reserved his cruellest, most cutting comments especially for her.

"Well, darling," began Kevin. "You always entertain us, there can be no doubt of that but whether you can dance is another matter." A cheer went up around the studio at his first comment and boos followed his second. Kevin looked scornfully around him, his disdain for the audience was well known. "Let me finish, please." He fixed his pale eyes back on Julia and she braced herself. "Julia dear, your posture is still dreadful despite this being the third week of the competition and we're nearly halfway through, your footwork is appalling and you're still letting Jan do all the work. On this performance I don't think you should go through to the next round, I really don't, darling."

At this, the audience actually hissed him. It was almost like a pantomime, thought Julia hazily, as Jan's arm tightened its hold.

Sonya, the sole female judge and the most venomous, piped up through the audience's booing. "I agree Kevin, it's week three now and we should be seeing some improvement but each week you've come out, Julia, and trotted out the same old stuff. And it's getting boring. You must listen to Jan; sort out your upper body and neckline and work, work, work on your feet."

Julia was tired, she and Jan had put in over seven hours training each day that week and she was exhausted. She felt her throat thicken and tears caught at her. This was ridiculous she thought and tried to hide her reaction but it was too late; her shoulders began to shake and tears ran down her cheeks making a trail through the thick stage make up. The audience, scenting blood, quietened. Charlie the compere made an aaahing sound and said something like, "There there," and then Jan dragged her off the dance floor. When they got to the back room he refused to wait for their scores and left Julia standing in front of Carol alone. Suni thrust a tissue into Julia's hand.

Carol wasn't quite sure what to say and stuttered a little until she got a prompt through her ear piece. "And now, after those shocking words from the judges, how do you feel?"

The fatuous question had what was left of Julia's rational brain dissolving and she broke down completely. Someone tallish and solid took her in his arms and led her away from the cameras. She vaguely heard Carol flapping in the distance as she tried to fill the air time.

Strong arms held her and a soft voice whispered: "Don't take on so, cariad bach, it's not worth it." As her sobs really began to take hold Harri took her through the doors, well away from any prying cameras which may have followed them and into the chilly corridor. He was now swearing quietly in Welsh – or at least that's what Julia assumed he was doing, there was real vitriol in the tone of his voice which suggested anger.

He took her outside, to the courtyard in the middle of the television studios. There was a low wall which bordered a small garden and Harri led Julia to it. He sat with his arms tight around her until her sobs lessened and she was calmer.

Julia blew her nose into the tissue Suni had given her. "Sorry."

"Uffern dan! What the hell for?" his accent sounded stronger and his voice was still full of anger.

"I'm such an idiot to break down like that. God, I must look like a mess."

"You're fine and it wasn't idiotic. They really slammed into you back there. I could've punched Kevin." Harri's hand fisted.

Julia laughed, a little tremulously, but it was a laugh at least. "Thanks for coming to my aid. I really don't think I could've coped with Carol or Jan …" she trailed off; the thought of having to face Jan was horrible. "God, I've really messed it up haven't I?"

"What, by crying?"

"No, by showing I couldn't cope with the stress." Julia added mournfully, "I can't see *Cabaret* coming my way now."

"Don't be so sure, cariad; in the face of what Jan's made you do, they may see it as gritty determination. And as for the crying bit I think you'll get the sympathy vote."

"I don't want the sympathy vote!"

"Do you want to stay in the competition?"

Julia thought about it. In some strange and possibly masochistic way, she did want to stay in the competition - if only to torture Jan. But she'd really like to prove to herself and the viewers that she could improve; that she could put two feet in front of one another without falling over. "Yes," she said, in a determined voice. "Yes, I *do* want to stay in."

"Well, there you go then. I think the viewers are seeing straight through Mr Moscow and can see how evil he's being and are voting for you."

"It's twisted!"

Harri laughed. "It's showbiz! Ready to go back?" He looked at her, concern in his dark eyes.

Julia took a deep breath and gave him a wobbly smile. She nodded. "Ready as I'll ever be. Bring it on!"

"That's my girl." He stood up and held out a hand. As he did so, a solitary snowflake fell from the cold dark sky.

"It's snowing. Oh, it makes me feel so Christmassy!!" Julia exclaimed, with all the wonder of a small child. "It's not often you get to see snow in the middle of London."

Harri looked up and followed the passage of another snowflake, making its way to the concrete. "It is indeed." He grinned. "It's a good omen for you!"

"You think so?"

"I know so."

Julia put out her tongue. She closed her eyes and reached her face up into the night.

Harri gazed at her and at the vision of her pink tongue held out in the hope of catching a snowflake. He moved towards her, without thinking and then stopped. He longed to capture that tongue with his own, to twist it with his and make it hot. For the first time in his life, he wished he were an ordinary bloke with an ordinary job and one who could simply make the next move.

And not somebody with this ridiculous clause hanging over him.

Julia opened her eyes and caught him staring.

"Oh Harri. This is amazing. You're amazing!" She flung her arms round him, her mood obviously restored.

For a long second, he returned the embrace and then disentangled himself. "Oh, I'm bloody amazing, cariad. Now, go back in, it's freezing out here."

Julia blew him a kiss and ran back into the television studios.

As he watched her go, he knew he couldn't risk making a move. Not yet. He had to be one hundred percent sure. Julia didn't seem the kiss and tell type but he couldn't risk his entire career for what might turn out to be a one-night stand. He just couldn't, no matter how big the temptation. And, oh boy, was he tempted. With a heavy heart, he followed her in.

Step Six.

And now it was, unbelievably, week four. And, she was still in, by the skin of her teeth. For some reason the public kept voting for her, even though the judges held nothing back and criticised her dancing remorselessly.

As Julia stood with Jan waiting to go on and do their Quickstep, her hardest dance so far, she thought it was inevitable that she would go out this week. She'd struggled all week to master the intricate and light steps and, despite putting in over seven hours training each day, was no more confident now than she'd been on Sunday when she'd begun learning.

Lavinia and Sam the comedian had followed Ted out of the competition and, while she couldn't pretend to feel sorry for the foul-mouthed Liverpudlian, she missed Lavinia's cheerfully diva-ish presence. The actress had become a good friend and since leaving had attended every Saturday night performance and had even dropped in on one or two of Julia's training sessions. Warren, somewhat bitterly, had been overheard to say she'd been in the rehearsal rooms far more since she left the show than when she was in training for it.

Julia took a deep breath and tried, unsuccessfully, to calm her nerves. Her only consolation was that the quickstep wasn't Jan's favourite dance either. He preferred the moodier, more sensual dances. Well he would, thought Julia.

Since surviving for the first weeks, the competition had really gripped her. She'd made great friends - with Lavinia of course but had also grown very close to Erica, one of the professional dancers who, since her partner Sam had gone out, had been doing some extra coaching with Julia and Suni.

And there was Harri of course.

Despite herself, Julia let her mind drift. They'd been out a few times, when they could find the time, mostly for a quick bite after training and once to a bar where they'd got shockingly drunk on Bellinis and had piled, insensible, into a cab to north London. He was as cheerfully friendly and encouraging as he'd always been but that had been as far as it went.

One memorable evening, Harri had waved some tickets at them all. It was an invite to a club night at a famous ice-skating rink nearby. It was his producer's birthday party, he'd explained. Did anyone want to come along? The others cried off but Julia and Daniel found themselves clambering into a taxi and speeding towards Snetterton House after rehearsals one night.

Julia couldn't contain her excitement. She'd longed to go skating at Snetterton ever since hearing about it but had never been able to justify the exorbitantly high price. In summer, the square in front of the Queen Anne building, housed a series of fountains but, in winter, a temporary ice-rink was set up. It was the latest must-go venue in the city. And its club nights were legendary.

She jiggled about on the edge of the pull down seat and gazed out of the cab window, willing the traffic to part before them.

"What?" she said to Daniel and Harri, who were sitting opposite and openly laughing at her.

"You're like a big kid," Harri said, but with affection.

29

Turning to him, her eyes shining, she replied, "Well, I've never done anything like this before and I've heard really good things about the club nights. The music's supposed to be fab." She pouted a little. "I suppose you've done it all before."

"Skating, yes. Not at Snetterton House though."

"So where did you skate, then?" Daniel asked.

"In Alaska. I did it as part of filming something for *Red Pepper*."

"Alaska? Wow!" Julia was impressed.

So was Daniel. "God, you've done some things as part of that job, haven't you? You're really lucky to have it."

Harri gave him an odd look. "I am lucky. Very. I work hard, mind."

The taxi driver put on his brakes suddenly. As the cab came to a violent halt, Julia slid neatly off her seat and landed on Harri's lap. She flung her arms around him. Any excuse to touch him, she thought.

"Oops, sorry," she giggled, embarrassed that Harri had had to take her full weight.

He hung onto her tightly for a second. "You alright?" he asked urgently. "Not hurt?"

Julia was content to stay where she was. "I'm fine." For a moment, she nestled in and allowed herself to enjoy his nearness. The scratch of the rough wool of his sweater stretched over his hard muscle and the smell of soap, and his leather coat – his very Harri-scent - was intoxicating. Then she began to disentangle herself, confused, as ever, by his proximity.

"Should have worn your seat-belt, babe," Daniel said. He bunched up nearer to the window. "Here, sit in the middle of us. It'll be a bit of a squash but you'll be wedged so tightly, you'll have less of a chance to slip anywhere."

As Julia moved reluctantly into the space he'd created, he looked out at the busy London night. "Traffic's come to a complete stop out there, wonder why?"

A blur of two-tone and blue lights, as an ambulance squeezed past the stationary cars, answered his question.

"Hope no one's hurt," he added.

The cabbie turned round and slid open the privacy window. "Sorry about that," he said, "Everyone okay back there? Bit of a hold up, accident I expect. I'll turn round when I can and try the other way."

Everyone assured him they were fine and, after a few minutes of silence, with the taxi still not moving, Daniel resumed the conversation.

"Yeah, I bet it is hard work," he said to Harri. "Still, a fantastic job. Something you'd want to hang onto for a few years, I imagine. Jobs as good as that don't come up very often in television. You wouldn't want to lose it, I imagine."

Julia sensed Harri shift away from her and was sorry. She'd been enjoying the warmth of the hard bulk of his thigh against hers.

"No," she heard him say in a distant voice. "I need to hang onto the day job for a while." Then he changed the subject as the taxi began to inch forward. "Oh good," he said with obvious relief, "We're finally moving."

When they got to their destination, they pushed through the crowds to the entrance, flaunting their 'Invite Only' tickets. As soon as they got through security, Daniel saw someone he knew and drifted off towards the bar.

Julia stood, for a moment, taking in the atmosphere. It was beautiful and, to her mind, completely lived up to its hype. A white marquee lined three sides of the rink and, at its head, with the magnificently lit Snetterton House as a backdrop, was the most enormous Christmas tree she had ever seen. This year, it was decorated with a mass of tiny white lights and had a huge silver star at its top. It was stunning and, what's more, she could smell the pine from here. Mingling with the aroma of mulled wine, wafting over from the bar, it spelled Christmas to her, with a capital C. Even the hard-core club anthems pounding out into the night added to the vibe.

"It's wonderful!" she yelled to Harri, over the music, and smiled up at him.

Before he could answer, though, three or four very drunk people staggered over to them.

"Hi Trevor," Harri said, as a tall man grabbed him in a bear hug. "Happy birthday. Sorry we're a bit late. Traffic."

This must be *Red Pepper's* producer. Julia laughed and stood to one side as Harri disappeared into the group, who greeted him with much backslapping and raucous humour.

By the look of them all, they'd been drinking for quite some time. Harri managed eye contact with Julia and, quirking his brows, extricated himself, making the excuse that they wanted to skate while the rink wasn't too crowded. He propelled her to one of the marquees, where they had to collect their skates.

Julia sat, trying to pull on her skating boots. "Are you sure these are the right size for me?" she complained.

"Come here." Harri tutted in mock exasperation. He kneeled before her and helped. "How much trouble are you?" He smoothed the thin leather boot onto her ankle, his cold fingers making contact with her bare leg making her yelp.

She leaned forward so that they were nose to cold nose. "I can be as much trouble as you want," she breathed huskily and then backtracked as she clocked his panicked expression. "On the rink, of course."

"Of course," Harri said, in relief. "You've never skated before, have you?"

"Nope." As Julia tried to stand, she fell onto him. "Whoops. Seem to be making a habit of this tonight. I'm glad I didn't have a drink first." She clutched onto his sweater, enjoying the feel of his erect nipples through the wool. "You'll have to hold me up, Harri."

"Looks that way, bach," Harri responded somewhat tersely. "Come on, let's get started."

As it happened, Harri had to hold onto Julia through most of their skating time. She proved to be as much a natural on the ice as she was in the dance studio.

"I just don't seem to have any balance for this sort of thing," she gasped and clung onto his arm on one side and the rail on the other. Past flirting now, Julia simply wanted to stay upright.

Harri was in mid-chuckle when the music abruptly stopped, to be replaced by the strains of 'Happy Birthday'.

Relishing a reprieve, Julia leaned on the rail, while everyone sang to Trevor who, judging from the racket coming from one of the marquees, was still ensconced in the bar.

When it was over, Harri looked her in the eye. "I think you're ready to try the middle of the rink out now."

"No way!"

"Way," he laughed. "Come on, you can still hang onto me. You can't stay by the rails all night."

"I rather think I can."

"Chicken."

Julia brought herself up to her full height. "No one calls me 'chicken' and gets away with it!" She glared at him and then slipped a little. "You will hold me up though, Harri, won't you? Don't let me go, will you?"

Harri laughed and put his arm round her waist. "Put your arm round my neck and you'll be fine. Oh, the music's changed again."

And so it had. The lighting changed too. To accompany the moody notes of Elvis' *Blue Christmas* the ice rink transformed from white to a greeny-blue. Dry ice shifted across its surface.

Harri and Julia made their unsteady way across the ice. It was as if they were moving underwater; it felt dreamy and romantic. Their limbs slowed to match the seductive rhythm of the old song.

Julia was only too aware of the man next to her. Although she knew she'd fall if he let go of her, she was certain he wouldn't. She felt safe.

She also felt as horny as hell.

She stopped and slid round to face him. With her sudden movement, he staggered a little. It brought his face next to hers, within kissing distance. She felt his breath, hot on her cold face.

He put both arms around her, to hold her steady. Feeling brave, in return, Julia slipped her arms round his waist, bringing him tight into her. She gazed up at him, willing him to kiss her. Where their bodies met, a heat burned, even through their thick winter clothes.

"Far enough, I think," whispered Harri but Julia knew he wasn't only referring to the distance they'd come on the ice.

"Better go back now, bach. Join the others."

Julia was shocked at how disappointed she felt. Not to mention the blow to her ego. "Okay," she said slowly. "If we must."

They'd joined Trevor and his gang in the bar, where she and Harri had spent the rest of the evening determinedly catching up on the alcohol intake.

Did Harri really like her, Julia wondered, as the Quickstep being announced brought her back to the present. She sensed a reserve in him, something holding him back. On occasion, she was sure he reciprocated her feelings. She vibrated with desire every time he came near her and his continued neutrality made her dry-mouthed with frustration. Maybe, it was that he simply didn't like her that way? The group were all very hands on; forever hugging and kissing one another. Callum, still in the competition and giving Harri a run for his money as the favourite, made the most of every opportunity to squeeze and stroke in nauseating fashion. Julia gave a shudder as she remembered how he'd pinched her bottom that very morning. If anything, Harri was more restrained than everyone else was and it was still causing problems in the infernal rumba that they were planning for the Christmas special.

"You. Alright?" Jan asked in his customary aggressive manner.

Julia sucked in a deep breath. If she were to stay in the competition and maybe, just maybe, find out what Harri's true feelings were, she needed to concentrate. Being able to see Harri most days in the training gym was a powerful incentive. She looked up at Jan. "Fine. I'm fine. Let's just get on with it."

Julia found herself backstage in what seemed like a matter of minutes, unable to believe what had happened. She had missed the dance off yet again and the judges had been forced to choose between Casey and Suni. Julia held her breath, hardly noticing that Harri had grabbed her hand and was holding on tight. A shout of relief echoed round when the judges voted for Suni. The whole gang, even po-faced Jan, leapt to their feet and cheered. Casey hadn't been popular and everyone recognised Suni's talent.

"Thank God for that. Come here, lovely girl and give me a cwtch!" Julia found herself wrapped up in Harri's powerful arms in a rugby scrum of a hug – the 'cwtch,' she assumed.

"Ooh," she managed as the air was squeezed out of her.

Harri dropped her immediately. "Sorry, got a bit carried away." His face was flushed Julia noticed and he seemed embarrassed.

As one, the remaining contestants milled onto the studio floor and gathered round Suni, Casey and even Charlie and Carol.

Julia found herself hugging Daniel Cunningham, Casey's professional partner. He was a lovely man she thought, tall and lean with floppy blond hair. "I'm so sorry," she yelled at him over the hubbub.

He hugged her back. "We'd gone about as far as we could," he said into her ear, his breath hot on her cheek. "Casey's got a modelling contract in the States coming up. She wanted out anyway."

Julia drew back aghast. "You mean it was fixed? The result was fixed?"

Daniel tapped his nose and grinned. "Can't say, but she didn't exactly have much time for training this week. Too busy on the phone – and it showed."

"But that's so unfair on you!" Julia said in a shocked voice. She knew how much the competition meant to the professional dancers, it was the source of Jan's eternal frustration with her.

"It's the way it goes," Daniel shrugged with a sanguine smile and Julia couldn't help but compare his reaction to that of Jan's in the same situation. Her admiration for this calm man increased.

He twisted his arms round her and held onto her more firmly. "I'll come and give you and Jan a hand if you like," he said smiling down at her, his green eyes glowing. "Apart from one or two show dances, I'll have plenty of free time. Maybe I can help you and Harri with your rumba, too?"

Julia thought of his presence in the training room, calming Jan and encouraging her. "Oh, yes please!" she said with more warmth than she meant to. "That's *just* want I need!"

Harri watched them over Casey's shoulder, as the girl hung limpet-like onto him. He scowled. So, that was the way it was. A shaft of jealousy speared his middle causing actual physical pain.

"Larry! We practise tomorrow. Nine on the spot!" Eva's voice irritated his ear.

"It's Harri," he muttered yet again, "and it's on the dot, not on the spot." He shrugged Casey off and went to congratulate Suni, keeping one eye on Julia and Daniel, still standing with their arms entwined.

Fuck these impossible restrictions imposed on his career. He'd have to make a move soon, or lose Julia. He'd just have to chance it. He just hoped it wasn't too late.

Step Seven.
The rehearsal wasn't going well.

Daniel had kept his promise and had come in to help practise the rumba with Julia and Harri. Jan and Eva were in the studio next door and, at first, Julia thought this would mean a more relaxed session – she was even looking forward to it. But she was wrong. Harri was tense and wasn't taking kindly to Daniel's suggestions. He seemed more reluctant to let go than ever and it was making the dance seem stiff. Even Julia could see it.

"Let me show you," Daniel said finally, after the third run through. He took Julia into the beginning hold and backed her gently down until she was almost touching the floor with her head.

"See, you have to make love to her, caress her." At this, Daniel held her with one arm and rubbed his hand electrifyingly down over Julia's breastbone.

Julia let out a startled yelp – Daniel's hand was hot and perilously near her breasts.

He lifted her up slightly and pulled her to him until they were nose to nose. His green eyes were mesmerising. "You never break contact, do you see Harri? You're always connected physically or, most importantly, emotionally. You've got to make the audience believe you're in love with this woman. And don't rush through it, take your time, linger over her."

Daniel pulled a disorientated Julia back to her feet and left her side. "You have a go." He placed Harri and Julia close together, far closer than they'd ever been.

Julia stared into Harri's dark eyes and willed her sympathy over to him; he must be finding this excruciatingly embarrassing. She was so close to him that she could feel his breath hot on her face; it smelled of toothpaste. She felt his strong arm come round her back and it seemed to burn right through her ballet top.

"Right, good, that's better." Daniel's calm and encouraging voice broke into the moment. "Now, back her down. Julia, you have to trust him like you trusted me, he's just as strong, he's not going to drop you. Release her hand now Harri and take yours down her body, that's it."

Julia could feel the muscles in Harri's arm tense against her back. "Look at him Julia, don't let him break that contact."

Julia did as she was told and was held in a spell cast by the warmth in Harri's brown eyes, he'd never ever looked at her in quite that way before.

"Now take your hand Harri and stroke it slowly down her. No use your whole hand, flatten the palm out."

Julia felt Harri's hand sear her body and felt it tremble slightly. And then, because she couldn't help it, because it was too much like bliss, she let her head arch back in ecstasy. Desire pulsed through her. She heard him whisper something in Welsh and let the husky words caress her – just as his hand was caressing her body from breast, over her stomach, to the where her legs met.

A beat began in the very core of her being, where Harri's hand lay. God, she was turned on! If she didn't have this man soon, she'd combust. Did he know the effect he had on her? She couldn't help herself; she bucked against his hand, making it press more urgently against her sex.

"Good, good," Daniel sounded surprised but pleased, "that's a good line. Hold it, then lift her gently up Harri and bring her back to the standing position and be ready to break away ... now!"

Julia found herself coming to without really knowing quite what had just happened. She was dizzy and her legs trembled. She still fizzed with unspent desire. Then she saw Harri breathe heavily and run a hand over his forehead, and she came back down to earth. He was sweating. Damn, she didn't think she was that heavy!

Daniel looked at both of them curiously: "We'll take a break now folks, but we've done some good work here this morning. Take twenty."

"Good idea," Harri mumbled and walked out.

Julia frowned at the towel she'd just picked up and muttered into it as she wiped her face: "I didn't think dancing with me would be so much of a hardship for him." She gazed up at Daniel in appeal. "I thought we got on so well."

He passed her a fresh bottle of water. "I think that's the problem, babe." He nodded to the door. "Think our Welsh friend likes you more than just a little bit."

"No!" Julia looked at him startled. "He can hardly bear to touch me. Today's the first time anything like that's happened and that's only because you were coaching us."

"Didn't look like that to me. Think he's gone to cool himself off, if you know what I mean." Daniel gave her a bawdy wink and grinned. "Don't sweat it – it made the dance hot, hot, hot!" He came nearer and swiped the bottle from her. "It'll be a show-stopper." He saluted her with the water bottle and drank thirstily. Screwing his eyes shut, he clamped down on his own burgeoning feelings for Julia. He'd seen the longing in Harri's face and knew he couldn't, maybe didn't want to, compete.

"Maybe he has to be careful," he added. "You know, in his line of work. People can be funny about the image children's television presenters give off. They have to appear a bit innocent, don't they?"

"What, still, in this day and age?" Julia glared at him.

Daniel shrugged. "Well, maybe. It's just a theory and Harri's serious about his job. He said the other night how much it means to him."

But Julia wasn't really listening, she stared at the door through which Harri had exited so swiftly and wondered what he had just said to her in Welsh.

"So, what did you say to me?" They were sitting in the pizza place again. Neither of them really wanted yet another pizza, it was simply a quick way to refuel their starving and hard worked bodies. The place was again packed with people celebrating Christmas. This time, *Mary's Boy Child* played on the sound system.

"What? When?"

"When we were doing the rumba this morning with Daniel." Julia, disconcerted by Harri's unusual disinterest, prattled on, mainly to fill the silence. "He was brilliant, don't you think? So encouraging and kind. He's exactly what I need. But what did you say in Welsh, during training?"

Harri looked down at his beer and reddened. "It was nothing."

"No, it *was* something. What did you say?"

"I said …"

"It sounded beautiful. I had no idea the language was so beautiful. What did you mean?"

A large group in the back of the restaurant erupted into laughter and began a chorus of *We wish you a merry Christmas*. Harri's eyes strayed to them and Julia thought she could see longing in his face. Was she really such dull company? "Well," she said a little huffily, "if you don't want to tell me I'm sure it's not important."

Harri flashed his eyes back to hers. "I said I loved you," he said abruptly. They held one another's gaze.

"Oh," Julia spluttered. There was a silence and the remains of their easy friendship fled. "You were obviously, erm, just getting into the mood of the dance then." She tried to say it without an ounce of hope or expectation.

Harri gave a huge sigh. "Yeah, that's it." He seemed deflated she thought. "Duw, I need another drink! Oh, look, it's Abi again, wouldn't you know it. Another Becks and more wine?" He busied himself with the order and the moment passed.

In the cab on their way home Julia tried to resurrect the companionship they'd shared by discussing Daniel's coaching skills. But Harri remained taciturn and, as it was so unlike him, she too lapsed into silence. The atmosphere between them was as frosty as the weather outside.

Step Eight.

Quarter-final week. Of all the dancers who had started only Harri, Callum, Suni and, unbelievably, Julia remained.

The show had begun to hit the papers, with Julia's story featuring prominently. As Lavinia said, it was all good publicity, even the focus on Julia's appalling dancing, but Julia wasn't happy being in the full glare of the tabloids. She and Harri remained friends but he continued to be distant with her. She blamed the increased publicity; she knew he had to be careful with any press coverage.

Daniel was as attentive as ever and, now that so many contestants had been voted off, it was good to find solace in his and Erica's friendship. They often went out as a threesome and her cosy pizzas with Harri became a thing of the past. Harri's position as favourite was slipping, the public were, in true British fashion, going for the underdog and Callum and Julia were increasingly tipped to win.

Julia, under Daniel's kind and patient tutelage, was blossoming. She was in no way as good as Suni but was really improving; even Jan had muttered reluctant words of praise.

It wasn't all rosy though. Now that Casey had left, Callum had fewer victims for his letching and Julia found herself constantly

40

having to dodge his roving hands. Fortunately, Daniel acted as a type of bodyguard and had the ability to diffuse tricky situations with an enviable grace and skill.

Julia wondered about Daniel. He was a quiet man, incredibly lithe and good looking but always seemed to be on his own. She had no idea if he was straight or gay; he seemed almost asexual. But she enjoyed his company and appreciated his friendship.

Bob, the producer, decided to throw a Christmas party on the night before the quarter-final show. Everyone had been working hard and the atmosphere was increasingly tense. He'd hired a ballroom in a local hotel and had invited all the original contestants, plus their partners and families.

The production team had gone to town. A host of purple and silver sequined banners fluttered from the ceiling, a tree stood to one side, groaning with purple lights and waitresses, dressed as silver mini-skirted fairies, dotted about, dispensing mulled wine and mince pies.

At the centre of the ballroom hung an over-sized silver glitter-ball, from which hung an enormous bunch of mistletoe, swagged with purple and silver satin ribbons.

It was all very over the top. And very *Who Dares Dances*.

As Julia entered, on Daniel's arm, the big band began to play.

"Bit of a busman's holiday this, isn't it?" she whispered to him and they laughed.

"Big difference between dancing for a competition and dancing for pleasure," he replied and pulled her into his arms for a foxtrot.

And he was proved right. Everyone let their hair down but the professionals really let rip. Julia, grabbing a glass of wine and using the time to get her breath back, watched in amazement.

Erica was doing a cha cha cha with Scott, Suni's irritable Australian partner. Alicia was smooching with husband Warren and Callum, true to form, was getting up close and personal with Casey.

"Quite a sight, isn't it?" Julia turned to see Harri's sweetly

41

familiar face next to her. They watched in silence for a few minutes as Eva and Jan outshone every dancer on the floor by doing moves that were definitely not recognised in any formal competition.

"Is she sober?" Julia wondered as Eva was whirled round by Jan and hoisted into a one handed lift. Eva had a glazed expression in her eyes and Julia had never seen the dancer look even slightly out of control before.

Harri laughed. "Don't know and don't really care." He emptied his glass.

Julia took two more from the table behind them and passed him one. "I haven't seen much of you lately," she said, almost afraid to bring it up.

"Busy filming," he shrugged. "We've got three Christmas specials of *Red Pepper* to go out and I've been doing those. I've only just got back from seeing Father Christmas in Lapland." Harri gave a short, "Ho, ho, ho. He says if you're a good girl, you'll get a present."

"Haven't they given you any time off?" Julia looked at him curiously. He had shadows under his eyes and was pale and drawn. He had a heavier work commitment than any of them but hadn't let it show until now.

"Some, and despite what the bookies say, I don't think they thought I'd be in it this long, see." He shrugged again and took another drink.

"Did you?"

"No," he laughed and finally met her eyes. "Did you?"

Julia smiled back. "You know I didn't. It's true that miracles happen at Christmas – you're looking at one."

Harri laughed again but this time more easily. "I've missed you."

"I've missed you too."

He gave a great sigh and put his glass down, as if coming to a decision. "Dance with me?" He held out a hand.

"Yes please," she said and took it.

They didn't take much notice of the demands of the music, just held each other closely. Harri put his head down and nestled into Julia's neck, breathing in her soft and familiar perfume. He tightened his hold on her, afraid she would escape him.

Daniel felt his eyes drawn to them and smiled sadly. He'd long known he couldn't compete with Harri. He'd come as close as he ever had to falling in love with Julia, maybe he really did love her. He admired her strength, her determination and her stubbornness in the face of continued criticism but he accepted that she was not for him. Perhaps no woman would ever be for him. But Julia had come closest. He turned away.

Harri and Julia stopped dancing and stood looking at one another. Harri looked up at the glitterball, still rotating slowly, showering everyone in a glittery light. A smile played on his lips as he noticed the mistletoe. He drew back and stared into Julia's eyes. He seemed to be silently asking her something and nodded in satisfaction at the answer written on her face. He didn't want to stop holding her, touching her. He'd made up his mind and he was going to act on his decision before it was too late – or before he lost his nerve.

"Do you want to get out of here?" he murmured finally.

Julia smiled up at him. "Not another pizza?"

"Not quite what I had in mind."

He looked at her and she was suddenly certain what he wanted – because she wanted it too.

"Yes," she whispered back. "Yes, I'd like nothing better than to get out of here."

He took her to a bar nearby. It was quiet and had high-sided booths lining the walls, which afforded them privacy.

After ordering drinks, he took her hand and stared at it intently. It was peaceful in here, a contrast to the party they'd just left. Julia leaned back on the cool leather couch, closed her eyes and listened to the soft jazz playing. She felt Harri smooth a finger over her palm and onto the sensitive skin of her wrist. He lifted her hand and then kissed her there, his mouth hot and demanding. Still she didn't open her eyes but let the sensations swirl around her,

43

jolting a shot a pure sex to her core.

"Harri?" she said eventually and opened her eyes to find his face near hers and her mouth captured.

For a first kiss it was pretty good. One strong arm held her to him but, while his mouth plundered hers, he did not relinquish his hold on her hand.

Eventually they broke apart, content simply to gaze into one another's eyes.

"God!" Julia said when she had her breath back. "Thank God," she said and meant it.

Now he did let go of her hand and ran a finger down her cheek. It was hot and he smiled, pleased that he had made her so.

"I've wanted to do that for a while," he said, his Welsh accent pronounced.

"Then why didn't you?" Julia found she was breathing heavily and her eyes dropped to his mouth. She wanted him to kiss her again.

He sighed heavily. "Don't get me wrong, I really wanted to but ... in my line of work I have to be careful. I can't go around, you know..."

"That's the silliest thing I've ever heard!"

"Do you know, cariad, I couldn't agree more."

"Kiss me again," she demanded.

He did so and then broke away to answer. "Besides I wasn't sure how you felt."

"I don't think I was sure. Until now." She traced a finger lightly over his generous lips. He had such a well-shaped mouth she thought, she hadn't noticed it until now and wondered why.

Harri smiled again, he couldn't seem to stop. "Well cariad, you were spending so much time with the lovely Daniel."

Julia straightened. "He's coaching me!" she said indignantly. "He's a really good friend. And I think he's gay anyway." She blushed.

"He didn't look very gay from where I was standing. Something tells me Daniel wants you as more than a friend."

This time Julia grinned. "You're jealous!" The realisation sent a warm glow spreading through her.

"You bet. It's been tearing me apart."

He raised a hand to the back of her neck and brought her close to him again. He was a little rough but Julia didn't mind, she found she was exhilarated and the sexual tug, deep in her soul, pulled at her again. Their mouths met and this time neither held anything back.

The sound of their drinks being clinked down on the glass table in front of them had them springing apart and giggling.

"Let's get out of here," Harri threw down a note. "Which flat's closest?"

"Mine," Julia said and grabbed her coat. They went out into the icy December night where the white Christmas lights turned them monochrome.

"Islington, please," she said to the taxi driver as they got into the cab. She was shivering violently but it wasn't with cold.

"Might take a while love," he replied, "traffic's terrible tonight. Crowds out to see the lights, I expect."

Julia and Harri didn't notice how long the journey home was, nor did they notice the spectacular Christmas lights; they were too busy kissing. They broke off just long enough to unlock Julia's front door and then it slammed behind them as Harri shoved her, none too gently, up against it. He took her hands in his and Julia felt open and vulnerable and incredibly turned on.

"I can't stop kissing you," he murmured, "I just can't stop kissing you." He tore her scarf away and kissed her neck, leaving a trail of fire. His knee nudged her legs apart and she felt him hard and demanding as he pressed against her. She'd never felt this sexually charged she thought incoherently, she was going to explode if she didn't have him. He searched under her heavy coat, and then slid two fingers into a gap in the front of her shirt. A button tore but neither noticed as Harri tugged the delicate lace of Julia's bra away and cupped her breast with his hand. Julia felt her knees give way, his hand was cold and the shock of it had her nipple zinging to life. Another button shot off and he took his burning mouth to her breast. The door rattled on its hinges under their combined weight and Julia would have been quite happy for him to take her there and then.

But Harri had other ideas, at heart he was a gentleman and it didn't seem right to be doing what they doing up against the cold glass of Julia's front door. And besides, he'd wanted her for so long that he was worried he wouldn't last much longer. He backed off, his dark eyes veiled with lust. "Bed," he managed, "where's the bed?"

Julia nodded wordlessly, took him by the hand and led him to her bedroom. As they stumbled along clutching one another, unable to let go, they paused to kiss frantically. They ripped off some more clothes and left a trail of winter coats, scarves, bags. Then they fell onto the bed and wrestled with one another's remaining clothes until they were skin on skin at long last. Julia was aware only of the erotic tickle of the soft hair on Harri's chest against her breasts and the feel of his needy erection pressing against her stomach. She gasped as Harri almost immediately rolled her onto her back and slid into her.

"Sorry, cariad, can't wait," he muttered. "Oh Duw, I've wanted this for so long!"

Julia's head arched back. She couldn't believe it, she was beginning to come already. Wave after wave of ecstasy spiralled through her, around her, over her. She felt Harri tense, hang over her for a long second and then collapse onto her, crushing her with his weight. "Rwyn dy garu di," he breathed. "I love you," He added, in his head.

Julia woke first in the morning. It was still dark outside but she'd grown accustomed to waking early to get to Jan's demanding rehearsals and today would be no different. She poked her nose above the duvet, shivered and pulled it round her again. She'd have to brace herself to go and turn on the heating. Funny how they'd not noticed the cold last night.

She twisted and gazed at Harri lying on his side facing her. He was frowning slightly in his sleep and had the quilt tucked up around his shoulders as if cold. His hair was sticking up any old how and he looked like a little boy. Julia smiled and remembered that he'd definitely not been the little boy last night. She giggled as she recalled how he'd woken her in the middle of the night and made love to her again, this time with a tender gentleness and at an agonisingly slow pace which had had her crying out in relief when he'd finally entered her.

She'd been right about him she thought with yet another giggle; he *was* a man of hearty appetites. He shifted slightly and gave a little snuffle. Julia got out of bed, loathe to leave him but desperate for some heat and a shower.

He was awake when she returned and greeted her with a huge grin on his face.

"You look very smug," she said but softened the comment with a smile and got back onto the bed.

"And you look gorgeous," he replied and tugged at the towel wrapped around her hair.

"Oh yes, I'm sure I do," she said as her hair fell down and flapped damply against her face. "I'm sure I'd win the public vote if I went on tonight looking like this."

"You get my vote every time."

"Corny."

"But true." Harri's eyebrows quirked wickedly in that expressive way they had. "Come here, I've got something to show you."

"We'll be late for training, Harri!"

He pulled at her dressing gown belt and the robe fell apart, revealing her breasts. He grinned at the sight. "For once, I've got something worth being late for. Come and see what I've got for you."

As the duvet was tented up dramatically around the area of his groin, Julia had a pretty good idea what he had in mind to show

47

her but she played along. "What is it?"

He grinned again and flipped back the duvet. "Dyma un a nes i'n gynharach!"

"What?" she said as he tumbled her into bed and covered her with his warm body.

"It's one I made earlier!" he said and he kissed her through their laughter.

"God Harri," she moaned a little later. "I think you've finally found your hip action!"

Step Nine.

In the car on the way to the studio, Julia snuggled up to Harri and whispered, "So, are you finally going to tell me what you said to me in Welsh?"

He rolled his eyes heavenwards and tutted in mock despair. "I told you, it means it's one I made earlier. It's a sort of a pun you know on … but honestly, if I have to explain my jokes all the time, this relationship is doomed." He stopped as she hit him.

"Not that! What you said last night, you know, as you erm –"

"Oh that!" He looked at her with amusement lighting his dark eyes. "You're not brilliant with languages, are you, cariad? Have you forgotten? I've told you what it means, already!"

Julia shook her head and grinned. "I'm about as good at languages as I am at dancing!"

"That bad, eh?"

She gave him another playful punch.

"And another thing, you've got to stop hitting me!"

"Tell me!"

"I will – but another time." He glanced at the driver who was obviously intrigued as to why he was picking up both Harri and Julia from the same address that morning. "Another time when we're alone, see."

And for the moment Julia had to be content with that.

Jan had been furious with her for being late but it hadn't broken into the bubble of happiness that she existed in throughout the day. She came across Harri often as he rehearsed with Eva and they made stupid little signs and gestures to one another.

"Me, I am to be sick!" announced Eva at the final dress rehearsal later that afternoon, as a comment on their behaviour.

"Tsk. Unprofessional," agreed Jan but he was secretly delighted that Julia, finally, was showing signs that she could actually dance.

The atmosphere in the quarter-final show was electric. The judges went wild over Harri's newfound confidence and, to Julia's amusement, declared that he had finally found his hip action. She'd caught his eye at that point and they'd had hysterics. Julia sobered up quickly when she found herself in the dance off, competing against Callum. Despite being the bookies' favourite, he'd performed abysmally in his quickstep; it just hadn't been a dance suited to big man like him.

The four of them stood breathlessly in front of the judges after the exertion of dancing yet again. Julia tried to console herself with the thought that getting as far as this was as good as it could get, to get to the semi-final would be a miracle too far.

As Charlie announced that the judges were about to declare the result, based on the best performance in the dance off, there seemed to be a buzzing in her ears and it was proving hard to concentrate. An ominous silence fell on the studio and after a wait of what seemed like three days the announcement was made.

A resounding cheer sounded around the studio and the entire crowd rose to their feet. In contrast, Jan fell to his knees beside her and appeared to be praying. Even for a Russian this seemed a bit of an over emotional response thought Julia and then Callum, gripping her in a bear hug, squeezed all rational thought out of her.

"Good on you," he yelled in his gruff Scottish accent and then took advantage of her confusion to give her a disgustingly sloppy kiss.

"Wha-what?"

He put her back on the floor and peered down at her. "Did you not hear? You've got through. You're in the semi-final!"

To Julia, it seemed as if everything exploded in a deafening riot of noise and colour. The other competitors, who hugged and kissed them with lavish excess, surrounded her and Jan. Then the crowd parted and Julia saw the person she really wanted: Harri, standing slightly apart, as he always did. She shot into his arms like an arrow finding its target and hung on.

"Da iawn, cariad bach," he whispered into her ear. "Well done!"

Step Ten.

Julia opened her front door at the first knock. She knew it would be Harri. After the celebrations in the studio, he'd gone home to get some fresh clothes with the promise to come back with the papers and to enjoy a lazy Sunday with her. She had coffee perking, croissants warming in the oven and was looking forward to spending some time with him. But as soon as she saw his face, she knew something was very wrong.

Harri stared around him cautiously, shut the door and grabbed Julia by the arm. He took her into her kitchen at the back of the flat, pulled the blind shut and threw his collection of papers onto the table. He sank into a chair.

"Harri, what's wrong?"

He looked up at Julia's worried face, she already knew him so well, he thought and there was little point hiding the news, she'd find out soon enough. He flipped open a red top and pushed it over to her.

"The heat is on as *Who Dares Dances* stars rumba to love!" screamed one headline.

With a sinking heart, Julia sat down and read on:

"*Who Dares Dances* stars Harri Morgan and Julia Cooper are getting some hot love action off the dance floor. Training to perfect their passionate rumba, has spilled into their private life. 'I could see them getting more and more intimate,' said one source, close to the couple."

50

Feeling sick, Julia pulled another newspaper over and opened it. Pictures of her and Harri were splashed all over the second page. There was one of them practising the rumba – a still from training footage and a photograph of them hugging one another after the quarter-final result. She read the beginning of the attached article:

"Harri, thirty one and Julia, twenty seven, have become increasingly friendly. An insider on the show said: 'They were seen getting very cosy at an after show party. They couldn't keep their hands off one another!'

"The couple have also been spotted sharing intimate late night dinners designed strictly for two. Our source added, 'It's become obvious they have strong feelings for one another and I think it's getting in the way of their training.'"

"Cheek!" exclaimed Julia, "we've both got so much better. Casey?" she looked questioningly at Harri, "Eva?"

He shrugged. "It could be anyone. It could even be Abi from the pizza place. Have you seen this one?" He passed her yet another tabloid.

She took it wordlessly and then gasped at the photos of her and Harri kissing passionately while they waited for the taxi home the other night. She got distracted for a minute thinking how gorgeous he was, in his long leather coat and black jeans and then realised just what the press coverage would mean. She looked at him, dismay on her face. "Oh, I'm so sorry Harri!"

"We haven't exactly been discreet, have we?" He rubbed a weary hand over his face and managed a weak grin. "I suppose it was inevitable that it would come out."

"Have you … has anyone contacted you from *Red Pepper*?"

"No, not yet. No doubt I'll get a call tomorrow."

"What will they do?"

Harri searched for her hand and found it. "I don't know," he frowned deeply, "they might not renew my contract, or give me the sack straight away." He shrugged again. "Who knows?"

"What, just for going out with me?"

He managed a grin at her outrage. "It's not so much that." He took an enormous breath, realising he'd have to tell her the truth. "I have this clause in my contract, see. They made me sign it." He searched for the right words. "I'm not supposed to form any personal relationships with anyone else on the show." He rushed on, ignoring her stricken expression. "I suppose it's really more of a case of being *seen* doing stuff like that, see." He nodded to the photograph of them kissing in public. "They don't usually mind me having a private life just as long as it's not seen happening – and doesn't get into the papers. Then they added this bit in the contract, just for this show."

"Oh my God," Julia said, as the truth of what he was saying dawned. "But that's so hypocritical!"

"You said it, cariad." He rose and came behind her, put his arms round her and kissed the top of her head.

Now it had happened, just how did he feel about it? Anxious and insecure for the future, yes but he also felt strangely relieved. There would be no more stumbling along until they tired of him; He'd *have* to find another career now. It was peculiarly freeing.

"You sound so calm about it all!" Julia twisted so she could see his face.

He kissed her quickly and laughed. "I suppose I've had a whole two hours more to get used to the idea. And in a way it might be a good thing. It's going to force me into action, it's going to get me out there and find out what I really want to do."

Julia nuzzled his stubbled cheek and wanted to cry. He risked losing so much. For her. Just to be with her. "But Harri, you've risked your job to be with me. Do you, do you regret – ?"

"What?" His voice reverberated against her skin and his breath was warm.

"Do you regret," Julia took a deep breath, "us?"

Harri went very still. "Do you?"

"No!" she said a little wildly, "of course not! But it's not my career that's been ruined."

"Bit dramatic, bach!"

Julia giggled weakly, despite herself. "I am an actor," she pointed out.

"True enough." Harri breathed in the scent of her hair and thought. He did feel calm. Would it scare her off, he wondered, if he said what he wanted to? That he had what he most wanted here, in this little kitchen, held in his arms. His career? Well, that would take care of itself; something was bound to turn up.

"I don't regret anything I've, I mean that *we've* done." He tightened his arms round her and kissed the only part of her he could get at – her neck. "You're the best thing," when she began to protest, he shushed her and went on, "the best thing that's ever happened to me. I wanted you from the very first moment I saw you at the *Still Life* party. And now I've got you I'm not letting you go."

Julia relaxed against him. She loved him, she knew that now. She loved his dark eyes and his wicked grin, she loved his beautiful body with its honed muscles. But most of all she loved his cheerful determination, his optimism, the steady way in which he tackled life's problems, whether it was mastering the tricky steps to a paso doble, or simply a fan asking for his autograph at an inconvenient moment. And she was confident that he'd face this crisis in his usual way - with steady fortitude. "So, you're not going to let me go, are you?"

"Not a chance, you have this habit of swanning off with tall good looking blond men every time my back's turned."

Julia giggled again, this time with more conviction and then frowned at a burning smell. "You're going to have to let me go I'm afraid," she said, with mock seriousness.

"Why?" Harri's voice was muffled; he was busy nibbling her ear.

"Because our breakfast's burning!" Julia leapt up and rescued the croissants. They'd been burned black and were beyond hope. She said as much to Harri, coughing and laughing and flapping a tea towel around the room so that the smoke alarm wouldn't go off.

He came up behind her and put his arms about her again.

"Cariad," he said into the nape of her neck as his hands caressed her breasts. "Don't worry, I've got another sort of breakfast on my mind. Come to bed ..."

Step Eleven.

Monday morning brought sheepish grins from the team at *Who Dares Dances*. Harri didn't know for sure just who had sold them to the press but didn't overly care; the way he and Julia had been carrying on it would've got into the papers somehow. The press loved Julia, they loved *Who Dares Dances* and they seemed to love him; they'd smelt a story and wanted more.

He'd rung his neighbour from the car on the way to the television studios. Apparently, there had been a few reporters sniffing around his flat all night. He was going to have to find another way of getting into it, he thought with a grin. He smiled at Suni and Scott as his mobile went off. He closed the door to his dressing room and, with his heart beating faster, answered the call from *Red Pepper*.

Still at home, Julia had picked up her mobile on its first ring, thinking it would be Harri with more news.

"Julia?" It was Bibi, her agent. "Julia? I've had the *Cabaret* people on the phone."

"And?" Julia tried not to hold her breath and failed.

"They want you, darling. Can you meet them later today? They're going to offer you Sally Bowles!"

Julia's first impulse was to ring Harri.

"I've got the part!" she yelled into her mobile.

"They're not going to sack me!" Harri exclaimed at the same time.

They both screamed simultaneously down their phones.

"I want to see you now," said Harri urgently.

"Can't, I've got a meeting arranged with the director of *Cabaret*."

"Uffern dan, I can't either, I've got to train with Eva. See you later tonight?"

"My place?"

Harri thought about the reporters nosing round his flat. "Think it might be better. Hwyl fawr am y tro."

Julia looked at the blank phone screen and clicked it off. She loved the man but she was going to have to learn some Welsh. She made a promise to herself to look up a Welsh dictionary online, as soon as she got home." Not knowing what he was on about half the time was driving her insane. Harri grinned as he flagged down a taxi to take him to the dance studios where he was due to rehearse with Eva. He couldn't believe life could be so good. *Red Pepper*, in acknowledgement of his previously unblemished record, had given him a warning to be more discreet and had let him off. They were so delighted with his unexpected progress in *Who Dares Dances* that they didn't want to attract adverse publicity by firing him. He and Julia just had to be very, very careful.

"Ah, so you are here at last!" Eva looked up at him from where she was stretching. "We work hard today Larry. We win!"

Even Eva at her most ferocious couldn't dent his happiness.

He took off his scarf, hung his coat up, and smiled at her. "Eva one thing, it's Harri, not Larry," and at this he took the startled Swede's face in his hands and kissed her fully on the mouth, "and another thing, I will win it. For you, for me and for the sake of international relations!"

Step Twelve.

On Saturday night, Julia stood before the judges once again. It was the semi-final dance off and she'd just competed against Suni.

She knew the result even before she and Jan had repeated their salsa. If the judges voted Suni off in preference to her it would make a mockery of the whole competition. Suni was, by far, the better and more consistent dancer. With meetings with the *Cabaret* people eating into her training time, Julia thought it was high time she bowed out gracefully.

She and Jan, and Suni and Scott stood in front of the judges as Kevin began to speak.

Here goes, thought Julia and braced herself for more invective.

"Julia darling. When you started out in this competition I thought you wouldn't make it through the first round, in fact I didn't think you *deserved* to make it through to the next round."

The audience began to boo, forcing Kevin to raise his voice. "You were bad, darling; sloppy feet, no heel turns, rotten posture but," at this Kevin paused for breath and the audience paused too, "in the last two weeks you have changed from being the comic turn, wheeled out by Jan to entertain us all, into," at this he paused again, this time for dramatic emphasis.

Get on with it you old queen, thought Julia and fixed a smile on her face.

Then Kevin suddenly stood up "A dancer! I salute you. Darling, you are *magnificent!*"

The audience took its cue from him and stood too.

Kevin shouted the last of his comments over the clapping and wild cheers. "I'm voting you into the final!"

Julia felt Jan clutch onto her, obviously he couldn't believe what was being said either.

After this, Charlie had to attempt to calm things down.

Eventually the audience quietened and Sonya spoke. "I'd like to echo what Kevin has just said. Whatever has got into you Julia," at this she leered slightly, "can I ask you to bottle it and give some to every woman here, including me? You've transformed yourself from a no-hoper dullard to a dancer!" The audience began clapping again. "Well done to you and to Jan, but darling, I'm going to have to vote for Suni."

Half the crowd cheered and half booed. Julia reached for Suni's hand and squeezed it. The tension was so tangible she could smell it.

"Arthur, as senior judge, you have the casting vote," yelled Charlie over the hullabaloo. "What a gripping semi-final this has been, a real nail-biter. Arthur, can I ask you for your decision?"

Arthur twinkled at Julia. "You know, love," he said in his earthy northern voice, "Kevin here got it right when he said you were a comic turn. You gave us all a laugh in those first weeks but now I've got a great big smile on my face for another reason. Judging on that last dance alone I'm putting you through to the final and -"

His words were lost in the uproar that detonated around them.

But it's wrong, thought Julia. It's wrong, Suni should have gone through. She turned to the woman and enveloped her in a hug only to be ripped away by a towering Jan. He picked her up and balanced her on his shoulder in a parody of the lift they'd done in their American smooth.

"Put me down Jan," she yelled but wasn't heard. "Oh, put me down you great big oaf!"

From her vantage point, Julia could see Scott stomping off, bitter that he'd lost his chance of winning the competition. Suni stood, obviously stunned, and alone until Harri and Eva came back onto the dance floor with Carol in tow. Harri put his arms round Suni and when Carol did the same he released her and came to where Jan was still holding Julia aloft.

"Are you planning on letting her down from there any minute soon?" he said to the giant Russian, "only I'd quite like to congratulate my girlfriend and rival, see."

Jan grunted and Julia slithered down his muscled body until she stood breathless and pink faced in front of Harri.

Oh God, *rivals* she thought, as the meaning of his words struck her. That could put a dampener on things. But she should have known Harri better; he simply grinned, folded her into his arms and whispered his congratulations into her ear.

Step Thirteen.
"You can't be serious!" Julia cried in dismay. She was at her first fitting for the dress she was going to wear in the Christmas Special. The one she would wear to dance the rumba with Harri.

Roxie, the most senior of the costume girls, paused and looked up from her position at the hem of Julia's short skirt.

"Why not? It's gorgeous," she said, through a mouthful of pins.

It *was* gorgeous. Julia was dressed up as a sexy Santa's elf. A very sexy elf, indeed. The tiny crimson top, the colour of which set off her hair to perfection was decorated with a sequined fur collar. She loved the colour – and the sequined strips hanging off the skirt; it was the bodice that was worrying her; it barely covered her breasts and was cut off somewhere above her ribs. The jaunty emerald green elf's hat didn't console her.

"Look," she said to Roxie, picking at it, "you can see more of me than the dress. I can't go on telly and expose all my flabby bits."

Roxie stood up and put her hands on her hips. It wasn't the first time she'd had an argument with a celebrity over a dance costume and it wouldn't be the last. The men were the worst; she could never get them to accept it was all about the bling, the razzmatazz and not about them looking manly.

She sniffed disdainfully and looked Julia up and down. She saw to her satisfaction that the girl was backing down already. She'd win this one. "What flabby bits, girlfriend?" Roxie tried to pinch some flesh and failed. "When you ever going to get abs like this again? Show 'em off. You got a pretty figure now hon, make the most of it."

Julia turned around in front of the mirror and peered at herself. "At least the dangly bits cover my thighs," she said and tried to tug what there was of the bodice over her tummy.

"Stop ruining it!" Roxie shrieked and slapped her hand away.

"Someone being murdered in there?" Daniel poked his head round the dressing room door and gave a wolf whistle. "My, my, that'll get the votes pouring in." He grinned wickedly.

"Hi Daniel," Julia smiled at him. "Do you really think it's okay?" She gave a little twirl. "You know what you're talking about," she added and ignored Roxie's, "Huh!"

"More than okay," he smiled, "it's heaven." He came in and gave Julia a kiss on the cheek. "And that's for getting to the final, babe.

I haven't had a chance to congratulate you yet."

Julia gave him a squeeze. "It's all down to you, you know. If I'd been left to that Russian, I'd have been gone long ago. You worked miracles with me. Thank you!"

Daniel looked down at her and found his eyes filling. "You did it itself Julia. You just have to believe in yourself a bit more."

"Look, I'm trying to fit a dress here. Get out!" Roxie bore down on Daniel with a pincushion and he fled, laughing.

"Now honey child," she turned to Julia with a menacing glare, "just a bit more off the bust line I think."

Julia blew out a breath and decided to give in. She trusted Daniel's judgement implicitly; if he thought the dress would do, then she would wear it. But she wanted something from Roxie in return.

Steeling her nerves, she said, "Roxie, if I agree to wear this, would you, would you do me a favour please? How long does it take you to sew on a few sequins?"

Step Fourteen.

Julia loved every minute of the final. She loved the return of the other dancers in a specially choreographed group jive; she loved the cheesy song and dance routine performed by some old group from the sixties; she even loved having to perform two different dances. In any spare second she'd have dialled Harri's number and voted for him. She wanted to give him a competitive final but, more than that, she wanted him to win.

It was going to be a long night. After the show, they were going to record the dancing section of the Christmas Special. It would be edited in with all the other bits and pieces, like outtakes and previously recorded interviews, later. And even then, it wouldn't be over, they then had the wrap party to look forward to.

In the break before the results came out, she and Harri managed to get together.

"I've just had Radio 5 Live ring me; they've offered me a sports programme." Harri was beaming. "And that's on top of the rugby commentary the BBC has offered."

She threw her arms around him. "Oh Harri, that's brilliant! Which one do you want to do?"

"I don't know." He grinned in disbelief at his good fortune and it lit up the chilly corridor in which they were standing. "I might do both. Why not?"

"I think you can do anything," she said as a response and kissed him.

Before the result was announced Charlie gave a little speech. He said it had been the closest final since *Who Dares Dances* began and that the series had raised a record three million pounds from phone votes.

In amongst the rapturous applause Julia sought Harri's hand and held on tight. They were both trembling a little and Julia's mind was whirling. She closed her eyes and prayed; something she did too rarely. She prayed for Harri to win.

"And the winner of this year's *Who Dares Dances* series is ..." then there was another of the over long dramatic pauses that so infuriated contestants and audience alike.

"Get on with it," muttered Julia with force and felt Harri shake with laughter as he heard her.

Charlie coughed and then shouted out, "The winner is Harri and his lovely partner, Eva!"

Then everything went a bit bonkers. Harri caught Julia in a hug that she thought was going to squeeze the life out of her. Eva uncharacteristically screamed. Jan punched the air and bellowed something in Russian that Julia had no desire to translate. Charlie, stinking of whisky, stumbled into them and caught them all in a silly jig while pyrotechnics went off in a shower of white light behind them. It was madness, wonderful madness.

And through it all, Harri's eyes never left Julia's. A different sort of madness and a much more welcome one.

***

When it had all finally calmed down, in the break before the Christmas Special filming began, Julia managed to catch up with one or two people. She found Lavinia having a sneaky – and illegal cigarette in the Green Room.

"Lavinia, you'll get shot!"

"I know darling, but it's the only way I can calm my nerves before having to do that dreaded dance. God, I was so relieved when I went out and then they made do that blasted jive. Now I've got to dance with Sam the terminally unfunny Scouser."

Lavinia eventually paused to take a breath. "And," she added in outraged tones, "they're *voting* for us! It's too much darling."

Julia grinned. "I know," she plucked Lavinia's cigarette out of her hand and threw it in the bin, "but that won't help." She pulled a sympathetic face. "At least it won't be too energetic dancing with Sam. He'll be lucky to get through the routine; he and Callum have already hit the champagne."

"Champagne, eh?" Lavinia's interest quickened. She glared at Julia for a moment and then relented. "I know, I know," she muttered mutinously, "but just you wait until you get to my age. It's the little perks that keep one going."

Julia laughed. "Lavinia, if I'm half the woman you are when I get to your age I'll be a very happy bunny."

Lavinia tried hard not to be mollified but then smiled. "Come here angel, I haven't told you how proud I am of you! In the final no less! And how is that studly Welshman you're seeing? No," she ignored Julia's attempt to answer, "don't tell me, I can see he's good for you. Good in bed as well, I suppose? Well, you only have to see him dance to guess that!" She gave Julia a hug and kissed her on both cheeks. "And *Cabaret!* So delighted! Oh Lord, there's Roxie, I'll have to go for my fitting. See you at the party later darling. Love you! Toodles!"

Lavinia swirled out in her self-made panic and the room settled and felt instantly calmer. Julia heard the rustle of silk in the corridor outside and ran out. It was Suni. She hadn't seen her since the semi-final.

"I feel awful," Julia said through their hug. "It should have been you out there tonight, competing against Harri."

Suni shook her head and smiled. "The public have been captivated by your story," she said, as graceful and dignified as ever. "They took a dislike to Jan and the way he bullied you." She put a finger up to silence Julia as she protested. "No come on, we all witnessed it, the man has been insufferable. You've been a saint to not rise to him or fail before him. And of course, the public loved the love story."

She leaned in closer to Julia and added: "So did I, you make such a perfect couple. Such love, such *love!*" and she sailed off, swaying elegantly in her turquoise sari.

"Ring me," Julia called after the retreating figure, she really didn't want to lose touch with Suni.

Suni waved a hand without turning round. "I will, I will. Happy holidays!"

Julia smiled to herself; she couldn't quite believe it was nearly all over. She'd miss all this she thought: the nerves, the tantrums, the rushing adrenaline, the friendship and camaraderie, the last minute costume glitches. Costume! Oh shit, she'd better get changed; it was nearly time for her rumba.

Julia and Harri stood waiting to go onto the dance floor, a peculiar mixture of tension and anticipation running through them.

Harri was resplendent in a pair of indecently tight red trousers and a green transparent glittery shirt, which revealed his muscles in all their glory. He too, had on a perky little elf's hat. But it was Julia's costume which was attracting all the attention.

Harri looked Julia up and down, his eyes lingering on her low neckline and bare midriff. "I can't believe what you're wearing!"

Julia, instantly on the defensive, said: "Why, what's the matter with it?" She tugged nervously at her hem.

62

He gave a short whistle of appreciation. "Nothing. Absolutely nothing." He scanned round quickly to see if any cameras were on them. "Come here," he said and then proceeded to kiss her extremely thoroughly.

Bob Dandry stood watching them. They made a very appealing pair and it was beyond luck that they had both made it to the final. It was a publicity dream come true. And now, even better, they were going to dance the rumba. He'd seen their training footage and this dance was going to knock people's socks off; he'd be lucky to get it past the watershed as it was so sexy. He chortled at the thought of the viewing figures. Since his little word to the press about Julia and Harri's affair they had rocketed.

He whispered into his walkie talkie to the camera director. The young lovers were still all over one another, God he could see tongues! He needed to get them on camera; the great voting public couldn't miss this.

Charlie was in over-drive. "And now ladies and gentlemen, boys and girls and everyone; it's what you've all been waiting for, our winner and runner up of this year's competition and our very own Santa's little helpers: Harri and Julia with their rumba!"

The curtain swung back on the couple to reveal them still kissing passionately. The audience roared its approval and leaped to its feet as the couple sprang apart.

"Keep smiling," muttered Harri, thinking on his feet, "hopefully they'll think it's part of the routine." He looked down and grimaced: "Thank the Lord these trousers are tight!"

Julia nearly lost it then, she blushed as red as her dress but then ran down the steps behind him and got into their beginning hold.

As the first chords of the old classic, the Carpenter's, *Merry Christmas Darling* rang out, the audience whooped and cheered. They were entranced by the romance and sexiness emanating from the couple who stepped onto the dance floor. And, as their rumba began, a collective sigh rippled round the studio. It was magic, sheer Christmas magic.

Step Fifteen.

"So, how does it feel to win both the final *and* the Christmas Special?" Daniel asked them at the wrap party later that night. He kissed them each in turn, lingering over Julia a little. "Congratulations," he said, one eyebrow raised, "your rumba had one or two additions but it was the hottest, sexiest dance I've ever seen." He laughed and lifted a hand in farewell. "Have a good night. Oh, and a very happy Christmas!"

Julia and Harri looked at one another and laughed too. They couldn't help it; they'd been laughing constantly since they'd finished their rumba to a cacophony of cheers.

"So much for being discreet, though," Julia said, in a more serious voice. She sipped her champagne thoughtfully. "I think you've lost any chance of working for *Red Pepper* now."

Harri grinned at her. "You know what? I don't really care. I've decided to take both the rugby and the 5 Live jobs."

"Does this mean you won't be flying off to Borneo to wrestle crocodiles then?"

"Don't think *Red Pepper* ever sent me off to Borneo," he replied and then got distracted: "Do they even *have* crocodiles there?"

Julia hit him.

"Look, I've told you before you're going to have to stop doing that, you're far more dangerous than any crocodile." He pulled her close; to his great pleasure, she was still dressed in her rumba costume. "Do you think Roxie will let you wear that to go home in? I'm having very wicked thoughts about peeling you out of it." He found the sensitive part of her neck and nuzzled it.

"There's not a great deal of it to peel me out of," Julia protested as she tried to concentrate on what he was saying. Harri kissing her neck did serious things to her equilibrium.

"Get a room, darlings," said Lavinia as she waltzed past with Ted.

They giggled and then Julia froze.

"What's the matter?" asked Harri in alarm.

"Roxie!"

"Julia love, I was only joking about the dress."

"No, I don't mean that." Julia put a finger on Harri's warm lips. "Stay there, just for a second, will you? Stay right there. I've just got to go and get something."

Harri did as he was told and was just beginning to feel a little self-conscious, standing on his own in the middle of the room clutching a warm glass of bubbly, when Julia returned.

She had on what appeared to be an oversized red t-shirt over her rumba costume. She looked faintly ridiculous as the shirt completely covered the dress apart from the dangling sequined strips hanging below.

But Harri wasn't thinking about Julia's peculiar choice of outfit, he was staring at the words that were emblazoned on the front of the t-shirt in sequins. Four words in Welsh, three in English glittered for all to see.

Julia came to him and whispered, "I remembered what the words you've been saying to me in Welsh meant and got Roxie to sew them on for me." She looked down and read with difficulty, "Rwyn dy garu di, Harri." She looked up at him and smiled through her tears. "I love you."

He caught her by the waist, too overcome to speak. Instead, he kissed her again with all the love that he had.

"Are you two *still* at it?" Lavinia's imperious voice floated into their consciousness as she sailed by again.

Harri lifted his lips away from Julia's and gazed into her eyes. He sighed heavily.

She cocked her head to one side and smiled, just a little uncertainly. "Haven't you got anything to say to me?"

He gathered her closer. "Cariad bach, I've got a lot of things I want to say to you and I intend to spend the rest of my life doing so, but I'd like the next declaration of love to be in private."

Harri looked at her and she thought she'd dissolve from the intensity in his dark eyes. She didn't need words after all, his love was there, plain to see. She reached up to kiss him. "Do you want to get out of here?"

"Pizza?" he grinned with a wickedly quirked eyebrow.

"Not quite what I had in mind," she said with a smile full of love.

He held out a hand and she took it.

End of Dance One.

The Waltz: a dance full of romance.

"The waltz really is the most romantic of dances. With the right pairing, costumes and music, it can transport you into a fairyland. How lovely to find your very own Prince Charming to hold you in his arms." Tabitha 'Whiz' Wisley, Tattin and Brownlow Literary Agency.

Step One.

Lucy sat back on a gilded chair and watched as the studio party got going. The ninth series of the ever-popular *Who Dares Dances* competition had just wrapped its first show – and *she* had been in it.

Her lips curled into a relieved smile. No one milling round on the famous dance floor, champagne in hand, could possibly know how much it had cost Lucy to dance that one short waltz in front of a studio audience of two hundred, and a television audience of, well, it was anyone's guess. Lucy tried not to think about the millions of viewers examining every fluffed move, every faltering missed beat that she had taken – for a recovering agoraphobic that was a dance step too far.

"Ready to join the party, Cinders?" It was Daniel Cunningham, her professional dance partner, bowing with theatrical extravagance and holding a hand out to her. Lucy leapt to her feet with a triumphant smile, ignored her sore feet and, once more, allowed

Daniel to lead her onto the dance floor.

As they reprised their dance, she couldn't help but think how lucky she was with her partner. Patient and kind-hearted, Daniel had been nothing but encouragement. The weeks of training had flown by and now, unbelievably, it was the launch show party. The show itself had passed in a blur. Lucy had seen it as though through another's eyes – it was as if she hadn't been there. She had no recollection of actually performing the dance, of even walking down the famous gilded staircase to the dance floor. But she supposed that somehow she must have done it. The judges remarked that her waltz had been competent, which she felt damned it with faint praise but *she'd got through*. It was only after the show had finished that she realised what she had achieved. And that was when her legs threatened to give way and she had sought out a quiet chair, away from the hubbub of the manic chatter and post- show analysis. Back to what she was good at – watching.

"You okay, Lucy?" Daniel peered down at her. "You're deep in thought." He swung her round and made her bend backwards, making her giggle.

"I'm fine. Better than fine," she grinned back at him. "I'm marvellous!"

As she straightened, one of the other celebrity contestants, Max Parry, captured her attention, not difficult considering he was six feet five or so. He was one of the loveliest men she had ever met, not that she'd met all that many. A gentle, shy man, he possessed an all too rare smile, which, if you were lucky enough to be a recipient, warmed you from head to toe. He'd spear headed the successful Team GB claim and had come home from the competition triumphant with an unbelievable three gold medals strung across his broad chest.

Daniel noticed who she was staring at. "Poor Max," he said. "He may be the world's fastest man in water but he's struggling on the dance floor."

Lucy and Daniel trained in the dance studio next door to Max and his beautiful American partner Lola, and Daniel was forever feeding her information about Max's progress. Daniel had taken the swimmer under his wing and was helping him as much as he could. Despite Max's lack of natural dance talent Lucy knew that, underneath the reserved exterior, there lurked a fiercely competitive streak.

Lucy apologised as she accidentally trod on Daniel's foot. "Max is working harder than any of us," she said hotly.

Lucy had lived a solitary existence until recently and had never had a proper boyfriend. Instead, she fell victim to intense crushes on actors on TV, characters in books – in short, on anyone so remote so as not to demand anything like a relationship with her.

"I know you've got a soft spot for him and I know he's working his balls off," Daniel said, as he steered them expertly around the dance floor, "but sadly, I don't think he's going to last long in the competition."

Lucy looked up at him indignantly. She was going to say something else in defence of Max but thought better of it. Since beginning *Who Dares Dances*, Lucy had broken the habit of a lifetime. She had developed a raging crush on Max Parry, lanky Olympic swimmer. The crush was a familiar feeling; that it was focussed on someone real; someone she had to encounter most days, was most definitely new. Her feelings were acutely and wholly distracting and Lucy sighed as she watched Lola glide Max across the floor in an easy waltz. He was chatting to his partner, obviously relieved at scraping through after being saved in the judges' vote off. Lucy continued to gaze, as she danced, allowing Daniel full control of where they were headed. She luxuriated in being able to gaze at Max undetected. He was in perfect physical shape; he had a typical swimmer's build, with wide powerful shoulders narrowing dramatically to a muscular pair of hips and long, long legs. A tan he had collected during the recent big competition emphasised every hard toned muscle.

It was just such a shame that he was gay.

Sensing his partner's concentration wasn't entirely on her waltz, Daniel suggested a drink. "Don't know about you but I'm gasping for one," he said as he led her to the bar in the corner of Fizz TV's studio one. Lucy took a last look at Max's elegantly shaped head as he was swirled around by Lola and then obediently followed her dance partner.

After their first round had been gulped down, Daniel excused himself and went to intercept Max, who had been released by Lola and was looking a lot happier for it.

As soon as he'd gone, Lucy called over the barman, asked for another drink and then nursed a cold lager shandy as she watched Daniel and Max while they talked. They made a striking pair. Both men were extremely tall and tanned and attractive. Her good friend and finalist from last year's competition, the actress Julia Cooper, had been delighted when Lucy had told her who was to be her partner. She'd raved about Daniel but had confided that he was probably gay. Looking at the body language as the two men strolled towards her, Lucy had a feeling Daniel might have made a conquest.

"Lucy lovie, ready for another yet? No?" Daniel peered at Lucy's glass with interest. When he'd ordered drinks before, she'd had wine. "You should've told me you preferred lager. How refreshing. Don't mind if Max joins us, do you?"

Lucy shook her head and indicated the empty stools at the bar. Daniel took the one to her right and she sensed Max slide onto the one on her left. She sensed it because she was too mortified by her suddenly hot face to actually look.

Daniel cheerfully summoned the barman. "Another pint, Lucy?"

"N-no thanks."

"Max, what would you like? Weak orange squash? Are you serious? Oh well barman, a G and T for me, with extra tonic and a pint of squash for my aquatic friend. Oh and nuts and crisps. I'm ravenous. Four packets of each, please."

Daniel turned to Lucy. "Got to say it's nice to see a girl enjoying a pint after a hard night's work." He was obviously amused.

Lucy knew she should have chosen something more sophisticated to drink but she'd been thirsty. Feeling foolish, she pushed her glass away.

"Great show tonight, wasn't it Lucy? Shame Lester had to go out." Daniel shovelled crisps into his mouth.

"Y-yes. He was a nice man." Lester Harris, the well-known and eccentric sports commentator had been voted off that night.

Lucy eyed the crisps desperately. She was starving but found it impossible to eat in public.

"Lousy dancer though, despite all the work he put in." Daniel turned and waved at someone on the other side of the bar. "Darlings, will have to love you and leave you for the moment. Just seen Kevin."

At that, Daniel gathered up his glass and two packets of nuts and disappeared in the direction of the show's harshest judge.

Lucy didn't know where to look. She couldn't look to her left as she hadn't got her face under control yet. Instead she stared at the pile of crisps and nuts that Daniel had left. She felt her tummy give a furious growl. She inched her pint nearer and took a tiny sip. It was deliciously cool so she took another.

There was a very long and very awkward pause.

Somewhere to her left she heard Max clear his throat.

"Don't drink much really," he said. He had a nice voice, light with the slightest touch of the north.

There was another pause.

"What with all the training I usually do, it doesn't fit in."

Lucy willed herself to say something. Something witty. Something funny. Blimey, it shouldn't be that hard, she was a writer after all.

"N-no, I'm sure it doesn't."

Was that it? Was that the best she could come up with? She dropped her head slightly and let her hair hide her face. Oh God, this was embarrassing. To have these strong feelings descend on

71

you was so *inconvenient*. And then to have to face the subject of your crush in person was simply mortifying. Get a grip. He's gay, she reminded herself, and he's just trying to be friendly, so make an effort. She blew her fringe out of her eyes and twisted on the stool, tensing herself to finally meet his eyes. But she needn't have worried as Max was staring into the distance, his drink untouched. Oh, but he was so beautiful she thought, a little incoherently. Given this rare opportunity to stare at close quarters, she gazed greedily. His thin face had a strong forehead and deeply set eyes. An aquiline nose swooped down to a firmly shaped mouth that had full, sensual looking lips. His hair was that lovely colour somewhere between blonde and brown and reminded her of the butterscotch Angel Delight she'd always had for childhood Sunday teas. It was cut savagely short in the way some gay men adopt and curled tightly against his head. Lucy felt her mouth drop open and hoped she wasn't drooling.

Max must have felt her gaze upon him because he met her look and smiled.

Her heart gave a sudden and painful lurch. Now Lucy was certain she was drooling. She felt a wave of heat spread through her and basked in his gaze. He had grey eyes, she noticed. Slate grey. Cool and clear.

"Lovely," she breathed.

"Sorry?"

Lucy shook her head. Had she really said that out loud? "The, erm, the show. It was l-lovely. The dresses and sequins and things." Oh God, this was getting worse. At this rate she'd get the Nobel Prize – for inanity!

Max's smile broadened into a grin and a deep groove appeared on his left cheek. It made the smile even more wonderful.

"Of course, you're *Who Dares Dances'* biggest fan, aren't you?"

"I am?" To distract herself from his mesmerising smile Lucy took a long swallow of lager. "Wh-what makes you say that?"

"I saw you in an interview. Last year sometime. You said you were addicted to it."

"Did I?" Lucy's brow furrowed in an attempt to remember. Since 'coming out' as she privately termed it, she'd given so many interviews it was hard to recall exactly what she said in every one. "Oh! Y-you mean, *Who Dares Dances Again*," she said, referring to the *Who Dares Dances* sister show. "I love that programme. Everything about *Who Dares Dances* is so minutely examined." Lucy gave a nervous laugh. "That's how I ended up here. Well, not here exactly," she waved a clumsy arm in the direction of the studio bar, "in the competition, I mean."

Max nodded and picked up his drink. "I remember you saying you'd like to be in it."

"Famous last words!" Lucy relaxed infinitesimally; he was proving easy to talk to.

Max grinned and took a sip of orange squash. "You were promoting your latest book. *The Black Lamp* was it? My nephew loves your Davy Jones books, he's got the whole set."

"Thank you." Of course, a man like Max would be close to his family. And, even in this day and age, it was still difficult for gay men to have children, so he must enjoy having nephews. Lucy beamed at him. "I'll sign a few for him, if you like. I'll dig out some DVDs as well, get them gift-wrapped as an early Christmas present."

"Oh, that would make Will's year, let alone his Christmas. Thank you." Max rewarded Lucy with another entrancing smile.

She grinned back at him, happiness at being in his company – and lager on top of the wine - creating a deliciously fuzzy feeling.

It was still wonderful to hear of a child enjoying her books. Since the first in her series of adventure stories had hit the best seller list, they had rarely left it. The film adaptations meant she was comfortable enough to indulge in little fancies like *Who Dares Dances*. Nowadays life was good. She had fame, fortune and a nice house in the country. Her life lacked very little. Well, maybe a man. She looked at Max who was tearing open a packet of nuts with very white teeth. Not likely to find him here either. But he might be a friend and you could always do with friends. And it was one of her new resolutions that she would make new friends. She felt herself relax just a little more and took another drink.

"So, are you still *Who Dares Dances*' biggest fan?" he asked. He nodded to the dance floor behind them, still thronged with party goers. "I thought you looked pretty good tonight, with Daniel."

Lucy leaned perilously back on her bar stool. Two years of therapy and a stepped progress of mini challenges had resulted in the biggest challenge of them all – entering this part reality show, part fierce dance contest. Maybe it was the alcohol, or maybe it was the kind expression in Max's eyes but she wanted to talk, to share her triumph, to make up for all the years living so solitarily.

"I love to dance," she began. "Always have, from ballet lessons at school to jiving around to the radio at home," she giggled. "But for the last six years, in between writing my books, I've only danced in private. The only audience being Basil." When Max looked puzzled, she added as explanation, "My cat."

"Ah," he said and settled back on his own chair, to listen, an intent look on his face.

"When *Who Dares Dances* started, a few years ago, I adored it from the word go." Lucy smiled, getting into her stride, almost forgetting it was Max she was talking to. "I loved the camp glitz, the frothy neon dresses, the elegance and excitement. But I never dreamed I could ever be part of it."

"Why?" Max frowned. He couldn't think of a reason that this gorgeous creature wouldn't be able to do anything she liked.

Lucy held up a finger to shush him. It wavered only slightly. "I'm just coming to that. The books got successful. I began to get invites to places." Lucy bit her lip as she pictured her mantelpiece, awash with cards inviting her to parties, book awards, literary lunches. She gulped more lager. "I couldn't go to any of them," she said, mournfully, almost to herself. "Nobody knew, you see, nobody knows now, it's a secret. Best selling writer Lucy Everett

74

didn't go out, didn't leave the house. The only people who knew the truth were my father, my best-friend Julia and Whiz."

Max raised his eye-brows. "Whiz?"

"My agent," Lucy explained. "Whiz by name, Whiz by nature." She hiccoughed a little and drained her glass. The barman, seeing it empty, swiftly replaced it with another pint.

"Erm, are you sure you want another drink, Lucy?" Max was disconcerted. He hardly knew the girl and she was getting very drunk. She was also telling him things she might regret sharing in the morning, when sober.

Lucy nodded. "I want to start living a little, Max. I haven't done very much of that so far."

"Well, okay, but have something to eat as well." He retrieved her forgotten packet of crisps, opened it for her and put it next to her glass. "Go on, eat. They might soak up a bit of lager. Look, let's grab some of these little sausages too and these mince-pies." Max slid a plate of forgotten bar snacks over to her. "It's supposed to be the season of indulgence and I reckon, after all that dancing, you've earned it."

Lucy made a face. "Very bossy."

"That's me." He took a crisp himself, and was mollified to see her begin to nibble too. "Are you happy telling me all this, Lucy?"

She nodded vigorously. "I know I can trust you. Don't know why, I just do."

Max took another crisp and eyed Lucy thoughtfully. Whatever was nagging away at her was desperate to come out. "Okay, let's hear the rest. And yes, you can trust me not to let it go any further. I'm all ears."

"Lovely ears," murmured Lucy and then shook her head. "Sorry. I meant you're a good listener."

Max grinned. "Come on then, I've only had half the story, I've a feeling there's more."

Lucy nodded and continued. "Once the film rights to the first Davy Jones adventure had been sold," she explained, "Whiz was determined that I should change." Lucy recalled her agent, in her no-nonsense, hectoring fashion, forcing Lucy to see the best psychotherapist in the country. As Whiz had said, money was no longer an issue. And what was the good of having money when you couldn't use it?

"So I went to have therapy."

"What was it? Agoraphobia?" Max asked.

"Amongst other things," Lucy answered, with a tight smile. Then she lapsed into silence as she remembered.

Progress in her rehabilitation had been slow, painful and erratic. And then, on one glorious spring day, a breakthrough had been achieved. She managed to walk from her father's Oxford home into the nearby park. Dr Frank Everett and Whiz had watched Lucy's stumbling hunched progress, witnessing her tense face and rigid shoulders. She had reached the park, paused, then turned and given two wobbly but triumphant thumbs up.

"After time, I began to improve and now there's no stopping me! Look at me, in *Who Dares Dances*."

Since her recovery, Lucy had gone onto greater things and had even managed a number of public appearances. She coped best if Whiz was on hand to groom her and coach her on what to say to whom. With the publicity, sales of the books rocketed even further. Whiz was ecstatic and Lucy found she could easily afford the house that she had bought in the Oxfordshire countryside which she shared with Basil, a nosy tabby with a penchant for garlic.

"Whiz has been amazing. A wonderful help. A really great friend. But I wanted to see if I could stand on my own two feet, so to speak," Lucy laughed. "I wanted to try something without Whiz or my father's help. When the invitation came to do this, I jumped at the chance."

It had actually been the third offer in as many years and Lucy, a great believer in the power of numbers, this time accepted.

"It's the best thing I've ever done." She smiled a little drunkenly, her eyes shining. "So I suppose, yes, you could say I'm the show's biggest fan!" Lucy took another long drink. The unexpected talking had made her throat sore.

Max stared at her. He wanted to react. Wanted to tell her how amazing he thought she was. His innate shyness held him back. Besides, he had a feeling Lucy still hadn't finished her confessional.

He was right. After ordering yet another pint of lager, Lucy continued to talk, this time almost to herself. It was as if she'd forgotten he was there. She told him about her lonely childhood in Oxford, how she had retreated from life once her mother had died, how devoted she was to her father. Throughout, his admiration for her grew.

Finally Lucy quietened. She slumped back on her stool, her chin sinking onto her chest in sudden exhaustion. The gruelling day of rehearsing, dancing and filming, and now this unburdening of her past had divested her of all energy. She felt emptied, purged but also strangely free. She turned to Max, grateful that he'd been her confessor.

Max gazed at her. Inside him something changed. Then his protective instinct took over. "Maybe it's time we called it a night?" he suggested, gently.

Lucy nodded at him and managed a small smile.

"And I don't know about you but I've got Lola rehearsing me at eight thirty sharp tomorrow morning. I need my beauty sleep. Come on," he continued, as he manoeuvred her off the high bar stool. "Let's get you a taxi and home to your hotel. Are you staying at the Artemida with the others?"

Again, all Lucy managed was a nod. In her head and heart though, the crush shifted and she knew she was in big trouble.

Step Two.

In her stuffy hotel room the next day, Lucy woke up with a raging hangover. She'd never developed a head for alcohol. As she lay there, willing the pain to subside and for her head to stop thudding, she thought back over the previous night. Once the first painful few words were over, Max had proved good company. He was shy, she'd heard he was, and self-contained, but he was good fun. He was an amazing listener and she'd found herself opening up to him in a way she hadn't for years, certainly not to a man, certainly not in a public place. Perhaps it was true that every woman ought to have a gay best friend! Tentatively, she raised her head and tested whether she was able to sit up. Mmm, not too bad. She eased herself into a sitting position and gulped the tepid water from the glass on her bedside table. She was sure she'd made a new good friend, she just wished she hadn't drunk so much.

She rested against the headboard and rubbed her temples, it always eased a headache. She really wasn't very good with alcohol. She frowned and thought back, she hadn't had that much surely? Only three pints; she wouldn't have had two or four as she mistrusted even numbers and it had only been weak lager shandy after all. Oops! She'd had a glass of wine too. That was what had caused the damage, she decided, blearily. Four drinks. Four was never a good number. She'd heard hangovers got worse as you got older but she was only twenty-nine.

Lucy allowed herself a smile, who was she kidding? She was out of practice with more than the drinking side of being with people; she was woefully inadequate at *talking* to people. Her youth, the time when most people went clubbing, drinking, meeting others, had been spent in solitude, writing.

She'd produced five books in six years. It was only when she'd 'come out' that her existence had become interspersed with the odd book signing tour, interviews and, once the film rights had been sold and developed into a series of smash hit films, a few premieres. She'd been steered through the nightmare of publicity by her agent Whiz. As she'd explained to Max, Whiz lived up to her name and whirled round Lucy like a literary tornado organising her, batting away the unwanted, in whatever form it might take, and coaching her to say just the right thing at just the right time to just the right person. The result was that Lucy's public persona was of a polished and professional person, beautifully dressed and smoothly coiffured. It couldn't be further from the truth.

She groaned again and just about managed to ring room service. Once she'd drunk about a gallon of tea, she slid back under the covers to welcome oblivion.

Sometime later, her mobile trilled into action making Lucy wake with a start. Eyes half open, she located it vibrating under her pillow. How it had got there was lost in the fog of last night's excess. She sat up cautiously. The tea and extra sleep seemed to have done the trick. The throbbing in her head had receded to a dull background ache. Pressing answer on her phone, she wondered if it was her new best friend, Max, ringing. She rather hoped it was.

"Hello Luce?"

Definitely not the slightly lazy voice, with its hint of a northern accent, from last night. This voice was throaty and female.

"Julia! Hello!" Lucy shook some sense into her head and settled back against the luxuriously padded headboard.

"Just thought I'd ring to say you were fab last night."

"Oh thank you! I was so nervous though."

"Well, it didn't come across and you've got a real sweetie for a partner so don't worry. Daniel Cunningham got me through last year's competition. Couldn't have done it without him. He's a dream, isn't he?"

"He lovely, so kind and encouraging. I love him already. Do you really think he's gay?"

Julia laughed. "Oh Lucy, you're not developing one of your famous crushes on him, are you? They'll get you into trouble one of these days!"

"No! Just wondered, you know."

Julia blew out a breath and Lucy could hear her thinking. "I never made up my mind about him. I never saw him with anyone, he never mentioned anyone. He just seems married to the dance world if you know what I mean. I don't think it leaves him much time for anything else. He *is* lovely though." She giggled suddenly.

"And I tell you someone else who caught my eye: Max Parry! Where's he been hiding all my life?"

This time it was Lucy's turn to laugh. "In swimming pools as far as I can see. I think he's part fish. He's such a lovely man though. I'm definitely half in love with him."

"Well, he's definitely gay. I told you before, Joe, a friend of a friend of Harri's went out with him."

"It *is* a shame – for women, that is! It's just what I was thinking. He was in the bar last night and we got chatting. He's unbelievably easy to talk to. I found myself telling him all about the weird kid I was and how difficult it is for me to be with lots of people."

"Did you come clean over the agoraphobia? You hardly tell anyone about that. Was that wise? He could run straight to the papers, Luce."

"What, Max Parry? No, He'd never do anything like that, he's simply too nice a man. Besides, he must have had his fair share of hassle with the press himself."

"Well, I don't know about that. I'd never seen anything about him before last night's show."

"Yes well, you're well known for reading the sports pages, aren't you?"

"I am now, Harri makes me." Harri was Julia's boyfriend. They'd met while competing in last year's *Who Dares Dances*.

Lucy laughed again. "Ah! And how is the Welsh Stallion?"

"Oh," said Julia lightly, "stallion like, you know."

"You lucky cow!"

"I am, indeed, a very fortunate girl. He sends his love by the way."

"Send back a big sloppy kiss please will you?". Lucy clamped down on her envy. Julia and Harri were a perfect couple and she wanted just a little bit of that for herself.

"Shouldn't be a problem. We're coming to next Saturday's show, did you know? Can you fix it for me to meet Mr Fish?"

"Shouldn't be a problem," Lucy echoed. "Daniel and I are doing the samba so watch out!" She stifled her unease. It would be her second dance. Number two. With an effort, she tuned out of her obsession with numbers and back into the conversation. "We're doing it to 'Santa Baby', you know, the old Eartha Kitt classic. I'm going to be done up as a Christmas tree, I think. Should be interesting," she added, sarcastically.

Julia hooted. "You'll be a picture! What will they think up next? Although, I have to claim a fondness for the Kylie version. Is Max doing one too?"

"Yup."

"I can't wait! Look, I must go, got that read through this afternoon."

"Good luck with it." Julia was just about to embark on filming the third Davy Jones adventure. It was how they'd met. "I hear the writer is rather good."

"Oh God yes but they're nothing but trouble, don't want the writer around." Julia teased her friend fondly. "But seriously, read throughs, they're always traumatic. Best over and done with. Take care of those two gorgeous men then. See you!"

"Bye, Julia."

Lucy clicked off her phone and tapped it thoughtfully against her lips. Had she really told Max all about her lonely childhood with her eccentric and elderly parents? Had she mentioned St Ursula's, the Spartan girls' school with its old-fashioned emphasis on Latin, Greek and etiquette and, luckily in the light of recent events, ballet? Had she told him about dropping out of Oxford, of being unable to cope with the impossible standards she set herself? Yes she had. Did she regret it, now she was sober? Not one bit, she realised, to her surprise and joy. She trusted Max. She may not know him well but she knew she trusted him completely. And if someone had asked her why, she simply wouldn't be able to explain it.

It was just such a shame he was gay.

Lucy glanced at the clock. She wasn't due for rehearsal for another three hours. She could just do a little bit of scribbling.

Since being more in the world, Lucy had developed an obsession with hotel rooms. One way or another she spent a lot of time in them nowadays. She liked the beige anonymity of them and the fact that, once you'd played with all the toys like the remote controlled curtains and sniffed the freebies in the bathroom, there was very little to do in them. And, when she had nothing to do, she wrote. After a spell in the writing desert, one that had lasted so long it had terrified her, she'd started something that very week. It was new and very different to anything she had written before. Whiz would hate it. From somewhere in Lucy's imagination, Davy Jones' older brother had appeared on the page. Tall and thin, with a serious face only enlivened by a heartbreaking smile, he had a mysterious past and was destined for a fascinating future.

With difficulty, she found out how to turn on the complicated music system and Radio Two flooded the room with, 'I'm Dreaming of a White Christmas'. Ooh, there was a thought, maybe she should set the next book in the winter. A Victorian, snowy Christmas, what could be more romantic?

As Lucy reached for her laptop, she felt the old familiar tingle begin again. She knew this book would be good.

Step Three.

It was the second Monday and Lucy was allowing herself to enjoy rehearsals. Entering this competition had been her own special challenge. Except for her few very close friends, all those around her assumed she was in it to publicise the latest and possibly last Davy Jones novel. And while it was true that the publicity wouldn't do any harm, it was hardly necessary. A Lucy Everett book went straight to the top of the best sellers list and stayed there. Aimed at ten-year-old boys, it was a lucky accident that their parents also enjoyed the exploits of young Master Jones, cunning Victorian thief and adventurer. With the addition of his older brother, Simeon, her books might just reach an even wider audience.

No, this was her own personal test: to see if she had finally beaten her agoraphobia and, more importantly, be her own person in public without the benefit of Whiz whispering what to do next in her ear. She was genuinely fond of Whiz but Whiz, true to her profession, had an eye to the dollar these days. Lucy was now selling well in the States and the agent demanded a heavy workload from her author. With the fifth book out in time for the Christmas market, Lucy really wanted to give Davy Jones a rest for a little while, maybe even permanently. She longed to concentrate on the more romantic novel she'd just begun but she knew Whiz would be reluctant to represent it. Just one more Davy Jones adventure, she'd wheedled, after book number three. And again after the fourth. Now the fifth was finished, Lucy wasn't at all sure Davy had anything left to do. The last book had resolved most of what she'd wanted and, apart from anything else, a *sixth* Davy book wouldn't do at all.

Doing something a bit mad like *Who Dares Dances* had had the desired effect, had got the creative juices flowing again and had inspired her. This romance had promise. And she thought she knew just the man to base her hero on.

As if on cue, Max walked into the rehearsal room with Daniel. Lucy put her hand up in greeting. "Y-you two look very cosy."

"Hey, Lucy!" Daniel waved back.

"Dan's been helping me with my samba." Max wandered over, a worried expression marring his beautiful face. "I just can't get it somehow."

Lucy grimaced in sympathy. "I know what you mean. I've got a horrible feeling I'm going out this week. I'm all arms and legs."

"God, you two, you make a right pair. Lighten up will you?" Daniel shrugged off his tracksuit jacket, wiped his face with it and threw it into a corner of the dance studio. He and Max had obviously been rehearsing hard; Daniel's usually floppy blonde hair was spiky with sweat. Max, in comparison, was looking completely fresh.

He must be so fit thought Lucy as she watched him move

gracefully to the water dispenser, there's not a drop of perspiration on him.

Again, as in the bar, as if sensing her gaze on him, Max turned and asked her if she'd like a drink.

"N-no thanks. Haven't done anything to deserve one yet. You pinched my partner!"

At this Max smiled and the deep groove etched his face.

So beautiful.

"You look cold, Lucy." He looked at her, concerned.

"Yes, it's freezing out there." It was. Lucy had run from the limo into the dance studios, to escape the cold blast of air which had hit her as she'd got out. She tried to focus on the conversation and away from Max's irresistible smile; it was easier to talk about the weather. She shivered, "They've forecast snow this week. And we're due the harshest winter since records began, so they say."

"Oh, they always say that," interrupted Daniel. "Now here's a thought," he continued, his mind obviously on more immediate matters, "why don't you stay and watch me train with Lucy? The two routines aren't all that dissimilar and I can show you how I do those voltas."

Max made a face at Lucy. "You know, sometimes I haven't a clue what he's on about!"

Lucy laughed. God, she liked everything about this man.

"But I don't know about me staying to watch, Dan." Max sobered and looked uncomfortable.

"Lucy won't mind, will you?" Daniel turned to face Lucy with a question on his smooth brown face. He'd seen the way these two had looked at one another. They were obviously attracted to each other but weren't acting on it. He sighed inwardly and wondered why he was in this position of matchmaker *again*. He'd been piggy in the middle between Julia and Harri last year. He hadn't done anything about those two though, he admitted to himself; he'd been too much in love with Julia himself. But Julia and Harri were very different people to the shy couple sharing the room with him at the moment. Max, he knew, was only truly at home with fellow sportsmen; he was struggling with the luvvie world of *Who Dares Dances* and didn't trust it. And as for Lucy, well Daniel had never met anyone quite like Lucy. She had some natural dance talent, honed by childhood ballet lessons, but he'd never met anyone with her peculiar obsessions, or anyone quite as socially awkward. Without a gentle shove, he couldn't imagine her ever giving Max any encouragement and he was certain Max wouldn't make a move without it.

"Lucy," he repeated as she hadn't replied, "you don't mind Max watching us rehearse, do you? It'll be me who he'll focus on. He needs to study my footwork."

Put on the spot Lucy did mind, very much. She hated people watch her do anything. She'd got through the first show in a blind and thankfully numbing terror. And somehow, dancing in front of millions of people was less daunting, less exposing than being watched in the intimacy of the rehearsal studio – by Max.

"I d-don't -," she stammered out.

"Look Dan," Max said kindly, rescuing her. "Lucy's not happy with it, so I'll go." Clutching his paper cup of water, he began to move to the door.

Oh Lord, it would be a miracle if he ever got these two together. Daniel raised his eyes to the heavens for divine intervention. "If you stay, we could all catch some lunch afterwards? The *three* of us," he added, for Lucy's benefit. She seemed to have this weird thing about the numbers three and five.

Max stopped and turned back to them. "It's up to Lucy."

"Well," Lucy began. Come on; make a decision the little voice in her head said. If you say yes, you can spend some more time with him at lunch. If you say yes, it's one more step towards fulfilling your goal of becoming a total exhibitionist. If you say yes, you never know, you might, just might - uh oh wicked, useless thought, you should be ashamed to even think it! - begin to get closer to him.

"Y-yes! I mean, well, alright but only if you think it might be helpful, Daniel."

"I do. Better get cracking then, babe. No more wasting time."

Daniel was suddenly all energy and efficiency. "Max, sit over there out of our sightlines. Don't want you putting Lucy off more than you have to and make sure you watch me and see how I push up from the feet to get the right hip action. And keep an eye out for the rolls. Lola's got you doing lots of those. Got it?"

"Got it," Max said, so meekly that it made Lucy giggle again.

Daniel turned to Lucy with a mock stern expression. "And you, young lady, are going to start believing in yourself. Oh yes, you are," he added as she shook her head. "It's going to be the best 'Santa Baby' samba since the show began. You're a strong, confident, sexy woman. Got it?"

"I'm strong and I'm confident. And sexy. Got it," said Lucy wide-eyed and giggled again. As she'd thought earlier, she was really beginning to enjoy this.

Max settled against a set of dumb bells in the corner of the room. This was a treat, having an excuse to watch Lucy freely. He smiled as she took off her red sweatshirt to reveal the lithe body underneath. The sight made his mouth water and his body gave off unmistakeable signals which told him just how attractive he found her. But Daniel was right, she really hadn't a clue just how sexy she was and that, if anything, made her even more appealing to him. She was tall and coltish, with long arms and legs. The thought that she'd make a good swimmer popped into his head. She verged on the thin side though and he knew that Daniel, as well as trying desperately to boost her confidence, was making her eat sensibly. Lots of protein for quick bursts of energy. Max knew all about that. He'd spent every waking hour thinking about how nutrition affected his performance since he'd entered competitive swimming at the age of twelve. He watched, half ashamed at the thrill it caused, as Lucy stretched upwards in preparation for rehearsal. The only part of her that wasn't slim were her breasts; they were full and lush. She really was beautiful but so different

86

to the woman who had caught his eye on the *Who Dares Dances Again* show last year. Will, his oldest sister's son, had insisted they watch it. Will, a huge fan of the reality programme, was an even bigger fan of Lucy's. Max fervently hoped the two cancelled each other out. He was too laid back to be judgemental about gay men but Will's Cerebral Palsy would be enough of a challenge for him, without having to face another prejudice. As they'd lazed on the sofa together, he'd had to admire Will's taste. On the television screen, he'd seen a bubbly woman with glossy brown hair and a shy smile that made his fingers tingle with desire.

"So who's this then?" he'd demanded, suddenly taking note of who was on the screen.

"Shut up Max and listen. I've told you, it's Lucy Everett. She writes the Davy Jones books."

So he'd shut up and they'd watched in silence, glued to the screen.

When it had been suggested that he enter *Who Dares Dances* - and after he'd stopped laughing, the dealmaker had been finding out that Lucy was a contestant too. He couldn't resist, and once Will had found out, he didn't have a choice. It was do the competition or be snubbed by Will for life. And only an idiot would risk Will's wrath.

And now, as he watched Daniel coax Lucy into the first moves, he couldn't help but compare the nervy stuttering woman he'd talked to a few evening's ago with the woman in the interview. And, after what she'd told him, he couldn't help but admire her bravery for taking part in *Who Dares Dances*.

He thought back over what Lucy had told him, that night in the bar.

Born late to academics, she had endured a solitary childhood being educated at home. When her mother became ill, Lucy had been sent to a school, which would have looked old-fashioned in the fifties. Clever Lucy had won a scholarship to her father's Oxford college but had left in the Michaelmas term. She just couldn't cope, she'd explained, with all those people, all those men. Scenting new blood, they sniffed around and hassled her and she hadn't understood why. Max thought that was when he began to have serious feelings for her - Lucy simply hadn't understood how irresistible she was. A home education by unworldly academics and a girls' school had hardly been the best preparation for a bunch of randy undergraduates. Lucy had dropped out. Her mother's death had forced a retreat into what Lucy trusted best: books. She read and read and when she'd run out of reading matter she'd begun to write. A chance encounter with one of her father's old pupils had secured a publishing deal and Davy Jones, and, in a way, Lucy Everett had been launched into the world. Into a world she hardly understood.

Max watched as Lucy tried to hold a pose and fail, wobbling on uncertain Bambi like legs. His protective impulse, always nestling near the surface of his personality, surged uppermost. Everything about Lucy was a puzzle. He'd enjoyed talking to her but at times it had felt awkward. Lucy was painfully shy and he wasn't much better equipped to deal with the world outside the narrow watery one of competitive swimming. It had been a stilted conversation conducted in fits and starts and only warming up after Lucy had become a little drunk. It had been more than nerves and shyness though, there had been something else constraining their conversation and he couldn't quite pinpoint what it was.

Step Four.
Despite their worst fears, both Lucy and Max survived their ordeal by samba.

"So you live to fight another day!" exclaimed Julia as she clinked glasses with Lucy at the after show party.

"I do indeed," Lucy beamed in response and downed her champagne in one swallow, relief that it was all over making her reckless. "Oh but Julia, I think it was worse than last week. I've never been more scared!"

"Well you hid it extremely well darling and," Julia broke off what she was saying as Max hurtled over and enfolded Lucy in an enormous bear hug. He had to bend down to put his arms round her and Julia was intrigued at the tender way in which he embraced her friend.

"We did it!" He picked Lucy up and whirled her round. "I really didn't think we'd get through this week."

"Oof. Max, erm -" but Lucy's protests were lost in Max's broad back and long arms.

Julia laughed as Lucy's gold dancing shoes swung into the air and her white-bobbled green dress slithered up to reveal slender legs.

Max put Lucy down eventually but still held onto her, as if reluctant to let go. "You were great!"

Julia watched as a blush stole over Lucy's usually pale complexion.

"I, w-well it's all down to Daniel really," she stumbled out.

Max looked into Lucy's eyes. "He got me through this too. Well, you and him really. Watching your training I mean. It was very, erm, inspiring."

Julia's romantic antennae prickled. How very fascinating. Here was this hugely tall man positively glowing. And he was glowing at *Lucy*. Just what was going on? Was it possible that Max Parry was straight? Julia thought back to what Harri had said. No, she remembered, Harri had definitely said Max had been out with a man called Joe.

"Julia!" called a familiar voice, "stop frowning like that babe, it'll give you wrinkles!" Daniel appeared from nowhere and kissed her on both cheeks. "Oh how I've missed you!"

"Daniel! How lovely!" All thoughts of Max's possible sexual orientation fled as Julia turned to greet her old friend.

"Fancy a dance for old times?" Daniel offered his hand in an old-fashioned gesture and a cheeky grin which definitely wasn't.

"Try and stop me!" Looking at Max and Lucy, who were still hugging, Julia grinned. "Shall we leave them to it?"

Daniel led her to the dance floor, making room for a boy in a wheelchair as he did.

"Oi Max, put her down. I'm here!" the boy yelled.

From somewhere below her Lucy heard a thin, slightly slurred voice. Reluctantly she stepped out of Max's embrace and turned to see a skinny boy, of maybe fourteen or so. The boy's head wobbled, as if too heavy for its neck.

Max leaped forward. "Will, me old mate! Did you enjoy it?"

Will raised an eyebrow. "Well most of it was okay." He nodded up at Lucy. "Are you going to introduce me?" he asked meaningfully.

Max laughed and did a half bow. "Of course. Lucy Everett, meet Will Tanner, my reprobate of a nephew."

Lucy hesitated; Max had never mentioned Will's disability. She found it difficult enough to talk to any teenager, let alone one in a wheelchair. The boy sat very still, a beady expression in his eyes, as if knowing exactly how uncomfortable she was.

Eventually she put out a hand and he shook it. "Hello Will. W-what did you think of your uncle's samba?"

"It was crap!"

She heard Max give a belly laugh.

"But you were wonderful," the boy continued. "You looked very beautiful. I love your dress. It was the sexiest Christmas samba I've ever seen."

"T-thank you, I think." Lucy was nonplussed and looked to Max for help. He winked back.

"Haven't you got something to say to Lucy, Will?"

The boy grinned. "Thank you for the books and DVDs. I got them yesterday."

"You're welcome."

"I've read all the books already, of course."

"Yes. Max said you had."

"So, I'll be able to sell them on e-Bay."

"Will!" Max said warningly.

"Only joking!" Will reversed his chair with surprising agility. "I really am your biggest fan, Lucy. I wouldn't dream of selling them." He gave his relative a pointed look. "Max might though, he doesn't read much."

"Well," said his uncle mildly, "the pages get all wet in the swimming pool."

"W-we're just off to get a drink," Lucy said, a little desperately. She wasn't at all sure how to take this alarmingly confident teenager.

"'Bout time. I'm dying for a pint."

Max cuffed Will's ear lightly. "The only pint you'll be getting is one of orange squash."

"Gross! Isn't it about time you drank a proper drink? What's your poison, Lucy?"

Max winked again but this time at Will. "Ah, Lucy *does* like a pint – of lager. First round on me? And is that your sainted mother I see over there, Will?"

"Yeah, she wants to know what your plans are for Christmas. Come on then, lead the way Maxwell the Mighty!" The boy cried. "You may dance like Rudolf with two broken legs but at least you've got the height to get the barmaid's attention. Follow on Lucy, I've got some ideas for another Davy Jones adventure that I want to discuss with you."

Max shrugged at Lucy in apology. "What can I do with him?"

Lucy trailed after them to the bar, listening to the banter between uncle and nephew and enjoying seeing Max in an entirely different light.

Step Five.
The days flew past in a whirlwind of dance rehearsals and publicity. Lucy was, ever so slightly, beginning to regret taking part. *Who Dares Dances* was taking over her life. She hadn't managed to buy one single Christmas present, or even write a card. More importantly, the novel, begun so enthusiastically, remained at thirty thousand words or so. She simply hadn't the time or energy to write very often. She had learned to loathe the long make up

sessions; the pan stick made her skin itch and the vast gallons of hairspray made her sneeze. She'd had no idea just how much hard work it would all be. It was one thing to dance along to Radio Two in the comfort of her own home, it was quite another having to endure Daniel's well meaning but strict tutorage. The one ray of light in a world of gruelling training sessions and nervy night-mare live shows was that she and Max had finally relaxed with one another. She regarded him truly as one of her closest friends. Any other feelings for him were squirreled away and, when she got the chance, written down in the form of Simeon Jones, the irresistible Victorian Rake with the mysteriously gained fortune. She'd left him tracking mysteriously dainty footsteps in the snow and was dying to get back to him.

Two hours after Friday night's dress rehearsal had ended, a frozen-looking Max returned to Studio One from Kings Cross saying that nothing, absolutely nothing was moving out of central London. He'd made a futile attempt to get home to his temporarily rented flat only to find the trains grinding to a halt and refusing to move until morning.

"The snow's really bad just north of the city and it's forecast to be heading our way. The underground and buses are slowly shut-ting down too. It's gridlock out there. I haven't a hope of getting a train from Kings Cross until the morning. You'd better get home now, before it gets any worse," he advised the few dancers who'd remained for a last minute practice. Rehearsals came to an abrupt end, as everyone scattered to pack up their belongings and speed off into the snowy night.

"What about your driver?" Daniel asked, as he buttoned his coat. "Surely he could've taken you onto St Albans? It's not that far."

"Who, Stefan? He's got a terrible cold. He was sneezing all the way back from the station this morning, so I sent him home."

"That was a mistake, mate. Where are you going to stay?" Daniel eyed Max as a mischievous plan formed. "You'll have to share with someone then. "'Fraid I can't put you up though, my old china." He turned to Lucy. It wasn't the most subtle of ideas but it might just do the trick. "Didn't you say your hotel room was quite, erm, roomy?" he trailed off, letting the thought sink in, an amused smile flickering at his lips.

Lucy looked at Daniel in horror. There would be room enough for the entire group, as Daniel knew quite well, but she couldn't share a room with Max. Could she?

"I , I d-don't think—"

Max, in his kind way, took pity on her. "It's alright Lucy, don't worry. I'll find somewhere to stay. Bound to be a room going somewhere."

Lucy thought otherwise. With so many people likely to be stranded, there would be very little accommodation going and certainly not at an affordable price. She and Max were good friends now; surely it wouldn't do any harm to let him stay with her? It wasn't as if he was interested in her in that way, after all.

She took a deep breath and made her decision. "That settles it," she said with unusual resolve. "You can come and bunk up with me at the Artemida."

Max looked startled. "Well, I'll come back to the hotel with you but it might be better if I get a room of my own."

"Are you kidding? Most of the other celebs are staying there as it is; it's been full since I've been living there. And with the snow storm, there'll be nothing to be had for love or ready money."

Max looked down at her, with a grimace. "Really?"

"Trust me. It's happened to me before when I came to town for the Sparklies Award."

Max looked blank.

"Sort of, um, the children's Booker prize," Lucy explained.

"Ah." He grinned. "Did you win it?"

"I did as a matter of fact."

She said it with a hint of smugness that he found very appealing so he grinned even more.

"We'd ... hadn't we, we'd better get going then, hadn't we?

Are you ready to g-go?" All of a sudden Lucy seemed nervy and flustered once again.

He could never understand what made her so. He helped her into her coat and waited patiently while she buttoned and unbuttoned it three times.

"Here, have my scarf. It's absolutely freezing out there. Quite literally." Max took it off and wound it round Lucy's neck. He noticed she flinched as his icy fingers made contact with her neck. He could never quite work out exactly how she felt about him. He bit down on his own feelings and withdrew, even though he longed to caress her bare, warm skin.

They made their way out of the Fizz TV studios, calling their goodbyes to the few remaining dancers, as they went. Daniel watched them go, a satisfied grin embellishing his handsome features.

Max and Lucy's attempt to flag down a cab failed. All those which passed were full of commuters making their desperate attempts to get home.

"Shall we walk, then?" Max asked, looking at the stationary traffic. "It'll be as quick." He glanced down at Lucy's flushed face and into her sparkling dark eyes.

"Why not?" She beamed up at him. "It's not as if we get any exercise nowadays!" He'd never know, she realised, how happy it made her, to be able to take a simple walk outdoors. It was something most people took completely for granted.

Max shouldered their bags easily and offered Lucy an arm. "It's not far, is it?"

"N-no, not that far."

"I know it's cold but it's a really beautiful night." He smiled and tucked Lucy's arm closer into his.

It was a beautiful night. This part of the city had fully embraced the Christmas spirit and had decorated the trees with masses of white lights. Beyond, against the black night, huge snowflakes fell silently, mostly blanketing any noise. With the traffic at a standstill, everything felt very unreal, and very unlike London. Some people were making the most of the situation and had crammed themselves into pubs and restaurants. As Max and Lucy slithered along, laughter and gusts of heat burst out as doors opened to let in more revellers.

"So what's your room like then?" Max asked, thinking of some of the places he'd put up with while travelling the world for competitions. Some of the London hotels rooms he'd experienced had been the worst: small and pokey and ridiculously expensive. "A bit grim?"

A vision of the suite with its Jacuzzi and vast plasma screen swam into Lucy's mind. "Erm, not exactly. Well, you'll see for yourself, soon."

"I'll check at reception to see if they've got another room, shall I?"

"Yes, if that'll make you happy then shall we grab something to eat? I'm sure you must be starving."

Food always made Max happy so he hugged Lucy's arm closer still against the cold. "Sounds like a plan."

They crossed the road, nipping in between cars with 'snow hats' and dodging around some brave cyclists. They found themselves at the entrance to the park opposite the main television studios.

"You know, it's so cold, even my face feels frozen," Lucy laughed. She took in a great breath and spluttered a little. "Not sure I'm too enamoured of the diesel fumes though." She glanced at the ornate park gates, their intricate patterns made magical with frost hoar and then gazed up at Max. "Shall we? It might be a short-cut, although my knowledge of London's streets is a bit hazy, to say the least."

"I'm game," Max replied and hoisted the bags further up onto his shoulder. He swung his arm around Lucy's shoulders and rested a casual hand on the back of her neck. To his surprise and joy, this time she didn't resist his touch.

Away from the heavy foot-fall, the snow in the park was deep and crisp. As they left the bustle of the street behind them, it was as if they were wrapped in their very own world of sparkling-white cotton wool. The only sounds being their crunchy footsteps and their cold gasps for air. There was no lighting along the path but the snow lit their way with a soft gleam and added to the dream-like atmosphere.

In the distance was the faint sound of music. Something Christmassy. As they rounded a corner, past a veil of whitened trees, they came upon a bandstand. It was lit with brilliantly white lights and, standing around a Christmas tree set up at its centre, was a group of musicians and a singer. A few hardy souls in the audience sat at benches, wrapped snugly in coats and hats. There were even a few couples dancing, their bodies made endearingly bulky by their winter clothes.

"Are we dreaming?" Lucy blinked and then looked again. No, the bandstand, with its tree, was still there. As were the dancers. There were streams of white lights stretched across from the bandstand to the winter-bare tree branches beyond, making a magical kind of canopy. Everyone was lit in an arctic white light and, underneath, the dancers drifted slowly across the snow in time to the music.

"Oh, it's so beautiful," breathed Lucy. "So completely beautiful."

Max looked at the band and then back to Lucy. "Shall we?" he asked, with a smile, his voice husky.

"Yes please!"

They made their way nearer. Max stowed their bags against one of the benches and stood expectantly, his arms in a waltz position.

With a happy sigh, Lucy fitted close against him and they joined the gentle sway of the dancers.

The singer crooned something sentimental and Christmassy, something about having a merry little Christmas.

From his position above Lucy, Max had never felt such content-ment, such a sense of being completed by another. He lowered his head, so that it rested on the top of hers and inhaled. Lucy smelled deliciously of strawberry shampoo and her hair lay soft and springy under his chin. Her body, where it touched his, warmed him to his very core.

Max closed his eyes and went with the moment.

But it couldn't last. Max lost all track of time but the band eventually stopped playing. There was applause, the clapping muffled by woolly gloves and people began to collect their things and drift off.

Max held Lucy close, unwilling to give up the magic, refusing to break contact, to let go of the heat coursing through him. He gazed into the distance, through the silhouetted trees and tried to imprint the feeling of her body into his memory.

The band started packing up. The instrument cases made a scraping noise, as they were dragged across the floor. There was a burst of laughter and chatter. It shattered the stillness.

"I suppose we ought to get going, Max," Lucy whispered.

He shifted slightly and looked down into her eyes. They were deep and unfathomable. He had no idea what she was thinking.

"Yes, I suppose we better had," and he broke the hold with the utmost reluctance.

Once at the hotel, as Lucy had predicted, there were no other rooms available. They rejected the services of a porter and wandered in the direction of upstairs. As they stood in the lift she was filled with a weird mixture of happy anticipation at the thought of spending time with her friend and the nagging disappointment this always brought her. From the corner of her eye she watched Max. He still held their two bags high on his shoulder, apparently not noticing their weight. He seemed lost in thought, staring at the panel of buttons, watching as the lights rose up to the top. She loved it when she caught him in this contemplative mood. His brows lowered over the grey eyes darkening them and his mouth pursed, as if on the verge of saying something vitally important. The action hollowed his already thin cheeks and made him look even more the Adonis the press had nicknamed him.

He was so beautiful she thought for the nth time. It was the only epithet which came to mind when describing him. He was beautiful, on the outside certainly but, far more importantly, on the inside too. It was just such a shame he was gay. She let out a sigh.

He smiled down at her. "You okay, Lucy?"

"Tired."

Max nodded. "Been a long day. And another one tomorrow. Show day."

"It's relentless, all this, isn't it?"

"What do you mean?"

Lucy thought of how she'd scraped through her samba last week. The judges had again said she was technically competent but lacked interpretation. She had no idea what that really meant.

"Well, you lurch from one thing to the other," she began, "and as soon as one dance is over and you have a nano second of relief and pleasure at getting through, you have to pick yourself up and begin all over again the next day."

Max rubbed a hand over his shorn hair in a weary gesture. "Thank God it's another ballroom dance tomorrow. Although it's a rumba next week."

"I'm dreading that one." Lucy shuddered. She wasn't looking forward to the rumba. It was a dance which demanded *interpretation*.

"Me too. Think it could be my ticket out."

"Don't say that, Max. Remember what Daniel always says: 'Keep positive and remember, we are all sexually charged animals!'" Lucy managed a laugh.

Max shrugged moodily. At this precise moment he'd much rather forget he was a sexually charged animal. Tonight, he would be caged in a small hotel room with someone for whom his feelings were threatening to spiral out of control. It was going to be a trial, far greater than any of his Olympic swimming ones. He stood back and let Lucy lead the way, trying not to notice how her bottom wiggled so appealingly.

Lucy let them both into the penthouse with the key card and stood back to enjoy Max's reaction.

He put the bags down and stood, hands on hips, for a long

minute. After his silence he turned to her. "Oh yes, this is a real dump." He pointed to the TV screen taking up most of one wall. "I mean, how could you put up with that paltry little thing?" He moved to the sofas and ran his hand over the upholstery. "And these, why they're positively shabby." He looked at the two doors leading off the main room. "Bedroom and bathroom I suppose?"

Lucy grinned. "Only a jumbo sized bed and a jacuzzi though, I'm afraid."

"Shocking." Max shook his head and adopted Kevin's lisping campness. "How have you managed to put up with all this squalor, darling?"

Lucy clasped her hands to her bosom and fluttered her eyelashes. "I really don't know how I've coped." She put a hand to her head and executed a mock swoon.

Max couldn't resist any longer. Taking her in his arms again, he led her in a swift waltz around the vast coffee table and then lowered her back into a dip. "Fantastic place to rehearse," he murmured. He pulled her back upright but held her in place and, for a moment, they stared into one another's eyes. His sensual mouth hovered above hers for a tantalising second.

Lucy panicked. On top of the all-encompassing romance of their strange interlude in the park, it was too much to cope with. He was doing things to her insides that no man ought to, let alone one who had no intention of following through. "F-food?" She pushed at him and he released her immediately.

Max got the message and regretted putting her in a position where she was forced to reject him. "Food," he agreed and tried to recover his composure. Being so close to her had shaken him.

"Room service?" Lucy passed over a menu.

Max smiled thinly. "Room service I think. Why bother with the dining room when we have all this?"

Lucy nodded relieved, she still wasn't happy about eating in public. "Have a look and see what you want. I'm going to, um, to have a bath."

She fled into the bedroom. Closing the door, she laid her hot face against the cool beech wood door. Was she going to be able to get through this? After a while and feeling a little more composed, she scuttled back out, went through to the bathroom and began to swish scented oil into hot water. That might relax her, that and getting into her M&S men's pyjamas.

They decided to slum it. Ignoring the six-seater dining table nestling against the balcony door, they commandeered a sofa each and ate off trays. Both wore the matching snowy white bathrobes provided.

Lucy just wished she thought Max had something on underneath his. To take her mind off the distracting sight of his attractively tanned legs she concentrated on her food.

"Y-you know usually I hate eating in front of people but I don't mind with you," she gabbled and took a slug of wine.

Max nodded, his mouth full.

"I always feel relaxed with you, Max." It was mostly a lie but sometimes Lucy *did* feel relaxed with Max. That was, when he wasn't settled on a sofa opposite her, with his long legs stretched out from under the white robe and the certain knowledge she had that he was wearing only skin underneath.

"Good." Max reached for his glass of wine and took a sip. He'd been very hungry and thirsty and the food was slaking one type of hunger, at least. The other would just have to remain unsatisfied tonight.

It was no good, now Lucy couldn't take her eyes off his naked feet; they were very large with long narrow toes, which for some reason, she found very sexy. "Is y-your, um, is your steak good?"

"Very. What about your salmon?"

Lucy looked down at her plate. So that's what she'd been eating. "It's fine." She shrugged. "I don't think about food much, I suppose it's just fuel." She trailed off as she saw the look of amazement on Max's face.

"But it's one of life's great pleasures," he exclaimed, "along with—"

"Along with what?" Lucy looked at him innocently.

Max thought fast, why did his brain keep doing a fast-loop back to sex? It wouldn't do. "Wine," he answered and set his empty plate on the floor. "I like to cook, Sarah my eldest sister taught me. It's a big part of my life. I have to eat carefully when I'm in training."

"I should imagine you do. I forget to eat at all sometimes, if I'm in the middle of writing."

Max shook his head; it was impossible to understand Lucy sometimes. He was a big man with an appetite to match. When he was in full training, he needed to eat every few hours or he just keeled over. She needed someone to look after her, he thought, as he watched her pick at her fish. And, he realised, he wanted to be the person who did it.

"I'd like to cook for you one day," he said. "I'll do my best to convert you to the delights that good food can offer."

"That would be really lovely. Perhaps we can ask Dan too?"

"Yeah, okay," Max said, puzzled. The three of them sharing a meal hadn't quite been his intention. It was no good; he really didn't understand what made this woman tick.

'Meet me in St. Louis' flickered on the TV as they made their way through the rest of the bottle of wine. Judy Garland began to sing the same song they had danced to in the park. They fell silent for a moment, listening to the yearning emotion. The memory of the feel of Max's strong body against her own hit Lucy with a punch. She felt empty inside, only filled with an aching need that would never be met. Not by him. "Tell me something about yourself," she insisted, in an attempt to dispel the mood.

So Max told her about the happy childhood home he'd shared with his three sisters. About Will. Of how close-knit the family was. Of his nomadic lifestyle entering swimming events all over the world. It had been lonely at times, he admitted, it made making any lasting friendships or relationships difficult. "Not that I've been a monk of course."

101

Lucy looked at him, at the strong tanned neck and broad shoulders. "No I'm sure you haven't been a monk. We've led very different lives haven't we? You and I, we're polar opposites."

Max shrugged. "In a way I suppose. But we both like to disappear, don't we?"

"What do you mean?"

"Well, you hole up and write your books."

"And where do you go to hide?"

Max grinned. "The water of course. I hide in the water."

"So you *are* part fish."

Max laughed. "Very probably, it's certainly where I feel most at home." He yawned and stretched and uncrossed his legs. Lucy tried not to focus on where the robe threatened to gape. It just wouldn't do to think like that about this man. He was out of bounds.

Sadly.

She put her glass down. "Y-yes, we ought to go to bed, it's getting late."

"I suppose I'm on the sofa?"

Lucy looked doubtfully at the cream settees. Although they were huge it was unlikely someone as tall as Max would get any sleep on one. She shook her head. "You won't be able to stretch out on one of those. You take the bed and I'll kip out here."

"Oh Lucy, I can't let you do that, it's your hotel room. *I'll* take the sofa."

"Well, that's madness. I'm much shorter, we've both got a long day in front of us tomorrow and we need our sleep."

Max frowned. "No, I'm not going to let you do that."

"But what's the alternative?" Lucy shrugged and spoke before thinking, "that we share the bed?"

"You did say it was a big one."

"It's enormous. It's one of those waterbeds, you know, like sleeping on a massive Lilo but more comfortable I'd imagine. I haven't ever slept on a Lilo, y-you understand." Nerves were making her prattle as always. "It's a fantastic bed," she added lamely.

"Shall we try that then?" Max paused, suddenly uncomfortable. "Lucy, you do know you're safe with me, don't you? I won't try anything. I promise."

Lucy managed a smile. "No, I know I'm safe with you. I trust you completely Max. It's not like that between us, is it?"

"Erm, no. No, it's certainly not like that between us." He tried to keep the regret from his voice.

Lucy stood up with sudden decision and smoothed down her bathrobe. "B-better go to bed then, it's past midnight."

"Better had. You go first."

Max watched as she left the room and wondered how he was going to get any sleep. He was sure she thought she looked as sexless as possible in her grey flannelette pyjamas and tightly belted robe but she was wrong. As wrong as she could possibly be. He dropped his head into his hands. He kept getting conflicting signals from her. They got on so well. Lately he'd felt as relaxed with her as she claimed she did with him, but then she would get all nervy and edgy and would back off like a frightened fawn. He simply couldn't read her at times. "Too long swimming with the fishes, Max my boy," he muttered to himself. "Perhaps this is what it's like in the real world? Lots of game playing." But, as he rose and busied himself by putting their dirty dishes back onto the room service trolley, he realised that Lucy wasn't like that. For too long he hadn't been part of the real world, but for even longer, Lucy hadn't been either. She was no game player. As a delaying tactic, he plumped up the cushions and tidied the sitting room. Living with three nagging sisters had left him with an ingrained sense of how to leave a room. It made him an unusually tidy man. With a last glance around, he snapped off the lights with the remote and went into the bedroom.

The bed was, as promised by Lucy, blissfully comfortable and so vast even he had plenty of legroom, even if he did have to lie at a slight diagonal. Exploring the cool sheets and enjoying the sensual movement of the water mattress he accidentally touched toes with Lucy. They both snatched their feet apart as if burned.

"G-goodnight Max," Lucy whispered.

"Night Lucy," Max answered and rolled as far away from her as possible. He wasn't sure if he could trust himself. But if he thought he would lie awake puzzling further over Lucy's erratic behaviour he was wrong. He fell asleep in an instant.

The wake up call roused him with a start.

Lucy awakened, bleary and a bit hung-over. She was hot and threw the duvet off and then tugged open the neck of her pyjamas, squirming as she did so.

"Don't do that!" said a masculine voice in her ear.

She froze. She had no idea how they had moved together in the night but now Max was on his side close behind her, his length curled protectively around her like a long comma. Her bottom was tucked securely into his groin.

"Why not?" It came out as a strangled whisper.

"Oh Lucy, don't you know?"

Lucy stopped fidgeting immediately. She'd had no idea that gay men found the bodies of women quite so repulsive. "S-sorry. So sorry. Shower? B-breakfast?" She was gabbling yet again.

Max let out a great sigh. "You go first. I'll order us something to eat." He watched covertly as she scurried out of the room pulling her robe round her. He tried hard to ignore the arousal pulsating through him. She was impossible. A peculiar mixture of the provocative and naïve. And he knew he was falling in love with her.

As Lucy waited for Max to finish up in the bathroom she couldn't help but notice how impeccably tidy the sitting room was. He'd cleared everything away so that the room service staff could simply collect the trolley and replace it with one containing their breakfast. She blew out a breath and her fringe shot upwards. It was one consolation she supposed, of sleeping with a gay man. He most definitely didn't leave the place looking a mess.

The show day sped past. Both Lucy and Max got through with their dances; for Lucy an American smooth and Max a fox-trot. Although Max garnered the fewest votes and was at the bottom of the leader board again, by some miracle the public rallied and kept him in. It was a close call though and Lucy could see it affected his confidence. He seemed newly defeated somehow. The dance off was between Angie, a star of musical theatre and Lenny Warrington, the rugby international. Lenny looked devastated to be sent home and a flash of guilt stabbed at Lucy at being able to stay in.

Step Six.

On Monday, Bob Dandry the producer, called a meeting in the main studio. After last year's twist, when the celebrities had to dance with one another in the Christmas special (Lucy had loved hearing Julia's account of how it had forced she and Harri together), the assembled gathering knew something was afoot.

"Just hope it's not dancing on roller blades," whispered Daniel in Lucy's ear making her giggle.

When she'd signed up for the series, she'd known something extra would be demanded of her but no one so far had any clue as to what it might be.

"Boys and girls, so pleased that you could all join me," Bob began, his head nodding in the way some pompous middle-aged men had. "I know you'll be dying to hear what this year's Christmas special will consist of and so I'll put you out of your misery right away."

"About time," muttered Max on the other side of Lucy.

He was looking strained today she thought, the thin face looked gaunt even and there were deep shadows under each stormy grey eye. With an effort, she tuned back into Bob.

"Right folks, this year we'll be asking you to learn the skill of one of the other competitors." Bob paused for dramatic effect.

He wasn't disappointed. An audible gasp passed around the room. They'd all assumed it would be some kind of *dance* challenge.

"Christ Almighty," breathed Max. "What the hell am I going to get? The only thing I can do is ruddy swim!"

"There will be, of course, a comprehensive programme of training available," Bob droned on, "but we will expect the celebrity you are partnered with to take on the majority of the work. Cameras will follow you round as usual and the celebrities who have already sadly gone out of the competition will take part too."

Lucy's mind was screaming. She thought over the options. Swimmer, stand up comedian, actress, rugby player, cricketer, television presenter; they all seemed equally awful and impossible. She was sure she wouldn't be able to do any of them.

"We've thought very carefully about how we paired you all up and we wanted to give you all a challenge that was completely opposite to what you normally do. So here is the list."

As Bob read through who was to be paired with whom Lucy barely took in the information, that was, until he came to her name.

"And now we come to our best-selling children's writer. We thought long and hard about this one but decided that the perfect challenge for our lovely Lucy was to train as an Olympic swimmer. Therefore, she will be paired with Max. Max of course will have to attempt to write a story! We'll let him off the full eight hundred pages but he'll need to produce at least a good length short story. Perhaps with a Christmas theme, Max? No pressure, though!

"And that's all folks. Any questions, just ask my assistant, Maria. Stay happy and remember: who dares, dances! Keep dancing everyone and I'm sure the Christmas show will be a Christmas cracker!"

A collective moan rippled through the room at the awful pun. The dancers and celebrities milled round excitedly, some stopping to share Lucy's panic. She looked round for the support she knew would come from Max and Daniel but they were nowhere to be seen.

Daniel had seen Max slink out of the studio. He could tell from the set of his shoulders that he was going through a low patch. It happened to them all, at some time or another. They all reached that point at which everything seemed hopeless. For Max, thought Daniel, as he followed him, it was worse than for anyone. Max had explained to him, without an ounce of arrogance, that he was used to being good at what he did. He was used to being the best, at coming out top. Holding last position on the leader board for three consecutive weeks did no one's confidence any good. Added to that was the fact that Kevin the judge reserved a special line in insults for Max and they were becoming increasingly personal. Max, not being from the world of show business, simply didn't understand such casual bitchery. He was one of the nicest men Daniel had ever met; he didn't deserve the treatment.

"You all right, mate?"

Max was sitting cross-legged on the rehearsal room floor, studying his laptop. On it was the film of Harri and Julia dancing the rumba in last year's Christmas Special.

Maybe that was it, thought Daniel, for a big man like Max the rumba would be difficult.

Max clicked shut the lid of the computer and looked up. "Yeah." The answer was unconvincing.

"No you're not. What's up? The dancing?"

"Yes and no."

Daniel handed Max one of the coffees he'd brought and sat down next to him. "Intriguing. You want to explain?"

There was a long silence and then Max spoke. "I - I don't know if I want to carry on with this anymore."

"With this?"

Max gestured to the rehearsal studio. "This competition."

Daniel shook his head. "Don't believe you, Max. You may be a gentle giant but you're a sportsman. We've never had a sportsman drop out. They always rise to the challenge. And you will too."

Max blew out an enormous breath.

"It's not the dancing, is it?" Daniel looked at his friend curiously. "Is it Lucy?"

"No. Well, yes … in a way."

Daniel made himself more comfortable. "You want to tell?" He shrugged. "I might be able to help."

Max looked at Daniel with a wretched expression on his face and scrubbed a hand over his tightly curling hair. "Don't think you'll be able to get me out of this mess, Dan."

After Bob's startling announcement, Lucy had to give an interview for a children's magazine and was late getting to rehearsal. She barged into the dance studio and stopped dead at the sight of Daniel with his arm round Max's shoulders.

"S-sorry. Sorry, didn't mean to interrupt." God, this was so embarrassing and she was making it worse. "I'll come back, Daniel, if you're busy."

Both men looked up at her. Max rose to his feet.

"No, you're okay. I'm calling it a day." He strode to the door. "I'll see you both tomorrow."

Lucy stared as he brushed past and disappeared. "What's wrong, Dan? Is Max all right?"

Daniel gathered up the empty coffee cups, a worried expression on his tanned face. "No babe, I don't think he is."

Step Seven.

The next week was ridiculously busy. Not only had Lucy to rehearse for the rumba, a dance that didn't come easily to her, she also had to cope with the publicity that Whiz had organised.

"Got to strike while the iron is hot, darling," her agent had said. "And boy, are you a hot iron at the moment!" She'd shown Lucy the photographs which had appeared in a national broadsheet. "Look, *The Telegraph* has adopted you! And that won't hurt. Any sign of Book Number Six yet?"

Lucy had fudged the issue but it was useless, Whiz always sensed when she had a book on the go. If only she knew the truth. Lucy was longing to return to the nineteenth century where Simeon had just encountered the Lady Clemency: society beauty by day and jewel thief by night. She'd been up until three that very morning, fervently tapping it all out on her laptop. And then she'd had to contend with Daniel in rehearsal, getting unusually impatient with her slowness.

And, if that weren't enough, she had to arrange a swimming lesson with Max and get him to a writing workshop. Daniel had shown interest in coming along too, as if he couldn't bear to leave his friend's side. Lucy would have thought it sweet, if her own raging lust for Max had abated. But the crush showed no sign of disappearing and Lucy had no idea how to cope with her feelings, never before having to face the object of her emotions on a daily basis. The cameras' incessant presence made it all the more stressful and Lucy was wondering just what she had taken on.

The crew followed her to the Crystal Palace swimming pool on Wednesday, where they were to film her first lesson with Max. The swimmer had a loyal female fan base, which Lucy thought ironic in the circumstances and the director of *Who Dares Dances* was keen to get as many shots of Max in his trunks as possible.

Lucy found travelling alone a great trial, so she concentrated on the breathing strategies she always used to get from A to B. "Just remember what Dr Froggatt taught," she muttered, as an incantation to get her from the hotel to the sports centre. She was so deep into her exercises that she forgot that, she too, would be practically naked in front of the television audience. But Lucy was ambivalent about her body. It was something to merely feed and clothe. She rarely gave it a thought.

She was preoccupied while tugging on her swimsuit. She hadn't swum since being at St Ursula's. She just hoped she could remember what to do. As she stepped out into the swimming pool and into a wall of heat, a solo cameraman with a handheld hovered to her left. She knew he was waiting for the moment when she removed the thin robe she had on. And then she saw Max, sitting with his legs dangling in the shallow end, and all rational thought fled.

He looked a different man in his own world. The self-doubt and lack of confidence she'd witnessed in him had gone. Wearing only a very brief pair of Speedos, he sat unselfconsciously talking to the teenage boy next to him. Max's back was ramrod straight showing off the lean muscles on his chest to perfection. He and the boy were in an animated conversation which ended as Lucy walked towards them. She'd never seen Max looking lovelier, or as comfortable in his own skin. Literally. It was about the only thing he was wearing.

Max spotted her. "Hi Lucy!" he said and then clapped the boy on the back and wished him good luck.

The boy eyed Lucy. "You too, Max. I'll be voting for you!"

Lucy watched as he sauntered off. She was puzzled; she'd thought the pool was closed to the public for this morning's filming.

"Shane Amory," Max said as he followed the direction of her gaze. "Next Team GB hopeful. Got bags of talent and only fifteen. He'll be at his peak for the next big competition if we're lucky. He's just finished a training session with me."

"Oh. I d-didn't know you trained people," Lucy managed, trying not to think about Max's glorious body currently on display. "Yourself, I mean."

"Best part of the job. I'd like to do more but I haven't the time at the moment. It's the most rewarding thing I do."

"What, better than winning all those medals?"

Max shrugged his broad shoulders. "Yeah, I think so. Passing on the skills. Seeing boys like that improve. He couldn't swim at all three years ago."

Lucy looked to where Shane was collecting his towel and waved. The boy grinned and waved back. "That's amazing."

"*Shane* is amazing."

"Perhaps it's more to do with his coach?" Lucy ventured a smile.

"Well, maybe." He laughed but without ego. "Are you ready?"

"Yes, well I think so. Maybe."

"You'll have to take that off, Lucy." He nodded to the scarlet robe that the girls in wardrobe had insisted would 'grab' the lens.

"What? Oh, yes." For the first time Lucy felt self-conscious. She was sure she'd be fine once in the water but would have liked some sort of teleporter in order to get her the short distance from the side into the inviting blue. The cameraman nosed in for the shot.

As if sensing what she was feeling Max turned away from her and slid in. He executed a graceful twist and then stood up. The water barely made it to the top of his thighs.

Lucy hurriedly averted her eyes from the water streaming down Max's muscles and shrugged off the robe. Making a swift decision, she held her nose and jumped in. She surfaced next to him and was very aware of the man's nearly naked body. She gulped, swallowed water and coughed violently.

"Are you alright?" Max asked. "You did say you could swim quite well." He held her under the shoulders to steady her. Like the rest of him, his hands were large and they brushed the side of her nylon-covered breasts. Lucy blushed pink and escaped his grasp. She did an ungainly and very splashy front crawl into deep water and then had to pause to get her breath back. Max swam after her, using half the energy and swimming twice as fast.

He trod water beside her. "Well, you've proved you can swim," he said with a grin, "but we'll have to work on your technique if you're to swim a couple of lengths of this pool."

Lucy nodded, not having the breath to speak. She'd thought she'd got this crush under check but it was threatening to go somewhere she didn't recognise. It wasn't simply that Max looked physically perfect – he did – it was the air of complete power and confidence that exuded from him today. He was in his natural element, where he felt most at home. Where, he said, he came to hide. Lucy thought back to how unhappy he'd looked the other

111

day and wondered what it was that he was hiding from.

He swam closer and eyed her curiously. "Are you sure you're alright Lucy?"

She nodded again. The crush couldn't be called that any more. She knew, without a doubt, that she was in love with this man. Tears threatened and she brushed at her eyes, hoping Max would think she was just getting rid of pool water. The love she felt so longingly for him simply couldn't be.

"Let's get started, shall we?" Max said kindly.

In the car on the way home, memories of her swimming lesson blanketed the anxiety she normally felt at having to travel without Whiz or her father. Max had been gentle and patient, even when she'd struggled to grasp the finer points of technique. Leaning back, as her driver negotiated the traffic, Lucy felt immensely warm and relaxed. As she lifted a hand to brush still damp hair from her face, she smelled chlorine. It brought back the vivid memory of how Max's huge hands had supported her hips while she practised the correct leg stroke. She could still feel his silky touch as he corrected her arm movement, his smooth wet body sliding over hers, showing her what to do, his hot breath murmuring encouragement in her ear. The bath-warm water had made everything seem slow and languid and dream-like. A breath caught in Lucy's throat. It had all been impossibly erotic.

Back in the swimming pool, Max reached the end of the lane, did a swift underwater turn and returned the way he'd just swum. He'd already done thirty furious lengths and the burning he felt for Lucy still hadn't abated. The swimming lesson had been disastrous; he wanted her all the more now. Why, he cursed himself, hadn't he stayed on the side and coached her from there? That's what he usually did when training someone. But he'd given into his feelings and it had been his undoing. He put new energy into his front crawl and ignored the knowledge that the lifeguards were waiting to open the pool to the public. Well, they'd just have to wait a little longer. For once in his life, Max Parry was going to be selfish. He needed to be.

Step Eight.

Lucy pulled at the dress but no matter how hard she tried, it just didn't feel comfortable. It had felt fine during the fitting but something had gone wrong since. The live Saturday show was due to start in twenty minutes and she and Daniel were to dance first. Lucy was dreading it. It was the rumba. And, to make matters even worse, her costume just wasn't right.

"Don't fiddle with it," Daniel said in a calming voice. "It's nearly time to get into the studio."

Daniel was on guard in Lucy's dressing room, as was his habit. He always did this in the hour before the live show began. He knew that, given half a chance, Lucy would slide out of the door and run off into the cold December night, faster than Santa with a forgotten present. And tonight, the chances of her doing this, were high. As the weeks had gone on, instead of becoming more confident, she was getting worse and tonight she was as jumpy as he'd ever seen her. She'd been muttering about it being the fourth dance but, for the life of him, he couldn't see the relevance. He glanced over as he saw her pick irritably at the shoulder strap. He suspected the cause of her nerves lay in her lack of confidence with her rumba. Technically, she'd picked up the steps quickly but she was too uptight to feel the *mood* of the dance.

"Dan, it doesn't feel right. I'm convinced it's going to give way halfway through and there's a lumpy bit sticking into my shoulder blade." Lucy heaved at the strap again. Her dress was one shouldered, but had been cunningly built around a bodice engineered with sections to support Lucy's not inconsiderable bosom. The problem lay with the flesh coloured safety strap that was cutting into her shoulder and making any arm movement stiff and awkward.

Daniel laughed but not unkindly. "Well, flashing your boobs should get a few votes coming our way."

Lucy poked her tongue out at him and tried to raise her right arm above her head. "I can't go on and dance in this!" Then she gaped in horror as a violent twang reverberated around the tiny room. Her right side felt suddenly very loose.

"Oh God, what have I done?" She twisted in front of the dressing room mirror to see what had happened. "It's snapped, the strap has snapped!"

Daniel sprang into action. "Get it off."

"W-what?"

"Get it off and I'll find Roxie. She's the only one who can repair stuff at this short notice."

Lucy glared at him. He might well be gay but she wasn't going to strip naked in front of him. "But I haven't got anything else to put on!"

"I won't be a tick and anyway it'll take you ten minutes to get back into it. No," he added, as she began to argue, "you haven't got time to find anything else to wear." He gave up. "Lucy, just take the damned dress off!"

"Turn your back then."

"Lucy!"

"Turn your back and hand me that towel."

Daniel handed over the only one in the room; a small hand towel and turned to face the door. He tried not to look but it was tempting. She may be as barmy as a basketful of kittens but the girl was built.

Getting the dress off was easier said than done. All the women's costumes were built around a leotard base that was very tight fitting. Lucy yanked and pulled but, without a dresser, it took an effort. At last it pooled round her ankles. She snagged it with the toe of her dancing shoe, kicked the emerald scrap of material up into the air and caught it. Under it, all she wore was a pair of tiny black briefs. Clutching the towel to her breasts, she handed the dress to Daniel who raced out of the dressing room in search of Roxie.

114

Lucy shivered. She felt very naked but, strangely also very freed. She pulled a face at her reflection. If Daniel couldn't find Roxie maybe they could dance later in the order, or better still, not at all? Miracles happened. She allowed herself a jittery giggle. It was the *fourth* dance that was the problem. To distract herself she examined her body more closely. She hadn't really taken much notice of it before. It had changed over the last three months. The regime of hard physical exercise and healthy food had had an effect. There were subtle muscles in her arms and legs now and a new curviness to her body that balanced her large breasts better.

"Not bad," Lucy stuck her tongue out again but this time to her own reflection. "Not bad at all." Then she caught sight of the bits that had escaped the fake tan sprayed on so enthusiastically by the make-up girls. Her white buttocks looked comically pale in contrast to her arms and legs. Lucy giggled again and then stilled as a knock sounded on the door.

"You didn't need to knock, Dan," she turned and then gasped. It wasn't Daniel Cunningham who stood there but Max. Lucy snatched at the skimpy towel and blushed furiously. Just as well he had a thing for Daniel, she thought, and hysteria bubbled up.

"Oh God, I'm sorry." Max stared, fixated on the luscious breasts, only just hidden by the towel. He tore his eyes away and looked at his feet. "Dan had to - I've just seen him in the corridor. He had to, um, here, he asked me to give you this." At this, he thrust the dress at her and crashed out of the room.

The corridor was thick with dancers, cameramen and runners so Max fled to the chill and quiet of the courtyard at the back of Fizz's TV studios. Apart from a lone refugee smoker, it was deserted. Max sank down onto a low wall and put his burning face into his hands. A vision of Lucy's naked loveliness swam into his head and sent heat surging to other parts of his body. He'd have made a move long ago, if only he thought it would be welcome. To be fair, Daniel had hinted as much. But, however friendly Lucy was, Max always had the sense that she held back. There

115

was restraint in her brown eyes, almost a sadness, and it made him unsure. It began to snow again, just a little, thin mean little flurries that probably wouldn't amount to anything. As he stared up into the unforgiving cold, he forced a laugh. She'd done him one favour at least, he wouldn't have to struggle for inspiration to sex up his rumba.

"Max?" said a low voice.

Max looked up, relieved to have a diversion from the images circling his brain. Bob Dandry stood in front of him, a cigarette glowing in his hand.

"So pleased to bump into you. I need to have a word with you, Max, would that be possible?"

Step Nine.

"So Max is out then?" Julia asked on the phone later that night. She always rang, too impatient to wait for the official results show the following day. "What a shame!"

Lucy collapsed onto a gilded chair at the back of the television studio and frowned into her mobile. She watched as crew, competitors and their guests milled onto the dance floor.

"I don't understand it. Max danced much better than Angie in the dance off. She fluffed her steps all over the place and she nearly fell over at the start." Lucy shook her head. "It's Kevin, I'm sure it is. He's had it in for Max ever since the beginning." She glowered at the three *Who Dares Dances* judges strolling off the set. Two out of three judges had ousted Max in the vote off.

"Well, you've got to admit that Max isn't the most natural of dancers."

"I know he isn't Julia, but he's worked so hard. He's put in over thirty hours of training this week and he really was the better dancer."

"Well, he's obviously got a fan in you! How's it going with you two?"

"There isn't 'an us two,'" Lucy said gloomily, "although, come

116

to think of it, we did have an interesting encounter earlier tonight. Perhaps that was what put him off his dancing!" She filled Julia in on what had happened in the dressing room, explaining Max's embarrassment and sudden departure. "He did seem to be admiring my boobs though," she added, as she remembered the look on Max's face as his eyes travelled down her body.

"Are you sure he's not straight?"

"Positive. He and Dan have got it together. I caught them at it in the dance studio the other day."

Julia sighed. "Ah, how sweet, they make a lovely couple."

"Well, maybe but I'd rather not think about the squelchy things that go on between them, thank you very much." Lucy said primly.

Julia roared. "Is that the green-eyed monster I hear? So who have you got the crush on then? Daniel or Max?"

Lucy ignored the sudden image of Max helping her out of the swimming pool, of how he'd held her to him as she'd slipped on the wet tiles. For one blissful second his long arms had enveloped her and her breasts had pressed against his warm, wet chest. And then he'd dived back in, his long lean body arrowing efficiently into the water.

"Lucy? Are you still there?"

"Yeah, still here. Look Julia, I've got to go. Max and Daniel are calling me over. No doubt for the usual post-mortem in the bar. Catch up tomorrow?"

Lucy walked towards the two men. Embarrassment flickered as she thought back to her dress disaster earlier that evening. She'd been practically naked in front of them both tonight, not that it mattered, she supposed. They were standing close together, talking earnestly. If they hadn't beckoned her over, she wouldn't have joined them; it seemed too much of an intrusion.

Max looked preoccupied. He must be disappointed to be going out, she thought. Any lingering unease fled. "I'm so sorry," she said and reached for his hand. "I thought you were the better dancer by far tonight."

Max leaned down and kissed her on the cheek. "Thanks Lucy, that means a lot, especially coming from you." Glancing at Daniel, he asked him to buy the drinks. "I just need a minute with Lucy, okay?"

Daniel nodded. "I'll be in the bar. A pint as usual, Lucy?" He asked it with a smile. It never failed to amuse him that she drank pints of lager.

Lucy put a hand to her face where Max's lips had touched. "What do you want, Max?" She followed him as he led them to the chairs at the back of the television studio. Her imagination went into overdrive. Maybe Max was going to tell her that he'd been mistaken, that he and Daniel had split up, it was Lucy he truly loved, after all. Nerves made her gabble as usual. "You know, we've still got to organise a writing lesson together, although I don't know when we'll fit it in. Next week's as mad as this one and Daniel said he'd like to come as well. Maybe I've got two budding writers on my hands?"

"Sit down Lucy. Please."

She complied and watched as he sat next to her, twisting towards her on a seat too small for him. He laid his arm along the back of her chair and lightly rested a hand on the nape of her neck. His touch made her shiver with anticipation.

"I'm out, Lucy."

Mystified, she was going to reply that it was a bit late to announce his sexual preferences and then she realised what he meant. "I know that, I've just been in the show!"

"No, I mean I'm completely out. No more dancing, no writing lessons, and no more swimming lessons I'm afraid."

"What? I don't understand."

Max gave an enormous sigh and took her hand in his.

Lucy looked at where they lay, entwined in her lap. Max's hand was almost twice the size of hers and was much browner. She tried not to get distracted by the sight of their fingers twisted together. She'd dreamed so often that they might sit like this, and now they were, she was filled with unease.

"They've bought me out," he said abruptly. "Remember the row there was about Angie and Lenny being in the dance off together the other week?"

Lucy looked blank.

"You must have seen it, in the papers and on the news? Fizz TV was made to feel embarrassed there were two black dancers in the dance off. People were trying to whip up a race row."

"I don't read the papers, or watch the news. I still don't understand Max."

He blew out another breath. "Angie would have gone tonight, should have gone tonight but instead they paid me off so that I would go and a black dancer would stay in."

"No!"

Max couldn't bear the look on Lucy's face. He hated that some of her unworldliness had disappeared. He could see her innocence fading as the significance of his news sank in. He hadn't wanted to tell her the truth but, as Daniel had pointed out, she would have wondered where he'd gone. And besides, Max felt that Lucy deserved the truth, however disillusioning.

Lucy stared at the chair in front of her. Most of its gilt had rubbed off showing the cheap wood underneath. That's how she felt about the show. It had been stripped of any glamour and charm it once held for her. She'd always thought that it was a proper dance contest, the one reality show that truly tested its celebrities. And now, thanks to Max, it had revealed itself to be -

"A f-fix! So it's all fixed then?" She paused, open mouthed. "The competition? They know who's going to win it, right from the start?"

"No, Lucy, not completely, but there are ways of getting people out if they want to. It happened with Dan's partner last year. Casey someone or other."

"The model," she said dully. "And I thought how lucky she was to get that big modelling job in America. I remember thinking it might make up for being voted off. God, I've been stupid. I bet that was the reason she wanted out!" She glared at Max; she couldn't believe that he too would be bought off so easily. Was he really giving it all up just for money? She gave a harsh laugh. "And you Max, why do you need to go? A modelling contract in the States?"

"Not quite that. I have other reasons."

"But you're not prepared to tell me them?"

Max took his hand away. "No."

"And how much have they paid you?" Lucy's voice was icy.

"A hundred thousand." He said it in an undertone but she might as well know all the sordid details. He felt her withdraw from him.

"Well, I hope you're happy." She got up. She'd been wrong about Max. He wasn't the gentle honourable man she'd thought; he was just as bent as the rest of them. She bit down the hysterical laugh which threatened. Bent! Yes, he was that as well. Why had she wasted so much time on this man? Daniel was welcome to him; in fact, Daniel was too good for him!

"Lucy, wait -"

"If you'll excuse me, I have to find my, my dancing partner. We have to arrange our training schedule seeing as *I'm* still in the competition."

"But Lucy, you haven't heard what I need the money for."

But Lucy had stalked away, leaving Max crouched on the uncomfortable chair, with his knees up round his elbows.

Step Ten.

It took all of her father's and Whiz's patient skill to persuade Lucy to go into training the next day. She refused to talk to them, just as she refused to talk to Daniel about anything other than the new dance they were rehearsing.

"No, let's just stick to what we need to do," she'd insisted. "Now how many steps do I need to take at this bit?"

And she'd worked them both into a sweat pushing even the very fit Daniel to his physical limit. He'd finally called it quits and Lucy had retreated to her hotel room, to stare glassily at the plasma screen playing music videos.

The week continued in the same pattern. She and Daniel were dancing a tango next. It was another dance she found difficult.

"Are you going to talk to Max?" he'd ventured during Thursday's rehearsal.

"Show me how to do that staccato turn again, please Daniel."

So Daniel had sighed and had gone over the move for the umpteenth time that morning. "Do it in front of the mirror," he instructed. "Without me. I'll stand over here so I can see where you're going wrong."

Lucy did so, counting the beat through the dance movement.

"That's better," Daniel called. "But try making that sharper, more aggressive. Remember to jerk your head. So *are* you going to talk to Max? He'd like you to, you know."

"One, three, five. Why Daniel? Whatever can he have to say to me?"

"Well, he might say he loves you for a start."

Lucy, in mid twist, jolted round to stare at him. "W-what?" Then, with a shriek heard throughout the dance studios, Lucy clutched at her left side and fell as if a lorry had slammed into her.

Cursing, Daniel ran to her. "Don't move, Lucy. I'll get help."

As she tried to stand and screamed in pain at the effort, he swore again and asked urgently: "Where does it hurt?"

"The b-back, the back of my thigh. Ooh Daniel, it hurts so much."

"Oh God, Lucy," Daniel said, his own face white with shock. "I think you've done your hamstring."

Step Eleven.

The Christmas tree, laden with decorations and its angel on the top, had been placed in pride of place next to the French doors. Cards hung on ribbons (arranged in groups of odd numbers, of course) and bundles of fresh holly sat on the mantelpiece. The fire had been stoked recently and was burning merrily and scenting the room with apple logs. The soundtrack was the quiet burble of seasonal songs coming from a CD. Lucy's favourite ornament, a childhood snow globe, sat on top of the television, as her family tradition dictated. It was a perfect Christmas picture. It was supposed to be the season of goodwill but Lucy wasn't feeling it. In any way.

She had everything she needed within range. The TV remote, a notebook, her laptop, her mobile and a glass of juice were all arranged neatly on the table beside the couch on which she lay. Five things she counted without interest. Most had remained untouched; she hadn't written anything for days. Whiz and her father had moved the sofa so that Lucy had a view of her garden. From where she lay, she could see the expanse of white which thickly covered the lawn. It had snowed most days since she had left hospital and the large raised pond at the bottom of the lawn was simply a white blob, gleaming in the dull light. A robin hopped onto the bird table, had a quick look round, gathered a bacon rind and flew off.

"Making the most of you being indoors, Basil," she murmured to the cat who slumbered on a nearby chair. The animal's ears twitched but it was the only movement in the room. Lucy took a moment to admire the irony of her situation. Once, this would have been her perfect day. Hiding in her house. Sitting. Thinking. Maybe writing. For too long it had been all she ever wanted. And now, when she was unable to walk very far, all she wanted to do was to run halfway round the world to the man she loved.

Daniel had visited her in hospital. He'd told her that Max was probably in love with her. Had laughed when she'd stammered out that she'd thought Max was gay. And then, had dropped the bombshell that the swimmer had gone to Miami to take part in a Grand Prix.

"Cars?" Lucy said, confused.

"No, it's some sort of swimming event, I think,"

"How long's he going to be away?" she asked, appalled.

Daniel shrugged. "Don't know, babe. You could ring him. Why don't you? It's about time you two got together, you know."

Lucy shook her head. She couldn't have that conversation over the phone. "I c-can't. Not after what I've - I'm too embarrassed."

"But you do like him?"

Lucy nodded and blushed. She looked away.

Daniel stared at her and then diplomatically decided to change the subject. "How's the leg?"

"Bit better," she said. "In between the massage and stretching exercises, I've got to rest it as much as possible. I even have a sports therapist assigned to me. They're sending me home tomorrow."

"Where to darling, the hotel?"

"No, my house. I live near Woodstock."

"That's the end of *Who Dares Dances* for you then."

"Yes and for you too. I'm so sorry Daniel. I know it meant a lot to you."

The dancer smiled and reached out a hand. "It's okay, as long as you're alright, that's the important thing. And who knows," Daniel gave a tight smile, "maybe one day I'll get to the final. Maybe next year I'll have someone to win with?"

"It was never going to be me, was it?" Lucy smiled apologetically. She knew she'd been technically proficient but had never been of a winning standard.

"There's always Julia?" Daniel raised his eyebrows in hope.

Lucy shook her head again. "She's filming in Scotland."

"Oh well babe, you get yourself better and do what the doctors say." He got up to leave.

"Daniel, before you go -"

"Yes lovie?"

"Max told you about the money he got for agreeing to leave the show early, didn't he?"

"Yes."

"What did he need it for?"

Daniel looked at her sheepishly. "Didn't he tell you?"

"He tried. I wouldn't let him." She bit her lip in remorse.

"He wants to set up a swimming programme at Crystal Palace."

Lucy remembered the boy Max was training before their swimming lesson began. "What, to train Olympic hopefuls?"

"No babe. To give youngsters like his nephew a chance. Disabled kids. You know, a bit like Riding for the Disabled but," Daniel shrugged, "in the water."

"Oh."

"You take care of yourself, now. I'll come and see you soon. Woodstock you say? Jot down the address, there's a love."

And now, lying on her sofa under a fleece and staring out at a snow-blanketed December day, Lucy remembered the shame that had flooded her. She'd misjudged everything about Max. His sexuality, at this her face burned crimson but, more importantly, his motivation for leaving. No wonder he needed the money. But one thing still puzzled her. An athlete like him, competing at the very top of his sport, surely wouldn't want just to quit like that. There must be something more to it. But whatever it was, Daniel, Julia and anyone else she'd discussed it with, didn't know.

Her mobile trilled. Picking it up, the hope ran through her, as always, that it might be Max. It wasn't.

"Julia, hello."

"Lucy darling! I couldn't believe it when I heard about your accident. How are you?"

"I'm fine. At home."

"Good. Who's looking after you?"

"A nurse. And Dad and Whiz pop in now and again, although Whiz is driving me crazy. She keeps banging on about another Davy Jones book. Daniel has promised to visit too."

"Oh, He's such a lovely man. No Max?"

"N-no, he's swimming in a competition in the States, Dan said."

"Those two still close?" Julia's voice was cagey.

Lucy managed a laugh. "We were a bit off the mark there, Julia. Max is straight and so, I suspect, is Daniel."

"Well actually, I'm glad you brought that up. I asked Harri about it again and, oh Lucy, I'm *really* sorry, but I got it wrong. Turns out it was a Jo as in J O that Max went out with. Not a man."

"Not a man called J O E then?" Lucy giggled weakly. "No, it's alright; Daniel told me Max is straight." She paused for dramatic effect that made Julia proud. "And, he also told me that Max is in love with *me*."

"Lucy!" Julia breathed. "I knew it!"

"How?"

"That after show party! You know, the one after you'd done your samba? I could so absolutely tell he was into you big time."

"You could have told me!"

"Darling, I'm sorry. Been a bit preoccupied lately. Been very selfish. I've got a bit of news, actually. Harri asked me to marry him."

"Julia!"

"I know! It's magical isn't it? Have no idea when we'll fit it into our manic schedules but we'll do it somehow. He told me about Max and Jo last week but, I'm so sorry darling, it slipped my mind."

"That's all right." Lucy felt she could be magnanimous in the light of Julia's engagement. "Congratulations. Oh Julia you'll be so beautiful."

The bride-to-be gave a dirty laugh. "I sincerely hope so! And I hope you'll be there to witness it as bridesmaid. I promise not to make you wear lilac polyester."

"Yes well, I wore enough of that sort of thing in *Who Dares Dances*. The costumes don't get any better do they?"

Julia chuckled. "You're not wrong there. But hey, what are you going to do about your gorgeous man Max? I mean, he's a looker."

"And the nicest, kindest, most gentle man you could ever wish to meet." Lucy added, defensively.

"Do I detect the feelings might be mutual, Ms Everett? Is this one of your crushes?"

"It's more than a crush." Lucy gave a great sigh.

"Oh Lucy! What are you going to do?"

"I don't know. I just don't know."

Lucy switched off her phone and stared again at the wintry scene in front of her. Yet more snow was beginning to fall. It looked likely it would stay around for the holiday. Her mood lifted a little; she loved Christmas, especially a white one. She couldn't do anything about Max now, but she could face up to another problem in her life.

"Whiz!" she yelled. "Whiz, can you come in here a minute? I need to talk to you about my next book."

Step Twelve.

In his tiny flat in Highgate, the sitting room lit only by the lights on his miniature Christmas tree, Daniel cruised idly through the channels on the television. A gossipy entertainment show mentioned Julia's name and made him sit up abruptly. Clasping a hand over his heart, because he felt it actually jolt, he listened as the breathy host of the showbiz programme announced Julia's engagement to Harri Morgan, ex children's TV presenter and last year's winner of *Who Dares Dances*.

"So it's ended," he whispered to the room. "I must now, finally, get over how I feel." He watched, as stills of Julia and Harri flickered across the screen. He knew he'd never had a chance with her, not as soon as he'd seen how she and Harri were together but, for a while, he'd hoped.

"Beautiful Julia. Congratulations." He blew a kiss at the TV and then added: "But if that Welsh bastard ever hurts you, it'll be me he answers to."

He snapped off the remote and sat in a sweet melancholy for a while. Then, with sudden decision, he reached for his phone. "If I can't have the woman I love," he muttered, as he punched in the number, "maybe someone else can have his." As he waited for the line to connect, he vowed to himself it would the last time, absolutely the last time, that he would play cupid.

"Hello Max! Oh sorry mate, is it still early there? Look, you've got to get your toned backside back to Blighty. Back to Woodstock actually. What? Yes, I'll explain."

Step Thirteen.

It was the day before Christmas Eve. The snowy weather hadn't abated and, out here in rural Oxfordshire, it was falling heavily. It had been hell getting a flight at this time of year but Max had managed it – at a price.

He hesitated before he lifted a hand to the lion head knocker. He looked about him. It was a big, secretive house. Victorian, he hazarded at a guess, with snow covered ivy snaking up the Cotswold stone walls and a carriage drive sweeping in a circle. It was a house peculiarly suited to the unworldly Lucy. A wreath decorated the front door and someone had put white lights in the towering conifer gracing the middle of the drive. It looked like the perfect Christmas card image.

He looked behind him as the taxi driver gunned the engine of the cab, skidded on the compacted snow on the drive and disappeared through the security gates. It had been nearly as difficult to persuade a driver to bring him out here, as it had been getting a flight.

"Committed now," he muttered and was glad the usual jet lag hadn't kicked in yet. It had been barely forty-eight hours since Daniel's phone call and any anger he'd felt had evaporated on the plane. It was an emotion that didn't live long in him. He was more intrigued now.

The door opened as an elderly man in yellow felt trousers and a tweed jacket came out.

"Ah, you must be Max," he said without ceremony. "We know all about you. Go in, go in, my boy."

Lucy's father, he assumed, as the man wandered off towards a black Range Rover tucked neatly to the side of the house.

"She's in the drawing room. Last door on the right at the back of the hall," said a female voice. It belonged to a tiny woman with fiery red hair. She emerged from the house in the wake of the old man.

She looked up at Max with open curiosity. "Simeon Jones," she gasped, "as I live and breathe."

"No, Max Parry," he said confused. Maybe the jet lag was hitting in after all.

"Tabitha Wisley – Whiz." The woman giggled. "Lucy's agent," she added, as he still looked blank. "How disappointing that Lucy hasn't mentioned me." She pointed a key at the car and the lights on it flashed as it unlocked. "I'm driving Dr Everett back to Oxford and then I'm going home. She's all yours." The last comment was said with asperity. "Let's hope you prove more inspirational than me. She hasn't written anything for two weeks."

It was all very unlike the welcome visitors got at his own family home. Still confused, Max made his way through the silent house. He knocked on the door he thought most likely to lead to Lucy.

"Is that you Daniel? Come in out of the cold."

He ducked into the room and stood for a minute, awkward, not knowing what to do next.

"Max! I th-thought it was - "

Lucy drank in the sight of him. He wore a black knee length coat, black trousers and carried a sleek leather holdall. A white scarf was wound several times round his neck. Her first thought was how well he fitted into the Victorian setting. He could be Simeon himself. She felt the cold sweep in with him and shivered.

"Hello Lucy," he said. "How's your injury?"

"G-getting better, thanks."

"Dan rang me."

Lucy looked up at him. In a flash, she understood what had happened. Daniel had been trying to sort things out.

"He explained one or two things." Max picked up a leather Chesterfield chair and placed it next to the head of the sofa. He busied himself by taking off his coat and scarf, shaking the snow off them and then laying them neatly on the back of the seat. Lucy watched him avidly. Despite the tan, renewed by the Miami sun, he looked tired. Finally, he sat facing her and took her hand in his cold brown one. Lucy had never seen him looking more beautiful.

"M-max, I'm so sorry. I'm so, so sorry."

Max's thin face creased into a smile. "What for, Lucy? For thinking I'm gay or for thinking I'm avaricious?"

"Are you, are you really angry with me?"

"I was, a little." He looked up to see her face crumple. "But I'm not now," he added. "Just curious. To start with, just what made you think I was gay?"

"Um, oh th-things." There had seemed lots of reasons at the time but Lucy couldn't think of one at this moment.

"Maybe it's because I don't go around in a testosterone filled rage all the time?" Max smiled slightly. "Or that I'm patently close to my family?"

"Maybe," Lucy racked her brain, she had never felt so stupid. "And you like to cook." Even as she said it, she realised how ridiculous it sounded.

"And that makes me gay, Lucy?"

"Well, you also seemed so close to Daniel." She tried hard not to sound defensive.

"I am. He's become a really good friend. And I needed one during *Who Dares Dances*."

Lucy felt newly ashamed – and humbled – at how easy he was making it for her. "Yes, I can see that," she acknowledged. Then she remembered what had started all of it off. "It was Julia really."

"Julia?" Max was startled.

"Yes, she said that you'd been out with someone called Jo."

Max frowned. "Jo?"

"I'm afraid, well, we all sort of assumed it was a J O E."

"Ah." Max laughed. Lucy looked so abject he simply wanted to sweep her into his arms. But he couldn't, not until the other matter had been resolved. "I wish you'd talked to me about it, Lucy."

129

"Y-yes. Me too. But that's easier said than done. And I think, once I'd got the idea in my head, I sort of saw evidence for it everywhere."

Max sighed. "I can't blame you entirely. For some reason, there have always been a lot of rumours about me."

"Why don't you deny them?" Lucy looked at him curiously.

"Why should I? What business is it of anyone's? It's my private life and that's how it should stay. I can never understand why it seems to matter to people so much."

"It m-mattered to me."

Max caressed his thumb over her hand. "Yes and I'm sorry for that."

"No, it's me who should be sorry, Max. I've been jumping to all sorts of conclusions. And I can't tell you how sorry I am about that conversation about the money you got for leaving the show. I should have let you explain."

"Well, maybe it wasn't the right time. I think you'd just had your vision of *Who Dares Dances* tarnished a little."

"Just a little." Lucy blushed.

They smiled at one another.

Max slid forward so that he was sitting on the very edge of his chair. He cupped Lucy's face gently in one long fingered hand. "We've got some catching up to do." He kissed her lightly on the mouth. "I've wanted to do that for a long time but I was never certain how you felt about me." He continued to kiss her, gently, tenderly, overjoyed and immeasurably touched at her shy response.

"Max?"

"Yes my love?"

"There's one thing I still don't understand."

Max sat back on his chair. The desire he felt numbed a little by creeping jet lag. He kept her hand in his and contented himself by simply gazing. "What?"

"I can see that the money was really *really* tempting, especially when you had such a good cause to donate it to but - "

"But?" He knew what was coming.

"You're an athlete," Lucy said in a puzzled voice, "an *Olympic* athlete. I know you found the dancing hard and I know the judges were vile to you, but I can't believe that you just -" she trailed off.

"What?"

"I can't believe that you just gave up," Lucy finished lamely, afraid she'd gone too far.

Max rubbed a tired hand over his face. "I've got something for you." He reached into the pocket of his coat and drew out a tape. "Play it will you?" He stifled a yawn. "And now, God I'm really sorry Lucy, but the jet lag always knocks me out for a couple of hours. I know this sounds rude, but do you think I could go and sleep it off somewhere?" He needed an excuse to leave the room. He couldn't be there to listen to the tape with her; he wouldn't be able to bear the disappointment on her face when she finally knew his secret.

Lucy smiled at him. "Of course you can. There's a room made up opposite mine. Top of the stairs on the left. It's a nice big bed so you should be okay." She crimsoned as her thoughts travelled back to their night together. If only she'd known then what she knew now!

"I'll find it."

He put the tape into the cassette player for her and then left quietly.

As he shook his head to clear the worst of the fug stupefying his brain, he heard his own voice trailing him up the stairs.

After the tape had finished playing, Lucy rewound it to listen again. She couldn't take in what she'd heard. When it had finished playing for the second time, it made more sense. She now knew why Max had been so desperate to leave the competition. It had been the writing challenge that had been the final straw. But Max had fulfilled his task. He *had* written her a story; or rather, he'd recorded one. For a dyslexic it was so much easier.

She switched off the tape player and stood and watched as

the last light stole from the garden. A low shadow slunk near the wall, leaving neat paw prints in the snow; Basil on a prowl. Snow cloaked the trees and everywhere was silent and still. But Lucy could hear Max's words reverberate in her head.

His story was all the more painful for being so common. It was that of a young boy bullied at school for being over six feet tall by the time he was eleven and misunderstood by his teachers who thought him simply lazy and disinterested. Then Max had found out, quite by chance, that he could swim for longer and faster than anyone else. He'd spoken in that deceptively low-key way he had, of how the water had saved him. It was something he could do, something that came naturally to him. Something where his height was an advantage rather than a weapon to be used against him. He hadn't minded the early starts, the long hours of training, the weekends given up for races. It released him from the bullying he'd endured and of the expectations of his teachers. It also gave him a reason not to do well academically. After all, he reasoned to his school, with his punishing training schedule, he couldn't fit in his homework, or even some of his lessons. And the more he swam the better he'd become. And at last, those who had bullied him were forgotten. Almost. He'd found a way of being himself, of being the best he possibly could be.

At twenty-nine he was pushing it to remain in top-level competitive swimming; most swimmers were finished long before they were his age. But he'd persevered, qualified for the Olympics against all expectations and then had gone on to win three medals. Gold medals. The time had come to retire, to go out on a high. And then he'd been invited to enter *Who Dares Dances*. He was persuaded that it might lead to something, although he didn't know what. He'd already been asked to do some presenting but had turned it down; he couldn't read an autocue, the words danced around on the screen. It had been Will who had finally made the decision for him. And he couldn't bring himself to refuse Will.

He'd enjoyed it at first. Lola had been a patient teacher and he was used to a gruelling training regime, used to being told what to do in order to improve. It hadn't seemed so very different to the coaching sessions he underwent for swimming. But the actual dancing, as he explained on the tape, was three minutes of sheer hell each week. Becoming more and more self-conscious about his enormous feet and huge hands, he was destined to fail in spectacular fashion. The more hours of training he put in, the worse it got and the judges' comments had taken him straight back to being bullied at school. Only this time it was worse, this time he was bullied in front of a television audience of millions.

Bob's announcement, that he was to write a story as his extra challenge, had come when Max was at his lowest. It had been the final indignity. His sisters tried to get him to back out but he'd never been the sort of person who gave up easily. But then came the offer of the money. It had been too tempting. He'd felt lousy about quitting but he knew he could start up something worthwhile with the money. It was time to go.

Going straight back into a swimming competition had been like a salve. He hadn't won but he was back in the world he knew and understood and felt protected in. What it hadn't done was make him forget the woman he'd grown to love. And then Daniel's phone call had woken him early one morning.

Lucy smiled through her tears. She'd once thought that she and Max were complete opposites but she knew the truth now. She understood his longing for a world that felt familiar and safe, of the strategies he used to avoid detection, of the risks involved of pushing oneself into a place where only failure might lie. She was like him in so many ways. A log shifted in the fire, making her jump.

Picking up her crutch, she turned to see Max framed once again by the doorway.

"So, now you know." His voice was low and lazy but she knew him better now.

"Yes."

"So, here comes the big question, do you think I'm stupid?"

"No!" She went to move towards him but stumbled.

He came to her and held her to him, safe in his strong arms. "A lot of people do think it's stupid not to be able to read and write."

"*I'm* the one who's been stupid, Max. If I'd had a brain cell, I would have realised why you left the show."

He stooped to nuzzle his mouth into her neck. "It wasn't just having to write a damned story, you know. *You* were driving me crazy. Half the time you flaunted yourself naked in front of me and half the time you kept me at a very long distance."

"Self-protection," she said enjoying the thrill of his stubble on her tender skin. "I was falling in love with you and didn't think there was a hope of it ever being returned. Not in the way I wanted."

Max went very still. "Are you, are you still in love with me?"

"More so now than ever." She lifted her face to his, to show him how much she cared.

His mouth crushed hers leaving her breathless. His long arms encircled her, lifting her up to meet his hard muscled body.

Eventually, after a long time, he released her.

"Oh Max, I didn't think it would be like this."

"Well, I've got a lot to prove haven't I? Got to dispel the last lingering doubts you might have that I'm gay."

"I don't think," she began to protest and then saw the gleam in his grey eyes. "Max I love you!"

"I love you too, Lucy."

"Even though I'm as mad as a basketful of kittens, as Daniel would say?"

"I can live with that." Max saw a frown cross her face. "What's wrong? It's true, I understand about your phobias, how could I not?"

"It's n-not that." Lucy buried her head into Max's solid warm chest and clutched the wool of his sweater. "I d-don't have, I don't think—"

"What is it, Lucy? You're beginning to worry me."

134

Lucy looked up into his beautiful face. "I've never actually, um, slept with anyone before."

Max's face relaxed into a smile, a kind one. "Oh, is that all? Well, if truth be told, I suppose I'm not all that experienced either. Never really had the time before." He grinned and the deep groove that Lucy loved so much appeared in his cheek.

She reached up and ran a light finger down it. "I love it when you smile," she said.

Her action seemed to galvanise Max. In one easy movement, he picked her up into his arms. Careful not to hurt her injured leg, he held her lightly as if she was no weight at all. "Perhaps it's time to find out if we're any good in bed?"

"Yes please," Lucy said, throwing her arms round his strong neck.

"Oh and Lucy?"

"Yes Max?"

"Shall we do it three times or five?"

"Don't mind," she said laughing and hiding her blushes in his neck. "As long as we don't do it just the once!"

"I think I can guarantee that," said Max and strode purposefully to the bedroom.

End of Dance Two.

The Charleston: a dance full of laughter.

"I've danced the Charleston at many a party, although I hasten to add I'm far too young to remember the dance in its heyday. One can dance it on one's own – but it's far more fun with a partner. As are most things!" Dame Venetia Denning, actor.

Step One.

Meredith left the stage in a kind of quiet despair. There must be more to life than this, she thought, towelling the perspiration off her brow. Once again, she'd died. Once again, the jokes she'd thought so funny when hunched over the laptop had raised hardly a giggle from a live audience.

"Not so good tonight then, Merry?" Del, the owner of *The Last Laugh Comedy Club*, caught up with her in the grubby excuse for a dressing room. He gave her a sympathetic smile.

"I'm really sorry, Del. I thought the stuff about being a ginger would go down a storm with them."

Del laughed. "You're so not ginger. Post-Christmas it's always a bit flat," he offered as explanation. "People are partied out. And there aren't enough students, and not enough booze in the ones who are here. This lot just want cheap mother-in-law gags."

They stopped and listened as the crowd rallied out of its stupor to greet Fred Loss, their favourite and a stalwart of the club.

"At least he'll get a laugh," Meredith bit out.

"I don't know what it is, Merry. I think you're really funny, always have." Del looked her up and down and raised his eyebrows. "Perhaps it's your obvious assets."

Merry put her hands over her not inconsiderable bosom. "What, flatten myself down?" She tugged at a lock of auburn hair despondently. "Shave my head? And I've tried every diet known to man – and woman." She looked down at herself. "I'm just built to be curvy."

Del blew out a breath. "It's always tough on women in this business and even harder if you're an attractive one. People say they don't find beautiful women funny." He shrugged apologetically. "As I said, I find you hilarious, but then I know you. Look Merry, I don't know how to say this." Del rubbed a hand over his face, embarrassed.

Meredith put up her hands in surrender. "Don't worry, Del, I'll spare you the speech. I quit."

"Well, it's that..." Del began.

"I know. I know. If the comic isn't funny, the audience goes home."

"And stays home." Del finished miserably.

"You've given me a chance in a lifetime. More than a chance. I can't thank you enough." Merry gave a tight smile.

The club owner grinned sheepishly. "Give my love to your aunt won't you? Fancy a drink later?"

Merry shook her head. "No, I'm shattered. Going home. I'll make sure I give your regards to Venetia."

Merry watched as Del hurried out of the door of the tiny room, towards the bar, clearly relieved he hadn't had to actually sack her. It had been his relationship with her aunt Venetia that had got her the job in the first place. Venetia had called in a favour from Del. She'd known him, when he'd been a die-hard Goth, back in their wild partying days. Venetia, now a respectable Dame and doyenne of stage and screen, was terrifyingly bossy. Few dared to say 'no' to her and live, or at least survive professionally.

"Well," said an annoyingly persistent voice in Merry's head, "I'll have to ring her up and admit I've failed. Again." She picked up her bag, hunted for her bottle of water and drank deeply. Once her thirst had been satisfied, she stuffed her things into her rucksack and swung it onto her shoulder. Giving a last affectionate glance around the cramped dressing room, she called goodbye to one or two people through the murk in the club and went out into the unwelcoming night.

It was icy. Cycling home past students, just coming out for the evening, she wondered quite why she was putting herself through this.

To keep her parents happy, she'd finished her degree in English Lit at Magdalen College, but had missed the hoped for first as she had been too busy appearing in Oxford Drama Society productions. The acting bug had bitten deep and hard. Encouraged by her paternal great-aunt, Merry had pursued a dual career on the stage as actor and comedian. Bits and pieces of acting jobs had come her way, mostly courtesy of fellow students, but they'd dried up recently. So, she'd begged a favour off Del and had appeared at the comedy club for the last week. She knew she was funny. She knew she was clever and witty, but somehow she could never get that across to her audience. Ever the optimist, she'd been full of hope that her wry, affectionate observations on life would go down a storm with the Oxford audiences. What she hadn't bargained for was that the combination of an alcohol fuelled audience and a woman under fifty simply meant catcalls and heckles to get her tits out. She'd died onstage every night. And every night she'd died a little bit inside too.

She was twenty six in six months' time. Her parents had been patient until now, letting her 'mess about with this comedy nonsense' as they termed it but her twenty sixth birthday was the deadline they'd set. Make it by then or give up and do something sensible. Something with a future, they'd suggested, something which can give you a pension.

Merry looked up into the neon-lit sky as cold sleety rain began to fall. She cycled harder in a vain attempt to keep warm.

Crouching over the one bar gas heater in her bedsit later that night she confessed all to Venetia on the phone, spurred on by the remainder of a Christmas bottle of Baileys.

"So I'm going to have to get a job. A proper one."

"Oh my darling, surely not?"

"I can't see any alternative, Venetia. Ma and Pa issued an ultimatum. I've got to get myself sorted. And, to be fair, you can see their point of view. It cost them a fortune to put me through uni. I've got to pay them back somehow."

Venetia huffed, "They've never understood what it takes to get established in this business. Your father especially, has no idea. After all, you've only just begun. A job indeed!" Venetia added, in scandalised tones. To her it was the ultimate degradation. Venetia had worked consistently throughout her long and illustrious career and did everything she could to ensure it was on her terms. She'd only picked those roles which she knew would serve her unique talents well. And it had worked. Admitting to seventy, she was a grande dame of the acting world, her appearance belying the wild excesses of her youth. She was also a firm believer in following your heart. The practicalities would follow. She said as much to Merry.

"Well that's fine, aunty, but I still have three weeks rent to pay and I haven't been able to eat today." Merry tried hard not to sound pathetic. It wasn't in her nature to admit defeat.

"My darling child, this can't go on."

"You're telling me. Now I've lost the gig with Del, I won't even be able to scrounge food out of the club's kitchen. I'll really miss those fajitas." Merry's stomach rumbled in memory.

"Merry, can you come and stay?" Venetia said suddenly.

"What, at Little Barford?" Merry said, referring to her aunt's country home in the Cotswolds.

"No, I've taken a flat in town. It's so convenient for my radio work." Venetia had recently been recording a classic series for Radio Four. "I've got an idea which may just save your career."

"Well, what is it?"

"Meredith child, you'll just have to reign in your impatience for once. Come as soon as you can though darling, won't you?"

Merry looked round at her tiny attic bedsit, with its single bed and lone window giving a smeared outlook onto one of Oxford's less attractive views. "Can I come tomorrow, aunty?"

Twenty-four hours later, Merry was blissfully wrapped in luxury in Venetia's Maida Vale mansion block apartment. She lay back on the cream leather sofa and stretched out her long legs.

"This is nice," she sighed, burying her toes in the thick carpet, which covered the floor of the glamorous sitting room. She looked around and admired the nineteen twenties polished cherry wood furniture. "It's so nice to be warm for a change. I could get used to this. I like Big Barry."

Venetia looked up from where she was pouring herself another glass of wine. "The doorman? He is a sweetie. A big fan of mine, you know."

Merry regarded her aunt fondly. "Everyone's a big fan of yours. Del sends his love by the way."

Venetia had the grace to blush ever so slightly. "Such a sweet boy."

Amused at the idea of Del being described as a boy, Merry snorted into her wine. He was in his mid-forties at least. "He's married now. His wife's expecting their first baby."

Her aunt shook her head. "I wouldn't have imagined him doing anything so conventional," she said incredulously. "And how is that club that he runs doing?"

Merry yawned and tried to make an effort to be sociable. They'd just eaten a delicious meal, and she'd drunk most of the bottle of Merlot her aunt had produced. She was feeling very mellow. "He's making a mint."

"By that quaint expression, I assume you mean it's doing well?" Venetia came to sit by Merry on the sofa.

"Yes Venetia." Merry laughed and gave in. Her aunt was obviously in a mood to talk. "So why did you lure me over here?" She gestured to their surroundings. "Not that I'm complaining. This is heaven."

Venetia smirked and Merry's heart sank. She knew that look. It was the one when her aunt had A Plan.

"I've got A Plan," Venetia said ominously.

Merry shifted uneasily. "I thought you might."

"Do you watch *Who Dares Dances,* dear girl?"

Merry shrugged and shook her head. "What is it?"

Venetia tutted. "It's a television programme."

"*Who Dares Dances?* Sounds like something you have to paint your face green and wear camouflage gear for."

Venetia looked mystified.

Merry waved her glass perilously. "SAS," she explained somewhat obliquely. "Isn't their motto, '*Who Dares Wins*'?"

"Very droll, my dear." Venetia raised her eyebrows in an attempt to humour her great-niece. "It's actually a sort of dance reality show."

"Don't watch much telly." Merry yawned again. Her only thought was to get into the vast bed in her aunt's spare room.

"Well, a weekly audience of three million viewers might disagree."

Merry sat up and only just saved her glass of red from splashing onto the sofa. How many?"

"Three million. A week." Venetia was satisfied she'd got her niece's full attention now.

"F - I mean, blimey."

"Quite. And just what is the capacity at dear Del's club?"

"Two hundred and fifty – on a full night. About five, if they know it's me on the bill. Three million though," Meredith marvelled. "The power of TV, eh? But what's it got to do with me?"

Venetia adopted an innocent tone. "I happen to know Bob Dandry who produces and directs the show. He rang me yesterday. One of their celebrity dancers has pulled out at the last moment, pregnant apparently." She paused and then landed the final punch. "I rang him back this morning and suggested you."

"What do you mean, you've suggested me?" Merry stared, slack-jawed, at her aunt.

"You are to report to Fizz TV Studios at ten o'clock on Monday next," Venetia said, triumphant. "To do the 'Big Meet,' as I believe they so quaintly term it, with your dance partner."

Merry tried to sit up straight, a difficult task on the slippery leather. "Venetia, what the hell have you done?"

"I've got you a job, darling. One even your parents won't mind; they're huge fans of the show." Venetia raised her glass and then took a celebratory sip of wine.

Merry slid back down onto the leather. "Wha - what?" One word sank in.

Dance.

She was beginning to wish she hadn't drunk so much. You needed a clear head to deal with Venetia in full sway. She sat back up again. "Dancing? Venetia I can't dance!"

"My darling girl, if you ever got your head out from that Oxford scented cloud and into the real world, you'd realise that is precisely the point."

"I don't understand."

Venetia looked down her long nose. "Patently."

"I suppose it's too much to expect you to explain?"

"Then I shall attempt to give you a potted history in popular culture," she said and grinned malevolently. "More wine?"

After rising to pour another glass for each of them, Venetia settled back and launched into an explanation about the phenomenally successful *Who Dares Dances*, part reality show, part dance competition. She told a befuddled Merry that its last series, however, had been dogged by vote rigging scandals and a race row. How the new series was a much shorter one, a special six week run leading up to the annual comedy charity fundraising event in television, *Jokes for Notes*. Some contestants were to reappear, including winners of previous competitions. The emphasis, Venetia went on, with this series was to be on the money the show raised for its pet charity, *Pennies for Pencils*, by the public voting to keep in their favourite dancers.

"So I thought, with you being a comedian, you'd fit right into it all. Luckily, Bob agreed. He owed me a favour after the fiasco that was *The Golden Egg*." Venetia referred to a doomed drama she'd been in a few years ago.

"Oh Lord," Merry said, "This Bob fellow didn't have a hand in that, did he?"

"He did, indeed," her aunt replied, through thinned lips. "So, he owes me *big time*, as you young people say. Of course," she added with her usual assurance, "I was wonderful in it. Just such a shame the leads were so awful."

Merry laughed and then stopped short. "So, to get this right then, I've got to learn to dance?"

"Yes, but it shouldn't be so hard; you had ballet lessons at school."

"Venetia, that was years ago!"

"Oh, it's better than nothing. And you have natural rhythm, after all. Inherited from me, of course." Venetia waved Merry's concerns away.

"Not sure about that," Merry said gloomily.

"Merry, do you want this job or not?" her aunt asked with asperity. "I had to twist Bob's arm most severely and the little weasel was very difficult. I think it's about time you took *something* a little more seriously."

"Oh aunty, don't get me wrong, it's not that I'm really grateful and so on, but I just simply don't know if I'm up to it."

"Merry, I know you and I know that underneath all that cheer and bravado is a mess of insecurity but I really think you can do this. I'm also assuming the thirty five thousand makes a difference?" her aunt added waspishly.

"What do you mean?"

Venetia gave an enormous sigh, "I feel as if I'm dealing with the hard of understanding. It's your fee, Meredith."

"You're joking!"

"I assure you I'm not in the least. In fact, my humour is being stretched rather thinly in this conversation. You should know that I never, *ever* joke about money."

"Thirty five thousand pounds!" Merry couldn't compute being paid such a huge amount of money.

"That would pay off your student loan, I assume?"

"And the rest."

"Then you'll do it?"

Merry looked at her aunt and admitted total defeat. "I don't have much choice do I?" she said in a mock humble tone and feeling the first stirrings of excitement. Despite what she'd said to her aunt (she didn't want to give Venetia her victory too easily, after all) she was someone who rose gleefully to a new challenge.

Venetia beamed. "Not really, darling girl. And, do you know what? I think it might just be the making of you."

Step Two.

In the intervening few days, before Merry had to report for duty, Venetia took her niece in hand. She provided a wardrobe of clothes to replace Merry's student rags, as she disparaging called them, and put Merry through an intensive modelling and posture course. She then treated them both to a day at a spa, leaving them preened, smooth skinned and primed for action.

While having their hair done, Venetia also gave Merry a few more details about the programme and its dancers.

"Apparently, there are a total of eight couples," she said, over the noise in the salon. "Celebrities partnered with professional dancers, as in the previous series. Each week there is going to be an elimination contest and there will be two couples in the final, in, I think, about two months' time."

"Well, the final's not something that will worry me," Merry said mischievously, in an attempt to wind up her aunt. She looked over to the next chair, where Venetia was giving imperious instructions to a harassed looking Alain, who was trying to wield a hair dryer.

"Nonsense Meredith. Have some faith in your ability. And it's simply a matter of getting the right partner, you know. You'll be fine if you get Daniel Cunningham. I knew his mother. She danced with the London Ballet at one point. No!" she cried and waved her hands at the hapless hairdresser. "I said quite clearly I do not want it looking too full. I told you to simply give it a little lift at the crown!"

Merry shared a sympathetic look with Alain and tried to distract her aunt. "Is there anyone you don't know, Venetia?"

"I shouldn't think so," she replied smugly and bent forward to finger her fringe into the preferred style. "I remember Daniel as a little boy. Tall and gawky with lovely straw blond hair and unusual eyes. Now, Alain, please concentrate on what I've requested." With that, Venetia turned her attention back to the matter in hand.

***

As Merry wandered around the television studio, on the following Monday, she felt, and looked, very different to the student-like comedian actor who had cycled so dispiritedly through Oxford a few days ago. Her hair had been given a treatment, which made the chestnut lights glow and gave it bounce and gloss. Her skin glowed from the facials and expert make-up lessons, and she held herself high after the posture training.

As she searched for the adult version of the gangly boy Venetia had described as being Daniel Cunningham, she felt excitement bubble inside once again. She might just enjoy this.

There were crowds of people in Fizz TV's Studio One; a mix

of press, family and friends, celebrities and dancers.

Merry recognised Harri Morgan from the photos of him in the gossip magazines that Venetia kept in piles in her apartment. He was even better looking in the flesh and she admired the boyish grin, which lit up his face as he laughed and joked around. He might be fun to get to know. Angie, an incredibly successful musical star (Venetia had prepped her) had won the last competition and was a hot favourite to win this special short series. Judging from the journalists flocking round her, the rumour-mill could be right. Angie was standing entwined with a sinewy man. Merry heard the name Scott mentioned and remembered Venetia saying to be wary of him, as he was foul tempered. She watched, amused, as the first meeting of Angie and Scott, who must be dance partners, was then stage managed by a small rotund man. He could only be Bob Dandry. She recognised the greasy ginger comb-over that Venetia had described in such cruel detail. Merry hid a smile as she saw the couple greet one another in apparent astonishment. It was a little strange, as she'd walked past them in the bar ten minutes ago. They'd been sharing a bottle of champagne and looking very chummy.

A woman in a stunning crimson sari strolled past and Merry recognised her as Suni, the celebrated Indian chef. A man with a hand held camera walked alongside her and another meet of celeb and pro was carefully orchestrated. This time, the professional dancer was a neat dark-haired man. He picked up the diminutive cook and swung her round.

"Suni," he said in a pronounced northern accent. "I'm made up that I've got you!"

"Warren," the woman gasped, "it'll be fun but put me down now, please." He did and they posed smilingly for photographs.

Merry leaned against a giant bright pink cup and saucer, a prop, she assumed. She watched and absorbed, fascinated. So, this was to be her life for the next couple of months. It was like a pantomime; carefully choreographed and larger than life. Merry gazed up at the cup behind her. That was certainly enormous. What on earth was it used for? Everywhere she looked she saw over made-up women, with hair piled high and sparkling with glittery hairspray. Some of the men were hardly any more butch. They walked with a bouncing step, on the balls of their feet, gesturing and exclaiming.

Mr Comb-Over rushed up to her. "You must be Meredith," he gushed. "How lovely to meet you. I can see the resemblance to your great-aunt, of course. If you would be so good as to come this way, I'd like to introduce you to your professional dancer."

Bob Dandry barely came up to her shoulder. Merry looked down at him and smiled. He blushed an unbecoming puce and then, to her complete shock, put a sweaty hand on her bottom.

Merry pointedly removed it. Venetia was one hundred percent right about you, she seethed inwardly. "How kind," she said aloud, through clenched teeth. "I'm dying to find out who I've got. This is such fun, isn't it?" She gave him an especially warm smile, amused to see him simper and sweat even more. How Venetia would love to hear about this.

"We're so thrilled you could join our happy band. Our family, as I like to think." Bob leered some more. He looked around. "Ah! Your dancing partner is sitting on the steps over there. Daniel Cunningham – the one in the white jeans and leather jacket. Let me just organise the cameras. If you'll forgive me Miss Denning, I'll be right back." He wiggled his fingers in a nauseatingly coy wave.

"Don't worry, I'll stay right here. Hurry back." Merry blew him a kiss and enjoyed the trembling hand across the brow it caused. "What a creep," she murmured and then turned to meet a pair of the greenest eyes she'd ever seen.

***

Daniel lolled against the most famous steps in television and decided he would try his damndest to win *Who Dares Dances* this time round. He had a habit of not getting very far in the

147

competition. Casey, the comely model, had gone out early a few years ago and last Christmas his partner, the weirdly eccentric but totally charming writer Lucy Everett, had been hospitalised. He didn't seem to have much luck with his celebrity partners.

The production team had told them all that this was a special series which had been commissioned due to the show's popularity. Daniel didn't believe a word. He didn't believe, either, the industry rumours about the new series trying to address the scandal of the last. He knew the viewing figures had shot up once the tabloids had an inkling of the race issue and the vote rigging row. Swimmer Max Parry, a contestant in the last series, had taken a payment to drop out of the competition early, to avoid leaving in just one black celebrity. Daniel was cynical enough to think the stories had been a carefully planted ruse to create publicity. Which it had done very successfully. He suspected any new scandal would be just as effective. He hated the way this business was making him so suspicious and disbelieving. Maybe it was time to get out?

At least some previous winners were making a return; that was good news. There was new blood too, in the form of some new pro dancers joining. Perhaps it would freshen things up. And he was really looking forward to having Harri back. It meant Julia would be a frequent visitor. His heart quickened at the thought and, as was his habit, he damped down on the feeling automatically. He couldn't go there; she was Harri's.

To distract himself, he pondered on what surprises were in store for this series. He felt sure Bob would have something characteristically evil to spring on them. In a previous series, he'd already made the contestants dance with each other and last year he'd made them learn each other's skills. It had caused his friends, Lucy and Max, a few problems. Writer Lucy had been fine learning how to swim like a champion but writing a story had been torture for Olympic swimmer, Max. Still, it had all turned out alright in the end. Daniel smiled. He wondered why he did it sometimes. It certainly wasn't for the money. The smile vanished. Thank God for the live shows; at least those padded out his meagre salary. No, the thing that drove him each time was the dancing. And this time he would win. It was his turn, surely?

It would all depend upon his partner. The only thing Daniel had heard was that she was an actress or comedian. The actress bit sounded alright, as most had had some kind of dance training at drama school, but a comedian? A vision of some well-known ones rose unfairly in Daniel's mind. And any hope of winning vanished.

He'd tried to interrogate Julia, but she'd been knee deep in cream tulle, bridesmaids' dresses and place settings; she was immersed in planning her wedding to Harri.

"You'll be fine," was all she said. "You knock most of us into shape eventually."

It hadn't done much to reassure him.

And now, here he was, geared up for 'The Big Meet' with his new partner, after which would come the inevitable press call and then the circus that was *Who Dares Dances* would begin all over again.

Sitting idly, watching the shrieks and carefully orchestrated emotions which accompanied the pro dancers meeting with their celeb partners, he became aware of a tall woman striding towards him. She had that wide hipped, loose-limbed quality that, for some reason, he always associated with Italian women. He guessed it must be the new Italian pro dancer joining them for this special series.

The woman stopped in front of him and smiled. It was an attractively broad smile, with full kissable lips and white, even teeth. Daniel also liked the luxuriant auburn hair and almond shaped eyes. She was dressed in carefully distressed jeans, red espadrilles and a linen jacket. She looked very elegant, very European and very desirable.

"Adelina?"

"No," the woman looked startled and then amused. "I'm Meredith Denning. Merry. I believe I'm your partner for this series."

Daniel managed to stand up and greet this gorgeous creature.

She was very tall, he realised, probably one reason why they had been paired up, he topped six feet by several inches himself.

"Daniel Cunningham. Erm, pleased to meet you." He found himself stuttering and his lack of cool surprised him. Get a grip, he chastised himself silently.

"Likewise. Can't say I've seen you in action but you come highly recommended," came the crisp reply.

Daniel had the distinct impression he was being laughed at. Then, the moment passed, as Bob bustled over and began to direct the cameras, so they had to repeat the encounter all over again.

Watching the footage later on, Daniel was amused to see the camera had picked up every nuance of expression which had flickered across his face: shock, surprise, embarrassment – and pure unadulterated lust. It made for an interesting start to Series Ten of *Who Dares Dances*.

Step Three.

As it was such a short series, training got going immediately. Merry was the only one of the celebrities who hadn't competed before, all the others had been involved in one series or another. But she soon got to know her fellow competitors and they made her feel very welcome. Suni she liked straight away, Callum a Scottish prop forward she could live without – she felt very sorry for Adelina, the gorgeous Italian professional dancer who had to put up with his 'accidental' gropings all day long. Harri proved to be as friendly and charming as she'd imagined and was partnered with Eva, a fierce looking Swedish dancer, who Harri explained he'd had to put up with when winning the eighth series. They seemed to have a love hate-relationship based on, as far as Merry could see, ferocious nagging on Eva's part. This, in his easy going way, Harri took good naturedly. He was often visited by his fiancée, the actress Julia Cooper, who was feverishly trying to organise the last few details of their wedding in between filming the latest Davy Jones blockbuster. Merry liked her too.

She had less to do with the others. Angie and Scott seemed to be determined to win at any cost and spent all their time training. Merry was intrigued by Casey, a model who wanted to act, but found her huge Russian partner Jan unnecessarily aggressive. Casey however, seemed to enjoy it. Whatever floats your boat, was Merry's opinion, who was nothing if not tolerant of other people's foibles. It amused her to see the clever, calculating Casey turn into a simpering dumb blonde whenever there was a man around. It was also obvious that she and Callum were having a raging affair. Merry hoped that Casey wasn't tempted by the idea of a threesome. She'd seen Casey flirt outrageously with both Callum and her Russian dance pro. She'd need a bed the size of an ocean to fit both men in. She reached for the tiny notebook she always had with her and jotted the thought down. There might be some material there. She licked her pencil and made some notes, giggling. She just wished other people found her jokes as funny as she did.

Merry was well aware she was at a distinct disadvantage in the competition, as the others all had months of training and some years of experience. But, what she lacked in ability, she made up for in enthusiasm and she intended to throw herself wholeheartedly into the competition. Merry was famous for her enthusiasm. It had got her into – and out of - all sorts of situations.

Early on, it had been decided they should all do a group dance and, after the first rehearsal of the merengue based number, it had become apparent that Merry's lack of experience was going to be a problem.

"Think I need some extra coaching," she said mournfully to Harri, as they took a break from the punishing routine they were practising. She leaned against the wall of the television studio, very aware of a camera filming her every move.

"Shouldn't be a problem, bach," he replied, as he towelled the perspiration away and gulped water. "I'm sure Daniel will help you out. He worked wonders for me and Julia. Kindest, most helpful bloke around."

And so, it was agreed that Daniel should offer her some extra lessons, where they could concentrate on getting Merry up to speed.

She was lucky that she and Daniel seemed to have taken to one another immediately. Venetia had been right, as always, and Merry somehow knew Daniel was going to make the ideal partner. More than that, she sensed she'd have some fun with him. And fun was important to Merry; she found it hard to function without it.

After one of the early group rehearsals, in the television studio, she and Daniel had gone to a nearby bar for a get-to-know-you drink. Merry was looking forward to a few hours off-camera. She found their presence disconcerting.

The bar was packed but Daniel, obviously a regular, was given a warm welcome by the maître d', who found them a secluded booth in a dimly lit corner.

"Oh, this is bliss," Merry cried as she slid onto the leather banquette. Lying her head back and closing her eyes, she was vaguely aware of a bottle and some glasses clinking onto their table.

"How are the blisters coming along?" Daniel asked, with a grin in his voice.

"Sadist," Merry said with feeling and, at the glugging sound of wine being poured into a glass, opened her eyes. "Is it normal to be unable to walk after only three rehearsals?"

"Pretty much." Daniel raised his glass. "Cheers."

She reached forward with difficulty as her muscles stiffened, and touched her glass to his. "Cheers."

"Now *this* is bliss," Daniel said appreciatively, as he drank.

"Couldn't agree more. Although I suppose I really ought to have some water too."

"Feeling dehydrated?"

"Just a bit. Hadn't realised how unfit I am. I worked up quite a sweat today."

"You certainly did," Daniel agreed and summoned the waiter again.

"So how long have you been dancing, Daniel?" Merry, having satisfied her thirst with sparkling water, was well down her second glass of red and feeling more revived.

"Since I was a little boy. Mum was a dancer, so I got hauled off to ballet and tap as soon as I was out of nappies." He grinned. "It was a great way to meet girls!"

"I bet! Do you think you'll stay with it, *Who Dares Dances*, I mean?"

"Well, for the foreseeable future. I'd like to win it before I move on."

"No pressure then!" Merry raised her eyebrows at him.

"None whatsoever," Daniel replied, with a wink. "What about you? What got you into the show?"

"My aunt. That is, to give her her proper title: Dame Venetia Denning," Merry said darkly. "No one has ever said 'no' to her and lived."

Daniel laughed. "Ah, the great Dame Venetia. I met her once. She terrified me."

Merry nodded. "That's her. She does that to most people."

"So, it was her idea, was it, that you do *Who Dares Dances?*"

"Yup." Merry took a sip of wine thoughtfully. "Although actually, do you know, I think it's one of her better ones." She pretend-pouted at Daniel. "You probably don't agree."

"I think you'll be great, once you get some basics nailed."

Merry giggled. "What, like knowing which is my left foot and which is my right?"

Daniel smiled. "That sort of thing, yes. Have you had any dance experience?"

Merry shook her head. "Not a lot, just a few lessons at school. And, as it was an all-girls school it was an *excellent* way to meet girls."

Daniel laughed. "Didn't you have any training at drama school? You're an actor, like your aunt, aren't you?"

"Ah, not sure that's quite how I'd be described." She screwed up her face. "I've only done bits and bobs of acting at university. Didn't go to drama school. My most recent stab at showbiz was stand-up. I wasn't very good at that either."

Daniel winced. "That's a tough road to go."

Merry saluted him. "It was no joke, I can tell you."

They groaned in unison.

"This dance show thingy is my last ditch attempt to make a name for myself. If I don't succeed at this, it's curtains for me – and not of the theatrical kind."

Daniel leaned back and watched as Merry poured out the last of the wine. She didn't seem at all fazed by her lack of success. In fact, she seemed quite cheerful. She was uncomplicated and optimistic. He liked that. A lot. In fact, he found he liked *her* a lot. "Another bottle?"

Merry beamed at him. "Now that sounds like a plan, Batman."

Daniel pursed his lips. "I've worn some interesting things for this show and, on occasion, haven't worn very much at all, but I've never dressed up as Batman. Does that mean I have to wear my underpants over my jeans?"

Merry raised herself, slightly drunkenly, to look over the table between them and made a show of scrutinising his crotch. "Now that," she said and held his gaze with wide eyes, "would be worth tuning in for!"

Step Four.

Merry was fortunate that one of the show's assigned rehearsal rooms was in a dance studio within walking distance of Venetia's flat. The other advantage was the cameras rarely bothered to venture out of the television studios. It meant she and Daniel could practise undisturbed. Hurrying into it, one evening, for an extra coaching session, she was taken completely by surprise by Bob Dandry jumping out at her. He was at his smarmiest best.

"Meredith, how lovely to see you and looking extra gorgeous, may I add?" He took both her hands in his clammy ones. "I thought

I'd pop in to see how you're finding your practice space. Must keep the members of our family happy, you know!"

"Bob, hello. Must dash, don't want to be late for my rehearsal, do I?" Merry replied, through clenched teeth, and tugged her hands away. "After all, I've got some catching up to do."

"Oh, not so hasty, my dear. I'm sure Daniel will wait a little longer for his beautiful partner. I just wanted to make sure you've settled into our little community and are being looked after."

"I'm fine, Bob," Merry said firmly. "Now if I could just get on."

Bob was not to be deflected. "You know, if there's anything, anything at all I can help you with, I'd be only too delighted. And I do mean anything, Meredith."

To Merry's utter disgust, he sidled closer.

"Here's my card," he said, with loose lips and a hint of drool. "I've written my personal mobile number on it too. Especially for you, I don't give it out to simply anyone. Just call me, Meredith. I'm at your service. Can't let the niece of my old friend Venetia go lonely."

With that, he pressed his body against hers and slid a hand round Merry's back, where it dropped to cup her bottom. He squeezed hard.

Merry jumped a foot. "Take your hands off me!" she yelped.

"Oh, come now Meredith. Producer's perks and all that." Bob's mouth flapped open like a just landed cod.

Merry gave the man a hard shove, so that he rocked away from her. "As you quite rightly say, my aunt – *Dame* Venetia Denning is known to you. Or, should I say, you're known to her." Merry pulled herself up to her full five feet ten inches and towered over him. "Take my advice, steer clear of me and never ever try anything like that again. Venetia has lots of friends in this business; she's a very influential woman. She could make life very unpleasant for you, if she ever heard about this."

Obviously, the mention of her aunt's name had resonance. Bob paled and put his hands up in mock surrender. He backed off further. "I'm sorry. Just a bit of fun, you know," he huffed, sounding not the least bit apologetic.

Merry stared him down. She didn't think she'd ever met a more unpleasant individual. "And now, if you don't mind, I need to get to my rehearsal."

Bob, still with his hands in the air turned and beat a hasty retreat, shaking his head as he did so.

Fuming, Merry stood, hands on hips and muttered, "Odious little man."

Suni, passing by, overheard. "He is indeed," she agreed. She looked up at Merry. "But be careful, my dear. He's a powerful one too."

"Well, this time he may just have bitten off more than he can chew!" With that, she turned on her heel and strode purposefully to where Daniel was waiting.

Step Five.
A pattern was quickly established. After they'd done any necessary group practices or filming in the television studios, Merry and Daniel would hurry off to the rehearsal rooms, near Venetia's flat, and continue to dance into the night.

During these one to one sessions, Daniel gave nothing but encouragement and positivity, something that Merry really liked about him. She sensed a preoccupation, though, and she thought she knew what or rather who caused it. Once, on an energy high from all the dancing, she'd gone out with Harri, Julia and Daniel. It became very apparent that Daniel was besotted with Julia Cooper. Over some shared tapas and far too much bubbly, Merry watched as Daniel hung on Julia's every word, laughed at all her jokes and kissed and hugged her whenever an opportunity arose. Harri seemed impervious to it, or maybe he was confident in his fiancée's feelings for him? Whatever the truth, it made for great people watching and Merry started forming material about the agony of unrequited love in her head. It never made it onto paper, though, for as soon as she hit the Egyptian cotton in Venetia's spare room, after the novelty of all the physical exertion, she was sound asleep.

Merry and Daniel started later than usual at the Maida Vale dance studios one night. The place was eerily deserted. And cold. They were going over the moves for the group dance for the umpteenth time before concentrating on their first dance for the competition proper: a waltz.

The merengue was still proving a challenge and Merry was tired tonight, her usual energy having been used up. She could manage the basic marching type steps, it was co-ordinating her hips and knees into the required sexy dip and sway that defeated her, especially after a long day's rehearsing with the group. School dancing lessons had never seemed so long ago.

"Focus, Meredith, you're drifting." Daniel's voice pierced the fog of her exhaustion. "Pull into me on the beat. No, more than that, you should be right into my groin."

"Any further in and we'd be committing an illegal act," she grumbled in response.

"Well, that's the idea, lovie. It's got to look absolutely filthy."

"And this goes out on primetime television?" Merry said between gasping for air, "it's obscene."

"Oh, the obscener the better."

"Is that grammatical?" Merry frowned as Daniel took her arm and twisted it over his shoulder.

"You're the one with the expensive education, babe."

"I must've missed the tutorial on *Dirty Dancing*,"

Daniel laughed. "Now, let's do those first few steps again. Your timing's really good but you need to push up from the floor more to give it some bounce."

"If I bounce much more, I'll give myself a black eye," Merry said, as she attempted to shove her breasts back down into her leotard.

Daniel watched with interest. "They are rather large aren't they?"

"Everything about me is large," Merry replied, with asperity

157

but wasn't displeased by the gleam in Daniel's eyes. It was the first time he'd shown interest in her as a woman and not just a dance partner.

"But perfectly proportioned," he added, with a charming smile, as if realising how ungallant his remark was. "No, keep your arm there so I can take my hand and - oh not again!" he cried as Merry dissolved into giggles at his touch. It was the third time she'd done so tonight.

"I can't help it, I'm really ticklish there. Ooh," she sighed, as Daniel increased the pressure and rubbed his hand down her side rather than lightly caressing. "That's better." She melted into him for a moment as the hand searched downwards. "Mmm. That's so much better."

"Then perhaps we'll do it like this," was the only reply he made.

Merry found she enjoyed looking Daniel over as, having declared a break, he strolled to the water cooler to get a drink. He was wearing his white jeans again and they showed off his long legs and tight behind to perfection. Until she'd started her training, Merry had never realised how fit you had to be as a dancer. Daniel was in about as good a shape you could be, with the strong lean muscles of the professional dancer and not an ounce of fat on him. She noticed he'd had his hair cut since yesterday and she preferred it to the slightly eighties look he'd sported when she'd first met him. Now his hair had a rumpled, just got out of bed look, which she knew meant hours in front of a mirror to achieve. Or, perhaps she was wrong? Daniel didn't seem as vain as the other dancers. Perhaps this was how he looked when he'd just got up. Merry felt herself blush inside. She knew what it was: sheer lust. She was developing a crush on Daniel Cunningham. And it was a wholly enjoyable and familiar feeling. She'd been famous at university for never falling seriously for someone. She flirted; it was as habitual to her as breathing and she'd had one or two flings, but she'd never really had her heart touched by anyone. Not seriously. But she'd had crushes. And she loved the excitement of them. As she watched Daniel gulp down water and then wipe his mouth with the back of his hand she felt a thrill go through her. She wanted this man.

"Penny for them?" Daniel offered her a cup of water.

Merry hoped the blush stayed where it had begun; deep inside. She turned on her smile, it usually had the effect she wanted. "Oh, just thinking how quiet it had got, now the aerobics class has finished." She took the water and drank gratefully.

"Had enough?"

"Oh no, I'm happy to carry on all night if we have to."

Daniel laughed. "That shouldn't be necessary. Want to have another go at the merengue?"

Merry thought about having slide up against Daniel's crotch and her tiredness fled. "Why not?" She picked up a towel and mopped her face. Despite the lack of heating, she was working up a sweat again. Must be the exercise. Or the ultra-close proximity to Daniel's presence. "You never know, I might even get it right this time."

"Miracles can happen, or so I've heard."

Merry snapped her towel at him but he was too quick on his feet and he dodged away, laughing.

"Seriously though Merry, you pick up the steps incredibly quickly. We can work more on the feel of the dance tomorrow."

"I like the sound of that. You know, I'm beginning to find this all rather fun. Where do I stand to begin? Behind you? Like this?" Merry got into position behind Daniel, with one hand on his shoulder and the other on her own hip. She admired their joint reflection in the mirrored walls. "We look good together."

"I'll choose to ignore that remark. Ready? Then I need to swing you round like this and we're face to face to get into hold."

Merry squeaked as Daniel took hold of her wrist and pulled her to him.

"Sorry, was that too rough? It ought to have an almost tango mood to it, quite vicious, passionate. That's what I mean about getting a feel for the dance."

Merry found she was getting quite a feel for Daniel. They were still in hold, faces inches apart and Merry was enjoying the view she had of his grass green eyes. Heat was coming off his skin and she relished the sensuality of having her breasts pressed against his hard muscled chest.

He broke away suddenly. "Right, that's good then. Just one more go through the steps into our lift, a quick once through of our waltz and then we'll call it a night."

"Whatever you say Dan, you're the boss. Just put me where you want me." Merry batted her eyelashes at him, coquettishly.

"Behave Meredith. We've got work to do. Beginning position again."

They carried on training until it was nearly eleven and then Daniel called a halt.

The studio's corridors were in darkness as they made their way to the exit and they could only by the glow of the orange street lighting outside. Merry hung onto Daniel, not because she wanted to flirt; she couldn't see a thing. And she was beginning to feel nervous.

"That's strange," she said, biting down on the old, never quite forgotten, panic. To say she hated being in dark spaces, would be an understatement. She felt her way along the wall. "Roger usually leaves the lights on for us."

Roger was the caretaker who, being an enormous fan of *Who Dares Dances*, didn't mind a bit having to wait for them to finish before he could secure the building.

"Oh God!" Daniel stopped dead and clasped a hand to his head. "I forgot."

"Forgot what?" Merry was annoyed at hearing a tremble in her voice. She vowed to keep calm. This time.

"It isn't Roger locking up tonight. It's his night off. They've got a relief guy in. I was supposed to ring down to the office with a finishing time."

They stared at one another.

"You don't think?"

"We can't be!"

They made the rest of the way to the main entrance in seconds. It was locked.

Daniel put his back to the door and slid down to the floor. "I can't believe it. We're locked in!"

Merry joined him, trying to force out a giggle. "Well, I did say we might have to train all night."

Daniel missed her veiled panic. "I'm glad you find it funny. Thinking back, it was odd no one came up to see how long we were going to be. Roger always does. What a stupid thing to do. How on earth did the other bloke miss us?"

"You can't see or hear our room from here," Merry pointed out. She was thankful she had someone with her; it made the claustrophobia a little easier to deal with. "We're through that linking corridor in the annexe. But you think he'd have checked throughout the building before he locked up." She concentrated on her breathing. Keep it regular and deep, said the voice in her head.

"What the hell are we going to do?"

Merry looked. Her eyes adjusted to the lack of light, and she could see better. And now she'd got her initial panic under control, she could think more clearly. It was a wide passageway, thankfully. Not too hemmed in. Offices and rooms led off the corridor. All its doors were shut, their glass panels reflecting a dull blue in the gloom. "Is there some kind of admin office along here, or does Roger have an office?"

"And then what?"

Merry poked him in the ribs. "I don't know. There might be a phone number we could call? Maybe the security firm? It's worth a try. Much as I enjoy your company Daniel, I'd like to get home to my bed."

"What about ringing your aunt? That's who you're staying with, isn't it? Couldn't she help?"

"Out," Merry replied. "She has a better social life than me," she added gloomily. "All I'm fit for is bed after you've done with me."

Daniel got up in one lithe movement and held out a hand. "Haven't even started with you yet, babe."

"Promises, promises," Merry said, almost forgetting her panic at the implied innuendo.

They began towards the nearest door. Despite being momentarily distracted, she found the place thoroughly spooky now she knew they were on their own. She clutched onto Daniel's arm again and this time with no ulterior motive apart from seeking comfort.

He patted her hand. "Ah, a big girl like you scared. What was that?" He veered round suddenly at an imaginary sound.

Merry let out an ear piercing scream and grabbed him round the waist.

Daniel burst out laughing.

"You bastard," she cried, her heart pumping and hit him, half giggling, half afraid.

He took her by the shoulders and, for a second, they stood close together enjoying the moment.

Daniel slid his arms around her waist and smiled down at her, realising he liked how much she made him laugh. Something that hadn't happened for too long a time. "This isn't getting us anywhere," he said, reluctantly releasing her.

"Oh, I don't know," Merry replied, in a small voice, loving the feel of his reassuring and very solid presence. Then she repressed a shudder, "But you're right. We need to get out of here." Using humour to ward off her fear, she added, "for one thing, I'm starving."

"You're always starving," Daniel complained but reached into his enormous leather holdall and fished out a banana.

"My saviour!" Merry cried dramatically, clutched it to her breast and then shivered violently.

Daniel took off his jacket and swung it round Merry's shoulders. "Warmer now?" he asked.

"Yes thanks," she replied. "My hero," she added but in a

completely different tone.

She followed him as he tried opening the various doors off the corridor. "It's no good," he groaned exasperated, as he rattled the third one. "I think they're all locked."

Merry's habitual optimism was beginning to desert her. The panic at the lack of escape route set in once more. She tried another door, only to find it locked, like the others. "What are we going to do?" She stamped her foot.

This time Daniel heard her desperation. "Don't worry," he said, trying to lighten the situation, "you won't have to spend the night with me." He put an arm round her shoulders and hugged her close. In terms of height, they were perfectly matched; Merry's head came up to just under his chin. She was trembling slightly, which surprised him. She always seemed so confident. He allowed himself to inhale the musky perfume of her hair and then felt her jolt as they heard a noise.

"What was that?" Merry's trembling increased.

"Don't know, but I think it came from the main entrance. Let's have a look. Game?"

Merry nodded.

He took her by the hand and they crept back towards the door. They jumped a foot as it was shaken violently, making the noise they'd heard. A flashlight shone into the darkened foyer, blinding them.

"Hey!" Daniel yelled, "Let us out." He banged on the door. "We're locked in!"

Merry could just make out a shadowy figure peering in at them. It didn't look like a security guard or caretaker. "Daniel, I don't think," she began to say but Daniel banged on the door again, drowning her words.

Then all went silent.

Merry went to the wall opposite and slunk down onto the cold lino. "This isn't funny anymore," she said morosely.

Daniel joined her and hugged her close. "No it isn't. I don't know who that was but I bet you anything they've gone to get someone who can help."

"Maybe."

"Or we could ring Bob?"

The thought of Bob rescuing them, and possibly demanding a greasy something as a thank you, made Merry even more miserable. "Think I'd rather take a chance on our mysterious door rattler."

She sounded disconsolate so Daniel racked his brain for something to distract her.

"So, you went to Oxford," he began, a little desperately. "Tell me what it was like. Did you have men falling at your feet?"

He felt her relax slightly and then heard a giggle. It was strained but it was definitely a giggle.

"Something like that," she replied. "There were a few. And I had an affair with my tutor in my third year."

"Really?" Daniel was intrigued.

Merry told him about Hillary MacDonald. "He's on the telly now, fronting a programme about the Romantic Poets on the History Channel," she said. "He was thirty seven when I met him, half Irish, half Highland Scot, glorious red hair and with a brain like a steel trap," she added, warming to her theme. "He took me under his wing, taught me all sorts of things."

"I bet," Daniel said drily.

"No it wasn't like that," Merry smiled at him. She peeled the banana he'd given her and broke it in half. "I was a girl from the suburbs, from a monied but otherwise ordinary background. The only exotic thing in my family is Aunt Venetia, the great actress."

Daniel nodded and accepted the half banana she offered. "She knows my mother a little."

"That figures. Venetia knows everyone! She's more than enough celebrity for our family. The rest of us are more down to earth. Hillary introduced me to so much: music, poetry, history. He gave me an education. We had to keep it quiet of course, but it wasn't sordid. It was good fun." Merry absentmindedly gave Daniel back the banana peel. He put it into the holdall without complaint.

"Not serious then?" he asked on a grin. He couldn't imagine Merry being serious about anything. She was too full of mischief.

"No, not at all. I don't think I'm made for anything serious." Merry giggled again but with more feeling. "Never felt like that about anyone, really. It's not in my make-up. Mucked up my degree though, that and my Drama Soc obsession," she continued. "I was supposed to get a First. Always keep your love life and your professional life separate is my mantra."

Daniel thought about Julia and agreed. "Good advice."

Julia was on Merry's mind too. "What about you Dan? You're straight, aren't you?"

"Yes, I'm straight," he said with a chuckle. "What made you think otherwise?"

"Well, a lot of the other dancers aren't," Merry pointed out reasonably.

"True."

"So, what is it about Julia that so fascinates you?"

Daniel shook his head. "Has anyone told you you're incorrigibly nosy?"

Merry gave a broad grin. "Frequently. Answer the question."

"What makes you think I've got a thing for Julia?"

"I've got eyes."

Daniel was silent.

"Did it start when you danced together?" As there was no answer, Merry continued. "I can see how it happened. It's such an intimate thing to do, isn't it? Dance with someone. And Julia is gorgeous. Intelligent and funny and talented."

"Oh yes. She's gorgeous, alright." It came out on a long breath.

"But getting married to Harri and they're devoted to one another."

Daniel looked down. "I think," he said eventually, "that it's become a habit. One that I can't break free of. I've tried." He took his arm from around Merry. She seemed perfectly relaxed now.

He was the one wrong-footed by the conversation.

"What about going out with someone new?" Merry persisted.

Daniel stared at the door and prayed for rescue. "I've tried that," he said, gruffly. "Went out with Eva for a bit."

"Eva!" Merry thought about the thin Swede with her glacial good looks. She shuddered. "Not the right woman for you."

"No?" Despite himself, Daniel was amused. "And what makes you so sure of that?"

Merry was on a roll now. "Well, for one thing, it's work again, isn't it? And another, she's too cold. Bet she was good in bed though?"

"Merry, I've never met anyone like you."

"It gets said to me a lot," Merry replied, with a trace of her aunt's smugness. "I *think* it's a good thing." She gave him an impish look. "But, back to Eva. Yes, she'd be good in bed: efficient, great technique but with no warmth, no feeling, no real enjoyment."

Daniel laughed again, he couldn't help himself. "You're so right."

"Always am," she said and yawned. She peered at her watch; it was nearly midnight. "God, look at the time. Do you think anyone will come and rescue us, Dan? Do you think it might be worth ringing the police?"

He shifted uncomfortably on the hard floor and slid his mobile out of his jeans pocket. Peering at it, he cursed. "I would, but my mobile's out of juice. What about yours?"

"Hang on a sec. I'll have a look." Merry hunted through her bag for her phone. Then she had an image of where she'd left it: charging its battery on the bedside table in Venetia's spare room. She turned to face Daniel, her eyes huge. "I've left it at home. God, I'm an idiot sometimes."

Daniel sighed. "Then we'll have to be patient and wait a little longer. I'm not sure we'd class as an emergency with the Metropolitan police, anyway, even if we could ring 999. Think they might have other things to do."

"I suppose so," Merry agreed. "Even in Maida Vale."

"Even in Maida Vale," Daniel echoed drily. "Oh well," at this, he replaced his arm around Merry's shoulders, as her mood had dipped again. "If we are to be stuck here overnight, we'll just have to go back up to the dance studio and kip on the exercise balls." He caught her look. "What? I'm sure they'd be comfortable enough, once you got used to rolling around."

Another half an hour passed, during which time Merry devoured two more bananas and a carton of raspberry smoothie.

"Never known a woman eat like you," Daniel grumbled as he handed them over. He searched through his bag for more food to distract her. "Here, have a cereal bar."

"It's your fault," Merry pointed out. "It's all this exercise you're forcing on me. It's making me permanently hungry. I'll be the size of a house by Easter."

Daniel snorted. "You won't put on weight, at least not fat. Might add a little muscle, though. Get you more toned up." He pinched her thigh, making her squeal.

A hammering at the front door made her squeal again.

It turned out that they did constitute an emergency for the Maida Vale branch of the Met. Rather, Bernie Solomon, walking his dog and being frightened out of his wits as he made his late night constitutional, had convinced them it was.

"I knew something was going on," he exclaimed, as his Westie pulled on the lead and barked at all the excitement of a policeman forcing open the door and letting out two very relieved and tired dancers. "I thought it was burglars. This lot," he nodded at the police officers, "weren't going to come out. But I insisted."

"Funny looking burglars," said one of the policemen. Then he turned to Daniel and gave an exclamation. "Don't I know you? You're one of those dancers on *Who Dares Dances* aren't you? I never miss a show. I suppose you wouldn't mind?"

He handed his notebook to Daniel who signed his name with a flourish. Merry could see him grinning in the neon light of the streetlamp.

"A pleasure constable," he said. "Least I could do to thank you for saving me from a night with this woman, she was eating me out of house and home."

"Oi!" squawked Merry and poked him in the ribs.

The police officer looked Merry up and down. "Can't say I'd share your concerns, sir," he said, on a friendly grin.

Merry felt herself blush. This was getting more and more surreal. "Thank you officer. I knew I could always rely on the chivalry of the great British police."

"You can do that, ma'am." The policeman tipped his hat.

Ma'am! Merry had never been called ma'am in her life. She filed it away for later, to use as possible material.

"This your new dance partner then, Mr Cunningham?" the policeman continued, shushing his colleague who was trying to get him to go to another call.

"It is indeed, officer," Daniel responded. "This is the raw material with which I have to work." He winked at Merry. "I doubt very much if we'll be lifting the trophy at the end of this run."

This time Merry kicked him. Sharply. On the ankle.

"Again sir, I have to say I can't see as I share your concerns. Think you'll both do alright. You'll get my vote at any rate." The policeman turned to Bernie. "And now Mr Solomon, do you want to get off home? And I'd be indebted if you could stop your dog from barking or we'll have more complaints."

Mr Solomon marched off, pulling a reluctant terrier with him and loudly proclaiming how the area had gone downhill since the new mayor had taken over.

The policeman shook Daniel's hand. "Well, good luck to you both." He nodded to the dance studio behind them. "We've been in touch with the caretaker. He'll be along shortly to secure the building. Night then." With that, he got back into the patrol car and it sped off to answer the next call, blue lights flashing.

Merry began to giggle and leaned on Daniel for support. He held her and joined in. It was amazing how fond of her he felt tonight. In a matter of days they'd become very close. It often happened with a dance partner, of course, you were forced into their company in a very intimate way. But this was extraordinary, unusual. He put it down to Merry. She was uncomplicated and fun loving, charming and naturally flirtatious. He wished he had her ease with people.

"Shall I walk you home?"

Merry wiped her eyes, still laughing. It was partly the relief at being out in the fresh air. "Oh Daniel, how lovely of you. No, it's alright, the flat's only round the corner and, as you know, I'm a big girl."

"It's late." For some reason Daniel wanted to prolong the evening.

Merry yawned. "It is indeed but I promise you, I'll be fine. And, if I'm not, I'll just shout for our friendly local police force to help sort me out! Or failing that, Mr Solomon and his faithful canine companion." With a wave, she strode off into the night.

Daniel watched as she went, fighting an urge to chase after her. Then he shook his head and went to flag down a taxi, shivering as he did. "Merry, you've still got my jacket!" he yelled after her but she'd disappeared.

Step Six.

Bob dropped his bombshell on the second week in, two days after they'd filmed the first show. The old hands tensed in expectation. They knew from previous experience that anything could be sprung upon them.

They had all been asked to meet, for a specially convened breakfast briefing, in a hotel in Bloomsbury. Along with the cameras, of course, which weren't missing a thing.

"This must be costing Fizz a packet," Daniel said, as he looked around at the faux art-deco interior of the banqueting room. "God knows what the bastard has in store for us this year."

Merry wasn't listening. "Will you look at the food," she said, pointing at the sumptuous buffet the production team had laid on.

"Exactly." Daniel had an instinct about this. And it wasn't a good one. "They've never gone all out like this before."

Bob and his assistant Maria entered the room. The babble of noise hushed, as all eyes turned to them.

"Hang on, our esteemed leader is about to speak. Brace yourself, this could take a while." Daniel pulled Merry away from the buffet, but not before she'd crammed a blueberry muffin into her mouth.

"Girls and boys, thank you all for coming this morning." Bob began. "And many thanks to the Artemida for being such wonderful hosts." He gestured to the hotel manager.

Maria led a half-hearted round of applause. Merry nodded enthusiastically, still chewing.

"As this special series of *Who Dares Dances* is linked to the *Jokes for Notes* campaign, our special request for you all this time is -" he paused dramatically, enjoying the tension on the faces before him, savouring being the centre of attention. One or two nervous gulps could be heard. "You will be asked to do a series of fundraising stunts. These will be filmed alongside our normal training footage, of course."

Merry sensed relief rippling round the collected celebrities and dancers. Some chatter broke out and Harri and Callum began to move towards the buffet.

Bob hadn't finished. "If I could beg your indulgence a little while longer," he raised his voice above the noise. "We'll be celebrating our hundredth episode, during this series." Again, Maria led a response. "And we plan to showcase the best of the filming in three, hour long specials."

Suni, Warren and Angie got distracted by a waiter offering them Kir Royales. Scott popped the cork on a bottle of champagne and began sharing it with the other pro dancers.

Bob was in danger of losing his audience. "If you could – "

"It can't be that simple," muttered Daniel in Merry's ear. He shook his head. "He always has something that catches us out."

Bob began to yell. "To make it a teensy bit more challenging. "

"Told you," whispered Daniel.

"Ooh, we are Mr Sharp-as-a-pin, this morning. Get out of bed on the right side?" Merry responded. "I'm not bothered what they ask us to do as long as I can get to those mini pancakes first."

"If I could have your attention for just one tiny second more," Bob shouted again. The room quietened. He tried to keep the glee from his voice and failed. "To make it that little bit more challenging, you will be asked to undertake something which taps into your fears. Your *innermost* fears."

"Duw, here we go," said Harri, on the other side of Merry. "He'll have us eating kangaroo testicles."

"Alright for you," laughed Merry, "you've had plenty of experience of doing daft things like that when you did that children's TV show."

"The worst this lot have had to face is running out of fake tan," Daniel added.

Merry stifled a giggle.

Bob was on a roll now. "For those of you with a thing about heights, we'll have you abseiling down The Shard, for those of you with a fear of water we've organised scuba diving in a tank full of sharks."

Angie and Callum gasped. Their phobias were well known amongst the team.

The reality of the situation was slowly dawning on Merry. "They've researched this, haven't they?" she said to Daniel.

"Oh yes," he replied. "Bob the Bastard has a streak named Evil running right through his middle."

"Meredith," Bob turned to the girl with a purely malicious smile. He hadn't forgotten how she'd treated him. "We had to find something extra special for you, as you joined the show so late in the day. But I don't think you'll be disappointed in what we have planned. I think you'll find it a real challenge, worthy of your talents. And of course, the harder the personal challenge, the more money the public will donate."

Merry swallowed. He couldn't possibly know, could he? It was the one thing in her gilded, easy life that truly terrified her.

Daniel glanced at his partner. She had gone a greenish-white. It was unlike the Merry he knew. "You alright, babe?" He put an arm round her and hugged her to him. "No matter what he wants you to do, remember you don't have to accept."

"That's the problem," Harri added and swore viciously in Welsh. "It was in the contract. We're obliged to go along with this farce."

"So, I'll let you digest it all at your leisure. Any questions, see Maria as usual. She'll give you some more information." With a cheery wave, Bob sped off, leaving his beleaguered assistant surrounded by anxious celebrities, keen to receive the packs of information which detailed their particular challenge.

"Shall I go and get ours?" Daniel asked but was reluctant to let go of Merry. In the few weeks he'd known her, apart from being momentarily panicked when locked in at the rehearsal rooms, she had only ever been fearless. He remembered her laughing off the judges' criticism of her first dance, a pretty awful waltz. She'd made a funny story of how she put Bob in his place when he'd groped her. She'd been all energy and enthusiasm – and charisma, so far. But now she looked so frail he thought she might fall if he let go.

"No don't," she answered eventually. It came out as a whisper. "If Bob is the devious shit you say he is, I know exactly the sort of challenge he wants me to face."

Daniel had never felt protective towards Merry before, had never seen the need to be. He looked down at her ashen face. "Don't worry lovie, we'll get through it together, whatever it is."

Merry clutched at his sleeve, watching as Harri took a blue folder off Maria. "You might have to help me Dan, if it's what I think it is." She gazed up at him, her eyes wide with fear. "You might have to help me through this a lot."

Daniel came back brandishing a thin folder. "Come on, let's go and get a coffee and have a look through this." He nodded to the breakfast buffet. "Do you want to go and get something to eat now?"

Merry shook her head.

"Must be serious if you've gone off your food," Daniel began to joke and then stopped as he saw the thin misery on her face.

They found a quiet spot in one of the hotel's sitting rooms. It had been decorated to look like a country house library, complete with fake leather bound books. Daniel ordered double espressos; he had the feeling Merry might need some caffeine. The blue folder lay on the low table between them, faintly accusing.

"Would you like me to?" he offered.

Merry shook her head again. But she managed to pick up the folder and open it with only slightly trembling hands.

Daniel watched as Merry read its contents. Her cheeks flushed and then paled, her usual mile wide smile absent. Until that moment, he hadn't realised how fond of it he had become.

"It's what I thought," Merry said, in a quiet voice. "I'm not sure how Bob's found out. Even if Venetia knew, she would never have told him; her opinion of him is lower than mine." Merry attempted a smile and it came out twisted. "My parents certainly would never have done so, and anyway, they don't know the whole story." She looked down. "I've got to be shut in a mummy's sarcophagus. For as long as I can. The longer I'm in there, the more money I'll raise. I suppose it's almost funny when you say it like that." Merry straightened her shoulders and looked Daniel in the eyes. She sucked in a deep breath.

"Okay," Daniel said, mystified. It didn't sound too awful; not when you compared it to swimming with sharks. But, he could see how difficult it was going to be for Merry. He didn't understand why, but her distress was genuine. Strangely enough, he could also sense a glimmering determination under the nerves and his admiration for her grew.

"You don't have to do it."

"Oh come on, Daniel. For one, it's in my contract as Harri

pointed out and, for another, I'm not going to let that slimy little low life beat me. Bastard." Her voice was pure vitriol. "Bastard, bastard, bastard!"

"Feel better?"

"A little."

"Look, here comes the coffee. Drink some."

"Bossy boots," Merry grumbled but obeyed. "God, he's scum. And if I don't do it, how will that look? Meredith Denning; couldn't even get in a stupid bloody sarcophagus for charity!"

"You won't get any arguments from me about the pond life that is Bob Dandry. And look Merry, while I can see this is going to be hard for you," Daniel began.

"Just slightly," Merry raised an eyebrow in humour.

"I don't understand why," he finished. He drank his espresso in one gulp. He didn't know about Merry, but he certainly needed the coffee hit. "Do you feel up to telling me?"

Merry looked deep into Daniel's kind eyes. He was a nice man. What a shame he was still so hung up on Julia. They'd had such fun in rehearsals and she didn't want that to change. She'd been enjoying this far too much to let this new development change things. She'd never told a soul about what had happened. Even her parents had only the haziest idea of the resulting phobia. She simply avoided any situation that was likely to cause her a problem. And if it did, she used humour, albeit of the blackest kind, to deflect from her distress.

Merry bit her lip. "I know I can trust you." And she realised she could. She'd been left with an abiding suspicion and distrust of most people but this man, who she had known for less than four weeks, she somehow knew she would trust. With her life, if necessary. It was a strange and wonderful feeling for Merry, who kept people at a distance if she could help it.

"Of course you can trust me." Daniel he took her hand. The urge to protect Merry overwhelmed him. Peculiar and unfamiliar, it was what he wanted to do. Protect her.

174

Merry let her hand rest in Daniel's comforting one. "Okay then." She grinned, it was a weak, watery one but it was definitely a grin. "But we may need about a gallon more coffee and a bucket load of that gorgeous food I spied back in the banqueting room! I've been bottling this up for years."

While Daniel went to load up plates with their breakfast, Merry let her head rest on the plasticky leather armchair and marvel at what she was about to do. It was her big secret. If she told him this, he would know her better than anyone. If she had to explain why it had to be Daniel, she wouldn't be able to. It simply felt right. He was the right man.

Daniel came back, laden with croissants, pancakes and more muffins and with the message that coffee was following. Merry gave him time to settle back down, watched as a girl brought a tray of coffee and set it down and then took a deep breath and launched in.

"I'd only been at boarding school for a week before some of the others began to pick on me," she began. "It started as a bit of plait pulling and knocking over my lunch tray. Nothing serious." She shrugged. "But then it moved onto something more. They had a ring-leader, this group of bullies." Merry took a deep breath. "Her name was Carly. Carly Jones. I've no idea what the motive was. Jealousy maybe? I'd made friends with one of her besties." Merry pulled a puzzled face. "Anyway, Carly came up with this initiation ceremony. It was claimed, so Carly said, that anyone new joining the school had to go through it." I know, Merry said, at the incredulous look on Daniel's face. "But I was eight and new and lonely. I probably would've done anything simply to get accepted into the gang." She took a gulp of coffee and continued. "They didn't tell me any details but, it was promised, I'd know what I had to do when the time came. Well, three weeks later – "

"Three weeks? You had to wait three weeks?"

"Yup and I was terrified the whole time. Didn't know what to expect, I suppose."

"Oh Merry!"

"It's alright, Dan. It's a long time ago." Merry patted his hand. "It must have been just before the first half term holiday, when it happened. I was woken up in the middle of the night. Even then I was tall for my age," Merry gave a weak giggle, "and hefty, so it took a fair few of them to tie me up and gag me."

"What?"

Merry smiled at him. "I know, it sounds really awful now. But at the time, I didn't struggle all that much, just went along with it. It was the promised initiation, you see? Anyway," she continued in a rush, as if now she'd begun, she wanted to get it over with. "I was carried quite some distance, I remember the girls huffing and puffing with all the effort."

"Serves them right."

Merry snorted. "Agreed. They shoved me in somewhere or other. I could hardly move, it was so small. I remember it smelling dusty. I heard the lock turn and I was left there. Alone."

Daniel rubbed a hand across his brow. "And there's me thinking girls are the gentler sex."

"Yeah right," Merry said, without humour.

"And then what happened?"

"I got my hands free, after a struggle, and then I could at least get the horrible, stifling gag off. It was a relief to be able to breathe more easily. I kept coughing to get the bits of fluff out of my throat. It was so dry. Then I tried to work out where I was. In some sort of cupboard," she added before Daniel asked. "It wasn't quite high enough for me to stand up. I tried and bumped my head on the shelf above. And it didn't matter how hard I banged on the door, it wouldn't budge."

Merry fell silent, thinking back. She'd hoped the cleaners would come along soon and release her. It was pitch black and she'd begun to get frightened. No matter how loudly she yelled, it seemed she was out of the hearing of anyone in the entire school.

"Eventually," she said, staring unseeing at the hotel bookcases, with their fake books, "I fell into a sort of fitful doze and when I woke up, I could see a glimmer of light creeping under the gap of the cupboard door. I was relieved. I thought someone would come and get me now. The cleaners maybe, or Carly? Then we'd all have a giggle about it and go into breakfast."

"But they didn't?" Daniel prompted.

"What? Oh no. Not for hours. Or that's what it seemed like. I was getting really panicky."

Merry recalled banging on the door and shouting again, only to end up bruising her knuckles and exhausting herself. She'd begun to get very frightened. And with the fear came cramp in her legs and the illogical certainty that the air in the small space was running out. She desperately needed the loo and the pain in her bladder added to the horror of it all.

She'd fallen into a daze, trying to take her mind away from the horror she felt. She concentrated fiercely on conjuring up an image of home: her cosy bedroom, her mother's delicious tarte Tatin, Jasper the Lab waiting with a waggy tail to see her at half term. She had been forced to let her bladder go. It had been was the most mortifying thing about the whole experience. She hadn't wet herself since a toddler.

"Then, miracle of miracles, I heard a key turning in the rusty lock. It was one of the cleaners. She wanted to put some dusters away, I think." Merry frowned, thinking how absurd it was that she could recall such a tiny detail. "Anyway, I fell out on top of her, much to her shock. Think the poor woman retired not long after. Had enough of the girls' high-jinks, I would imagine."

Daniel drank another, now cold, slug of coffee. "I would imagine," he echoed drily. "Then what happened?"

"After being squished up for so long, I couldn't walk, so Matron was called and I was put in the San. The school's medical room," she added, seeing Daniel's questioning look.

Merry fell silent again. After being cleaned up, a yet more humiliating experience by a Matron who clearly thought Merry should be old enough to control her bodily functions and said so in no uncertain terms, she'd spent two days recovering in bed.

Merry didn't breathe a word about what had happened. Some kind of survival instinct told her that telling the truth about the bullying would be suicidal. In fact, she remained mute for the entire forty-eight hours afterwards. An unsympathetic Matron gave no encouragement so Merry took it all within herself, where it festered and magnified.

Looking back, Merry supposed she had been in shock, or possibly had some kind of mild post-traumatic syndrome. She was offered no help of any kind though, and after catching up on her sleep and having a cursory medical examination by the doctor, she was returned to lessons and the dormitory.

Daniel, looking at her face, knew she wasn't telling him everything. She was miles away from him. Then he watched as she tried to pull herself together. She shook herself, drank more coffee and ate a morsel of cold, flaccid pancake. She looked up to see him staring, concerned.

Merry smiled and shrugged. She continued her story. "One consolation, I suppose, was a grudging acceptance from Carly and her gang. We never became friends though. We circled warily round one another in a sort of mutually agreed but unspoken distance. It was still fairly horrible at school until Carly was found guilty of one bullying act too many and she was expelled."

"But you never told?"

Merry shook her head. "Would have made things worse for me. Or maybe it would've got rid of Carly sooner? Who knows, maybe it was a kind of misguided pride? Still, hindsight is a wonderful thing and I was only eight, remember. It was only when she'd gone that I could relax a bit."

The truth was she'd never really relaxed since. The experience had left her with an abiding and deep-seated fear of being trapped in small spaces. And, being five feet ten by the age of twelve, it wasn't difficult to keep finding herself stuck. Then later, when older, lifts, basements, tunnels - anywhere with no obvious exit was added to the list of places to have to deal with. Merry hated large crowds too, when she felt penned in and was jostled and she even found queues hard to deal with. She never gave up, though. She'd used her humour and fierce intelligence to hide the truth. By the time she left the school for Oxford, she was one of the most popular and well liked of pupils. She often wondered what had become of Carly.

When she finished, Daniel sat back on his chair. Some fresh coffee arrived, so he poured them both another cup. "And you've really never told anyone about this, at school or afterwards? And you've never had therapy or counselling?"

Merry smiled and shook her head. Trust Daniel, with his showbiz background, to think of that. In her matter-of-fact, middle-class upbringing, the most sympathetic phrase, when-ever things went wrong, had been: 'Worse things happen at sea.' Therapy, or any kind of counselling, didn't exist in her parents' world. Perhaps she should've considered some? It had been a huge relief to share the experience with someone after all these years. Well, most of it. She'd missed out the more humiliating aspects. A thought occurred. "You mustn't tell anyone, Dan. Please."

"Of course not, if that's what you want. Some of it is bound to come out when – if – you do the challenge, though. That's part of it. So, don't you think you ought to tell someone in the production company about it? I mean, I know everyone's going to have to face some kind of fear but this is a real phobia, from what you've told me."

"No!" Merry was adamant, her eyes blazing. "I'm not letting anyone else know how much it affects me. I'm not giving Bob the Bastard that satisfaction. I'm going to do this, if only to see that self-satisfied smirk wiped off his face."

Daniel pursed his lips. "Well, okay, and you know you can count on my support." He chased a croissant flake around his plate, a frown spoiling his smooth good looks. "One thing puzzles me, though."

"What?"

"If you've never told anyone about this, how come Bob has found out?"

Merry shook her head, thoughtfully. "I've absolutely no idea but I'd be very interested to find out." She stood up, with a sudden new energy. "And now Mr Cunningham, I've had enough of all this introspective rubbish. The clock is ticking and I have a tango to perform this week. Hadn't we better get down to some practice?"

Daniel grinned up at her, enjoying her sudden change of mood. Besides, the full length Meredith was an impressive sight. "You're such a taskmaster," he complained.

"You bet, and you ain't seen nothing yet." Merry gave him the benefit of her mega-watt smile. "Come on lazy bones. As Jan would say, 'Ve haff vork to do'!"

Step Seven.

Their tango, the following Saturday, was met with a much higher score than their abysmal waltz. Unusually, the judges were unanimous in their praise of Merry's ability. Daniel was pleased too. He'd known she had the capability to pick things up quickly but what he really admired was her hard work and her persistence through even the most painful of blisters. Being so tall, she'd told him once, she'd never needed to wear heels, let alone *dance* in them. She seemed too, to have shaken off the momentary melancholy that had accompanied sharing her phobia. Meredith Denning was back on form – and how!

In the television studio bar after their triumphant tango, Merry glugged back her first drink with all the thirst of one stranded in a desert. The image of John Mills sinking his pint in Venetia's favourite film, *Ice Cold in Alex* came to her. "Oh boy, I needed that."

Daniel smiled indulgently and motioned to the barman for another round.

The others crowded round briefly to congratulate them but soon drifted off. Daniel liked it when it was just the two of them. Merry was so gregarious, she always had a flock of people around her. It wasn't often, out of rehearsal time, that he had her to himself.

"You were so good tonight. I was really proud of you," he said, as he passed her a fresh glass of wine. "Well done!"

"All down to you, Batman," Merry replied, a wicked gleam in her eyes. "I'd never have the self-discipline to do this on my own."

"Oh, I don't know, Merry, I've a feeling you could do anything you want, if you really put your mind to it. You know, you're really beginning to move like a dancer."

Merry giggled. "Must be all those tap and ballet lessons at that excuse for a boarding school. If we'd done something really awful, they made us do country dancing in the summer, complete with a Maypole." She snorted. "I always had to lead being so tall. Maybe I would've taken ballet more seriously but I could see the teachers never thought I'd have a future in it, once I'd gone past five eight and ten stone. I've forgotten most of it."

Daniel shook his head. "Nah, you never forget all of it. You make some fantastic lines with your hands and feet and your posture's brilliant now. And, I for one, am very pleased that you didn't join the world of ballet. It would have been my loss."

They clinked glasses.

"To us," Daniel cried.

"We are bloody marvellous, aren't we?" beamed Merry.

"How lovely it is to see you all getting on so well," came a snide voice. It was Bob standing behind them. "Don't have too much to drink now, boys and girls, tomorrow is the first day of the challenges, remember." He wagged an admonitory finger at them.

"And don't forget," said Merry, echoing his singsong tone. "It's only Angie being filmed." She raised her glass and drank deliberately deep. "You look cheerful tonight, Bob. Has someone died?"

Bob glanced from her to Daniel, aware he was being made fun of. "Well, no need to take that attitude," he huffed. "Only doing my duty and reminding you not to drink too much. We've got a hard week next week. Two dances to learn, after all."

"We're hardly likely to forget that," Merry replied and pointedly turned her back on him. "Where were we Dan? Oh yes, a toast. A toast to our partnership. Raise your glass."

Daniel did as he was told and Bob slunk away.

"Not sure it's all that wise to goad Bob like that."

Merry drained her glass. "Probably not. But, what else can he do to me, Dan? He's already got me stuck in a ruddy mummy's case. He's a—"

Daniel thought it wisest to humour her. "I know; he's a bastard."

"I'll drink to that." Merry peered into her empty glass. Well, I would if I had anything to drink." And, with that, she summoned the barman and ordered another round.

Step Eight.

Merry was running late, but something stopped her from pushing open the door to the now familiar rehearsal room in the Maida Vale dance studio. She could see movement through the glass panel and paused. She could also just about hear the strains of some unfamiliar music.

Flattening herself against the doorjamb, so she wouldn't be seen, she watched as Daniel danced alone. He was doing something complicated that she'd never seen before; one of the routines the show asked of its professional dancers, perhaps? She watched, enraptured. She recognised a few Paso movements and there were shades of a tango too, but really this was more freestyle. It was as if Daniel was dancing for the sheer love of it.

Daniel pulled himself to his full height, lifted up his elbows and twisted in a leap across the floor that had Merry gasping. She really hadn't thought him capable of such balletic action. He appeared to hang in the air for a second before landing and then jerking back into a classic bullfighter's pose. He was magnificent; expressive and lithe, sexy and elegant but utterly masculine.

Merry was in a quandary. She knew she was late and also knew every second counted. The more she danced, the fiercer was the hunger to win. She wasn't bothered too much about winning for herself; she wanted it for Daniel. But still, she held back. She didn't want to go in and break the magic Daniel was creating. She held her breath and prayed he wouldn't spot her, that she could watch some more. All too soon, though, the music stopped. Daniel held a pose, on his toes, before collapsing onto the floor.

Merry let go the breath she'd been holding, waited a moment longer, and then pushed open the door.

Daniel was wiping his face with his towel. He reached for his bottle of water and gave a casual salute with it before drinking deeply.

Merry found she couldn't speak. Those few seconds watching him dance so freely, so completely without reserve, had changed how she thought of him. It was the sexiest thing she'd ever witnessed. She gulped.

"Ready to tackle the quickstep?" Daniel said and grinned. He knew she was dreading it. It was always tough for the taller celebrities to get that fleet of foot needed for a really good quickstep.

Merry swallowed. She wanted to rush into his arms but it wasn't dancing she had on her mind when she got there. This was no lazy college crush. This was going places her heart had never taken her before and she wasn't sure if her brain could follow.

Daniel frowned. "You okay, Merry? Too much wine last night?"

Merry nodded. "Fine," she squeaked. "Erm, just worried about the steps."

"You'll be wonderful, babe. You are in the hands of an expert after all. Come on in, the water's wonderful, as my pal Max would say."

Merry put down her bags and shed her fleece. "I can do this," she muttered to herself. "I can do it." But she wasn't sure what 'it' was – and hoped it was purely the dance.

Step Nine.

Their salsa and Merry's dreaded quickstep went well on the following weekend. They were just pipped to the top spot by Suni and Warren's supremely elegant American smooth. Merry didn't mind too much; she liked the quiet Indian celebrity chef and loved the delicious samosas that she often brought into the television studios on show nights even more.

Now they all had a week off, wonder of wonders. Fizz TV had won the rights to an important darts competition, of all things, and that was taking precedence. It was just as well, as it was Julia and Harri's wedding on Friday and most of them had been invited.

The wedding day dawned clear and cold, one of those rare English winter days when the air is frozen into a perfect, hard blueness. It was going to be a traditional affair, or as much as it could be, with the bride a film star and the groom a high profile television presenter. Despite being offered thousands, Julia and Harri hadn't sold the picture rights to any gossip magazine and wanted to protect their privacy as much as they could. The guest list, date and venue had remained top secret until the very last minute.

"This is so exciting!" Merry whispered to Daniel as they scurried from their car to the church, under the cordon of white umbrellas protecting guests from the unwanted press attention. Despite all efforts to the contrary, some information must have leaked out.

As they waited to be directed to the right pew, she tugged at the neck of her silk wrap dress and pulled her pashmina more tightly round her. It was cold in the porch of the old church in Julia's home village and Merry felt both chilly and self-conscious in her formal clothes.

"Have I said how lovely you're looking today?" Daniel murmured.

"No you haven't," Merry basked in the glow created by his compliment, the icy weather forgotten. Then her usual humour reasserted itself. "Must be the shock of seeing me in something other than footless tights and baggy T-shirts."

Daniel hooted. "You might have a point. Can't say understated

184

elegance is your thing during training."

Merry adjusted her hat and pulled a face. "I should think not. Don't want to get all my nice togs sweaty." She tugged at the brim again and asked him anxiously, "Does this look alright? I borrowed it from Venetia and her style is a bit more over the top than mine. Don't think I've ever worn a hat so enormous!"

"You look beautiful, Meredith." It was another compliment but Merry had the distinct impression Daniel's mind was elsewhere.

"We must be sitting here." He stopped at the end of a pew, decorated with white lilies. "You know, I can't wait to see what Julia's dress is like."

Merry looked at him, in mock reproof. "Sometimes Daniel, you are just too camp for words." But she felt the same. Julia's wedding dress had been the hot topic of gossip in *Who Dares Dances* circles all week. She slid along the polished wood a little way and inhaled happily. There was nothing like the smell of a village church filled with white lilies. The scent from the flowers and wood polish was underlain with the faint aroma of old damp. Gorgeous. She waved at Harri, who stood, looking nervous, at the front and then sat back, enjoying the buzz of quiet chatter against the sound of a string quartet playing in the background. The organ wheezily fired up with the familiar strains of the *Arrival of the Queen of Sheba,* announcing the main event.

Merry craned her neck to get a first glimpse of Julia, as she made her entrance on the arm of her father, a distinguished looking man in silver grey morning attire. "Oh!" she sighed and then was silenced by what she saw.

Julia looked wonderful. Utterly beautiful. Merry's sigh was echoed in a soft wave of sound throughout the church, as the congregation absorbed the vision coming its way. Julia wore a silk whisper of a simple cream dress, with a cowl neck and long train. She didn't wear a veil but had a wreath of yet more white lilies crowning her hair.

Wedding dress aside though, what made her look truly stunning was the happiness glowing in her face. As she walked towards him, her eyes never left Harri's.

Merry felt Daniel stiffen at her side. She heard him gasp and came right down to earth with a bump. This must be torture for him, seeing the woman he loved marrying Harri. Someone with whom she was so obviously besotted. Merry felt for Daniel's hand and took it in hers. She squeezed in what she hoped came across as a friendly, sympathetic gesture but she was sure Daniel didn't even notice.

The ceremony was followed by a similarly traditional wedding breakfast in a discreet and upmarket hotel. The speeches made everyone cry, the happy couple looked ecstatic and couldn't keep their hands off one another and everyone basked in their reflected bliss. The atmosphere was helped along by generous servings of Krug.

Then it was time for Julia and Harri to dance their first as man and wife. All who gazed on were amused and touched to see the tune chosen was the same to which they'd danced their infamous rumba. At its finale, after the cheers and clapping, guests drifted onto the floor. It was too early in the evening for any cheesy sing-a-long tunes, for the moment, the music was sentimental and romantic.

Daniel and Merry sat at their table trying not to catch one another's eyes. 'It's fine' Merry thought, 'I'm not going to get bored or self-conscious just because everyone else is up on the dance floor.'

She watched Daniel covertly. He looked thoroughly miserable and uncomfortable. His usual easy-going demeanour had fled. She understood how hard today was being for him. But she missed her friend Daniel. The one who made her laugh, the one who made her work so hard that she had bleeding feet most days. He wasn't that Daniel today. Besides, she liked a party. She liked dancing. And she was more than a little desperate to dance with Daniel this evening. If he didn't ask in the next five minutes, she decided, then she would haul him up onto the floor, whether he wanted to dance or not.

Daniel watched as his old dance partner Lucy and her tower of a boyfriend Max Parry took to the floor. He and Merry were now the only people under eighty not dancing.

He cleared his throat and turned to her, holding out a hand. "Would you like to dance?"

"Well, we hardly ever get the chance to dance together, do we, Mr Cunningham?" Beaming, she shot to her feet. "I'd love to dance."

The thought that somehow this was different flashed through Daniel's mind. It wasn't like the rehearsing they did, the rush through the steps, the panic about learning them on time and the concentration on the dance. This would be for pleasure. And some pleasure. He clasped Merry in his arms and felt her melt against him. She matched his slow step immediately. She always had. She picked up the steps quickly, tuning into him and what he wanted from her.

Oh, but this *was* different. The woman he'd allowed himself to love unrequited for far too long, was a few yards away looking radiant. Even through his misery, he was aware of the cliché but that's how Julia looked, dancing in the arms of her husband. And it wasn't him. He'd thought he was over Julia but her loss twisted in his gut more strongly today than for a long time. He'd said it so often to himself but enough really was enough this time. It was time to move his heart on. Time to accept Julia would never be his.

Daniel's arms tightened around Merry and he brought her nearer. She was wearing her trademark perfume, something musky and animal. He felt her attraction. Strong and straightforward, warm and real. And available.

As the music stopped and the familiar and insistent beat of ABBA's *Fernando* began, he backed away from Merry a little and gazed into her face. He saw her intelligence, her humour, her sense of uncomplicated fun. She'd once said she never took anything too seriously. Perhaps, for once, it was time for him to do the same?

"Let's get out of here." His words were throaty with lust and Daniel could see the same need in Merry's eyes.

He took her by the hand and led her to the cool, dark corridor outside the ballroom. Backing her against the wall, he pressed himself urgently against her voluptuous body, enjoying the exciting curve of her breasts and the heat flaring from her skin.

Merry took hold of his cravat and tugged him even closer. Daniel's eyes dropped to her full lips and he had the crazy idea to kiss them.

So he did.

She responded instantly, grabbing the back of his head and pulling him in for more.

Eventually, he lifted his mouth off, rested his forehead against hers and whispered, "I want you. Now."

He wasn't thinking straight. Didn't want to think straight. He knew what he was doing and, from her response, so did Merry. They were both consenting adults, both without any kind of commitment. The one thing he wanted to commit to at this moment was her.

Wordlessly, Merry led him to the room she'd booked for the night. It was above the dance floor and the beat of the music thumped through the floor. Outside were the sounds of people yelling and laughing, a car horn hooting and driving off. Julia and Harri must be leaving. But it was all in the background. All she could focus on was the hunger in Daniel's green eyes.

With gentle fingers, he undid the soft belt of her dress. Merry sighed, enjoying the sensual caress of the silk as it slid off. Daniel removed her clothes with the utmost precision, his eyes never losing the veiled look which now darkened the green to black. He didn't speak and avoided touching her skin, which Merry found it unbearably exciting. He unfastened her bra and held the straps delicately between finger and thumb as he slipped them down her shoulders and over her arms with a deliberate slowness.

When at last she stood naked in front of him, she resisted

the temptation to cover herself and stood proudly. Only then did Daniel touch her. The skin to skin contact made her gasp. One long finger traced across her collarbone, down between her breasts, circled her navel, flirted with her hipbone. Tantalisingly slow. Merry forced herself to remain still. She watched, fascinated at the look of almost grave intent on Daniel's face. It was as if he were painting a picture with his finger, one that needed the utmost concentration and care. Merry felt herself melt inside, her legs trembled with the effort of staying still. She let out a whimper.

He laid her on the bed, his eyes never leaving hers. He still hadn't taken off his clothes. As he covered her body with his, the buttons on his jacket, the smooth wool of his morning suit abraded her skin. It was the most erotic thing she'd ever known.

Daniel was gone when she woke in the morning. Merry was glad. The perfect night didn't need any early morning awkwardness to spoil it. She stretched like a cat and an aftershock of pleasure shot through her. She smiled her mile wide smile. Daniel had been as controlled making love as he'd been when undressing her – and as skilful. Afterwards though, he'd held her close, stroked her tenderly and they'd fallen into an untidy, champagne fuelled sleep.

And now it was the morning. And in two days' time she would have to face him in training. The mile wide smile vanished.

***

It was just as well Merry had some time to compose herself before she had to see Daniel again. What had happened between them had been so spontaneous, so unexpected, so *extraordinary* that she needed to think it over. It was hard to do though, through the hideous hangover that dogged her for an entire day afterwards. Whether it was champagne or guilt that made her feel so sick she couldn't decide. And, although she'd had the occasional one-night stand and had never regretted walking away afterwards, this was different. Different in so many ways.

She tried to analyse the situation. There was no question that she was deeply attracted to Daniel. Attracted to him more than to any man she'd ever known. She was also certain that Daniel had acted while still in love with another woman. Maybe, *because* he was in love with another woman. She'd seen, in the church and at the reception afterwards, how tense Daniel had been, how his eyes followed Julia. And yet he'd chosen to sleep with Merry. It didn't make much sense.

Unless.

Unless Daniel was one of those people who simply grabbed sex when and where he could. Lots of the other dancers did. They took advantage of the quick intimacy that sprang up in the dance studio, with their celeb partner. Merry frowned. But Daniel wasn't like the other dancers. He was far too nice a man to be like that. Or had she mistaken his personality so completely?

Step Ten.

On the morning of the next rehearsal she was no nearer sorting out the whys and wherefores of what had happened and decided that her only option was to play it as cool as the winter weather.

As she strode through the iced Maida Vale streets, to the rehearsal studios, Merry tried to clear her head. She didn't suit being unhappy and tired of it quickly. It had been a wonderful night. Just one, electrifying night and she was determined it wouldn't happen again. She was too near falling dangerously deep for Daniel, and her pride wouldn't admit to her being the rebound girl.

Daniel watched her through the glass wall separating their rehearsal room from the corridor. As she changed into her dance shoes, Merry looked happy and relaxed; much as she had done throughout the time he'd known her. He rubbed a hand across his forehead. He was consumed by guilt. Guilt that he'd come onto her so strongly, guilt that he'd panicked and left her sleeping in the morning. But, most of all, guilt that he'd slept with her in the

190

first place. How had that happened? Never mix work and pleasure, she'd told him.

And, oh but it had been pleasure. Pure unadulterated, uninhibited joy. He could still sense her long, newly toned body beneath his. He could feel her breath against his skin, her hot and eager tongue, hear her laughter, her simple joy. Maybe it had been so good because it had been a long time since he'd slept with a woman. He looked up as Merry entered. Or, maybe, it was because it had been Merry.

Shit, this was going to be harder than she thought. Merry ignored the shrivelling feeling inside, painted on a bright smile and flung open the door. She'd glimpsed Daniel from the corridor and, apart from seeming a little preoccupied, he appeared back to his usual calm and pleasant self. She was so close to really falling for this man but couldn't let herself. Not when she was so sure he was still in love with someone else.

"Morning me old mucker," she called out. "Brass monkeys out there." And it's pretty frigid in here, she added silently. When Daniel didn't answer, she prattled on, his silence making her nervous. "So, what torture have you got in line for me today? Have we got to work on the Paso? Well come on then, shake a dancing leg or two, we haven't got all day."

Daniel decided to take his cue from her. After all, she'd said she'd never treated anything, or anyone, that seriously, hadn't she? She was young; they took one—-night stands in their stride. Didn't they?

He stood up and, with an effort, smiled. If she was going to treat it so casually and ignore the fact they'd slept together, then so was he. But something inside him died a little as he forced out a grin and said, "Well then Meredith, we'd better get a move on, hadn't we. The Paso isn't your strongest dance, is it? Go and warm up, please."

As Daniel watched Merry stretch and limber up, his heart spiralled downwards. He could love this woman. Really love her, more so even than Julia. His feelings were running out of control. This realisation shook him to the core. But what if she was just another he was destined to love and not have that love returned? He sought refuge in his professionalism. It was his only protection now.

When Merry was ready, he put her into her starting position, loathing and loving being able to touch her again. "Right, the Paso. Think Spain. Think bullfighting." He warmed to his theme. "So, you've got to be the cape, I'm the matador."

Merry made a face. "Naturally. Of course, the woman couldn't be the aggressor, could she? Macho rubbish. You know, I'm not sure I'm going to enjoy this dance as much as the others."

He ignored her. With a grim expression, he strode over to the corner of the studio, fetched his practice cape and stood with it high behind his shoulders. "This dance has to be full of passion, fight, anger and sex. Got it?"

"Got it." As Merry stood in front of him, her arms held back and high, she realised there wouldn't be any problem whatsoever with that.

Step Eleven.
"So what's the little weasel going to get you to do?" Venetia enquired later that week.

Unusually, both women were in the flat at the same time and were making the most of it, drinking wine and catching up with one another. They were ensconced in Venetia's opulent sitting room, enjoying a rare moment when they could relax together.

Merry repeated what she had just told her aunt. "Bob's got hold of some sort of Egyptian mummy sarcophagus and I've got to stay in it as long as I can." She suppressed a shudder at the thought.

"How ridiculous! Where on earth has he got hold of something like that?" Venetia, distracted by opening packets of snacks, didn't notice Merry's unease.

"It's only a fake one, I believe. He's got some kind of contact in

192

the magicians' world. Somebody called the Great Jessie?"

"Oh him," Venetia huffed. "Never a man so aptly named. Complete and utter idiot." She focused on her niece. "Twiglet darling? I shouldn't, so bad for the waistline but I simply can't resist them." She poured some into a bone china bowl. "Oh, it's lovely having you here, you know. But I've hardly seen you; you've been working so hard."

Putting down the bowl of Twiglets on the coffee table, Venetia sank onto the sofa, next to Merry. "I'm delighted you've got Daniel as your partner. You're both doing so well, darling. The papers are full of you." She patted Merry's knee affectionately. "And you're such a brave little thing, you'll rise to this nonsensical challenge, I'm sure."

Venetia didn't notice how Merry stiffened at the mention of Daniel's name. Something was obviously on the Dame's mind, as she just couldn't keep still. She rose, muttering something about finding the bottle of wine she'd opened.

As she topped up their glasses, Venetia came out with what had been preoccupying her. "Oh Merry, I'm opening up Little Barford," she said, referring to her main house in the Cotswolds. "Got a bit of location work for the new '*Persuasion.*' Goodness knows why people feel they have to keep remaking Austen but they do. The director liked the Lady Catherine I did a while ago and thought I'd be ideal for the Viscountess Dalrymple. Can't imagine why." Venetia primped her hair and smirked. "But darling, it's work and they've very kindly offered to pick me up and drive me to Bath each day which means I can live at home. Couldn't be easier, so I couldn't very well refuse."

She looked at Merry properly. "You'll be fine though, won't you? Keep an eye on things here for me? I'll only be gone for a week or so." She stared more closely. "Darling, I hope you don't mind my saying but you look awfully peaky. You don't mind being here on your own, do you? Big Barry will look after you. I'd quite like to keep the place on, you know. So handy to have a place in Town."

When Merry didn't answer but simply shook her head and gave her aunt a wan smile, Venetia took action. "I think, young lady, you've been overdoing it. Too much training! I shall have words with Daniel. You look exhausted. Early night for you. Go and pop yourself into bed and I'll make some hot milk. How does that sound?"

It sounded wonderful. Merry wanted to make the most of having her aunt around. Not usually so feeble, she wasn't looking forward to coming home to an empty flat each evening. She let herself be tucked in and fussed over, and thought how good it felt to be spoiled a little. Not that she deserved it. She pulled the duvet over her shoulders and burrowed in.

It had been much harder than she thought to ignore what had happened between her and Daniel; to carry on as normal. Venetia was right, Merry was exhausted but it hadn't been because of the hard physical training; it was carrying the burden of her feelings for Daniel, of pretending she didn't care about their shared night. It was that which was taking its toll. It had surprised Merry as she thought herself more resilient. Her only consolation was that Daniel seemed to be ignoring it too.

She now knew all about the *Who Dares Dances* phenomenon where working so closely together built up an intense closeness between partners. It was inevitable that it often spilled out into their personal lives. The show was full of gossip about who had slept with whom. In her aunt's luxuriously appointed spare bed, Merry flung herself onto her back and gazed up at the ceiling. Despite her physical and mental fatigue, sleep was a long way off.

She'd have to chalk this one up to experience, she decided. It was obviously what happened all the time in the showbiz world. But it didn't help her sore heart and aching head. And it didn't help that she knew she was falling in love with Daniel. Deeper than with any man she'd ever met before.

She thumped the duvet in frustration, switched off the bedside light and pulled the covers over her head. Maybe, in the morning, the mess she'd made of her life would go away.

At least there was one part of her life that wasn't such a disaster. From being the late addition to the competition, Merry found herself the hot new favourite and, not only in the broadsheets but a tabloid sensation too. In Venetia's absence, she now began each day by scanning the online gossip pages of one particular newspaper that had taken her to its heart. She simply couldn't help herself. It was such a novel feeling that the big world out there had suddenly taken notice of her. She was described as a 'hilarious new talent,' 'clever and witty: the new Miranda Hart.' She was even trending on Twitter. Merry now found herself regularly besieged by reporters and photographers who snapped her arriving and leaving Fizz's television studios, turning up for rehearsals and even leaving Venetia's flat, no matter how early the hour. Big Barry the doorman had a hard time defending his territory but assured her that no journalist would ever get past him. As he was six feet tall and nearly as wide, Merry chose to believe him.

Even her parents had joined her fan club. They'd requested tickets for the filming of that week's show. For the first time since she'd gone up to Oxford, Merry felt she was doing something of which her parents approved. It was another new thing to contend with. It all added to the pressure and made Merry unusually anxious.

Step Twelve.

It was Saturday night, filming night, and she and Daniel were waiting backstage for their cue to go on. They'd done their pre dance interview earlier in the day. Daniel had been extremely complimentary about her dancing. Had praised her to the hills, even. He'd been far warmer about her and to her in front of the cameras, than he'd been all week. They'd had a quick practice in the corridor after warming up and were now waiting for Suni and Warren to finish their waltz.

Merry shivered and fidgeted like a racehorse before the Grand

National. She hopped from toe to toe, scratched at where the cheap lace of her costume irritated and rubbed her nose where the pan-stick make-up suffocated her skin.

"Merry, are you alright? You've got the jitters. It's not like you to be so nervous." Daniel looked at her properly for the first time since the wedding. Her face was strained and white, even with a layer or three of fake tan.

Merry didn't answer immediately. She waited until Bob had gone past, pulling herself in to avoid any physical contact with him. He revolted her. "Don't know what's wrong tonight. Just feel so nervous." She clenched and then unclenched her hands.

"Is it because your parents are in?"

Merry peered round a stage flat. "And right on the front row, I see." Merry pulled at the neck of her skimpy costume. "Oh I don't know. I think it's just that I've realised there are expectations of me." She sucked in a deep breath. "High expectations. I'm in all the papers all of a sudden and now my parents are sitting up and taking notice." She looked up into Daniel's eyes. "This isn't just for fun, is it? It's getting seriously competitive."

Daniel grinned. "Oh, my darling Merry. Have you only just cottoned on?"

He put an arm round her and hugged her to him. It was their first non-dancing contact since they'd slept together and Merry's senses burned. Then she clamped down on the inevitable disappointment which followed: this was strictly a brotherly gesture. No more.

"Behind all the sequins, the slap they insist upon, what passes for the glamour," Daniel began, "lies the blisters, the hard work and the ambition." He nodded to Eva who wandered past in a daze. The judges had just awarded her and Harri a paltry score of twelve for their salsa. With the wedding, Harri's rehearsal time had been curtailed and it had showed. "The celebs are in it for a variety of reasons but the pro dancers; they're in it for the kill." He hugged Merry closer. "Have I disillusioned you, babe?"

Merry attempted to shake her head. It was difficult as it was pressed against his chest but it was so good to feel his hard muscles that she didn't mind a bit. "No. I don't mind all that. I've just realised how much I want to win this."

Daniel released her but then took her hands in his. He swung her back so that he could take a proper look, from head to toe. "Then, my darling Meredith," he grinned, "win we will!"

As they gazed at one another, they heard Charlie the show's compère, yelling, "And now we have actress and comedienne Meredith Denning and her partner, Daniel Cunningham! Give them a big hand everyone!"

"Ready Merry? Ready to dance for your life?"

"Ready for anything, Daniel," she replied and the voice in her head added, 'I'd be ready for anything life threw at me, as long as I had you,' but contented herself with just a wink.

She flicked out her hair as she got into her Paso character and they stalked onto the dance floor to uproarious applause and a standing ovation.

It seemed to Merry that it was seconds – or hours – or minutes later when they had finished their dance. She had no sense of time when she danced.

Something came together for their Paso. The hours of gruelling training, the exhaustion in their limbs, the emotional battle they were fighting – and the love each was hiding from one another. It all came together in one glorious dance. Passion, fire, anger, musicality – all matched by Daniel's clever choreography to create something very special. Merry knew it. Dan knew it. The audience knew it. They were on their feet for the entire time, clapping along, cheering and whistling, sighing at the quiet controlled parts, whooping when it became passionate.

It was one of those times that Merry had heard about, had read about. One of those rare, magical happenings that Venetia had once explained between audience and performer. When each feeds off each other and makes a far more precious whole than any of its parts.

As they stood, breathless, in front of the judges, waiting for their feedback and scores, Daniel held Merry so close she could feel his heart racing, almost feel the blood coursing through his body.

"Please let us be good," said the voice in her head. "I want this so much for Daniel. I want to win this for him."

Sonya was first to begin. "Well, Daniel and Merry. We knew from the start that there was something special about this partnership and tonight you have excelled yourselves." She paused as the audience cheered its agreement. "I can find no fault with your performance tonight, so it's a ten from me."

Daniel hugged Merry even closer as the audience went wild. Charlie raised his hands in an attempt to quieten things.

Kevin, the most outspoken judge was next. He frowned. The audience held its collective breath. "I could say that this dance was disappointing, that your footwork was appalling, that you're shaping was shoddy," he began. "I'd quite like to say that, darlings." The audience booed him good-naturedly. Kevin was the judge people loved to hate. "I could say that but it would be completely untrue. You were fantastic, darling!" He half rose to his feet and those watching gasped. Usually Kevin barely moved a well-Botoxed facial muscle, let alone his body. "I have no score to give other than a tempestuously terrific ten!"

Again, the hysteria in the audience swelled and again Charlie had to try to gain control. "Quiet now please. QUIET! Let's hear what our last judge has to say. Arthur, over to you. Could it be a ten from you too?"

The audience indicated precisely what it thought and Arthur, head judge, simply shrugged, grinned and over the roar of approval held up his sparkly ten score.

Charlie yelled. "Well, that's a perfect score of thirty for our Paso Doble-ing pair, Merry and Daniel. And that takes them straight to the top of the scoreboard and into the final!"

Merry and Daniel didn't hear a word. They didn't even hear

the racket from the crowds around them. They simply hugged one another close. The only sound – to them – was that of their hearts beating as one.

"Merry that was wonderful!" At the after-show party, Merry's mother ran up to her and gave her a hug. "Darling, I had no idea you could dance."

Merry laughed. "I'm not sure I can."

"Rubbish, Merry. I've always told you, you can do anything you set your mind to," her father added.

It wasn't quite what he always said to her, but Merry chose to take the diplomatic route and stayed silent on the subject.

"What a shame Venetia is away working and missed this. You will get us all tickets to the final, won't you, darling?" Mrs Denning said, while looking around. She was obviously star-struck. "Oh my, is that Scott? I love him. And Suni the Indian chef? I made one of her veggie curries just last week, it was absolutely delicious." She turned to her daughter. "Do you think she'd mind if I went over for a chat? I do so adore her cookery programmes."

"I'm sure she wouldn't, Ma. Suni is one of the nicest people around and everyone likes to be congratulated on doing something well."

Merry's sarcasm went completely over her mother's head. She watched, as Mrs Denning, wearing unfamiliar high heels, tripped over to Suni. "Mum's enjoying herself."

"She certainly is. She's always loved this show, it's a real treat to get these tickets and on the front row too! Ah, Daniel, old boy," Merry's father added, as Daniel joined them, bringing champagne. "Sterling work, may I say. To make this lump of a daughter of ours dance like that takes real talent. The choice of the Adele track was a masterstroke for a Paso."

Daniel kissed Merry on the cheek and handed over a glass of bubbly to her father. "Oh, I think there always has to be some latent talent in a celebrity. It's just a question of exploiting it." He raised his own glass in a toast. "And it was Merry's idea to use that song." He winked at her. "An inspired one, if I may add."

"Thank you, Daniel," Merry said, demurely.

Merry's father huffed. "Yes, well. It's just good to see you stick at something for a change. You've wasted enough time since leaving Oxford."

Daniel saw an uncharacteristically defeated look on Merry's face and wondered how she'd grown up so carefree with a father like this. "Mr Denning," he said brightly. "Who can I introduce you to? I know you and your wife are big fans of the show. Maybe our esteemed executive producer and director. Have you met Bob Dandry?" He steered Merry's father away, leaving her to be surrounded by the other dancers. She disappeared into a cloud of congratulations, champagne and hugs.

Step Thirteen.

Merry's euphoria at getting into to the final was short-lived though: she had her fund-raising challenge to get through first.

For the entire week after the semi-final, Bob pestered Merry. He took any and every opportunity to brush past her, to snake a hand around her waist, to whisper vaguely threatening remarks to her about her challenge. Merry bit her lip and tried to ignore him, muttering curses all the while under her breath. She even flirted with the idea of sticking pins in a plasticine doll. Venetia had assured her she'd once tried it on someone and it worked. The man was truly loathsome. She missed her aunt's lightening presence. No matter how revoltingly Bob behaved to Merry, she'd always had Venetia to help her laugh it off. Even though they hadn't really coincided in the flat all that often, it had been comforting to know someone else was occasionally available to chat over things. Someone who understood the tribulations of the showbiz world. Things were still awkward with Daniel, and any conversation she had with him was restricted to training matters. She missed him too.

Merry was also preoccupied by the dances she and Daniel

had to do in the final. As well as a free dance, where, he told her, anything went, they'd decided to reprise their Paso. It had been one of their most popular dances, both with the judges and the voting public. Daniel explained that now they had two weeks of training in front of them, they could add some more exciting details. Knowing Daniel as she did now, Merry was more than a little anxious about what he had in mind.

She soon found out.

***

She and Daniel began their fortnight of intensive rehearsing at eight am sharp on the Monday morning. Merry had barely shaken off her hangover from the party on Saturday.

"So," Daniel said, the minute Merry walked into their favourite rehearsal room at the Maida Vale gym, "I thought we'd give them some really thrilling lifts."

"Lifts," squeaked Merry. "I'm five feet ten and weigh a ton."

"Merry, it's not about how big you are, it's all about technique."

"Oh, that's alright then. After all, technique is what I've mastered after, oh yes, all of five weeks training."

"Don't be so defeatist, Meredith," Daniel said brusquely. "Would I ask you to do anything I didn't think you were capable of?"

"Yes."

He laughed. "Go and get some water. You'll need it when I've finished with you today and then we'll get started."

"Yes Daniel," Merry replied meekly.

Daniel caught her look. "I'm going to suffer for this, aren't I?"

"Oh yes, Dan-Dan the dancing Man." Merry turned her back on him to fill her water bottle from the dispenser in the corner. "And you have no idea how much." Concentrating on her task, she bit her lip. "But not as much as I'm suffering now," she murmured to herself.

It was true. Merry was finding it impossibly difficult to work so closely with Daniel and be neutral about her feelings. It got worse every time she saw how patient he was with the other dancers, how he helped out with their training whenever he could, how painstaking he was over every detail, how he never minded how many times Merry trod on his feet. And she couldn't, no matter how determined she was, forget that one magical night they had spent together. Her mind loved his dedication and kindness and her body raged for his touch. Oh, she was in trouble.

She turned back to him. "Thanks for sticking up for me on Saturday. At the party I mean." She still couldn't look him straight in the eye. "With my parents."

Daniel shrugged. "Nothing like a well-meaning parent to know how to stick the knife in where it hurts the most. My mother does the same." He quirked a brow, held up his water bottle and quoted: "When are you going to stop wasting your talent and join a proper ballet company?" He grinned. "And now, are you ready? Have you stretched yet? Let's get warmed up properly. We'll need to, we've got a hard day in front of us."

Merry blinked back the sudden tears which threatened. She hardly ever cried, and never over a man. She wasn't about to start now. She took a swig of water, straightened her shoulders and turned to him with a wide smile. "As ready as I'll ever be. Do with me what you want, Dan. I'm yours for the day!"

No matter how hard Daniel worked her, Merry couldn't completely forget the ordeal of her challenge that was to come. Bob had taken far too long and had got far too close to her when he explained about it. He'd turned up in Maida Vale, unannounced, one evening.

"The TV studio is booked for Thursday, Meredith," he simpered as his hand 'accidently' brushed her waist. "It'll be a closed set, just you and me and the crew of course, to allay any nerves you might have." His hand ventured lower and Merry moved away.

"I want to be there too," Daniel interjected.

"I don't think there's any need for that," Bob blustered,

202

wrong-footed.

He took a step away from Merry and she began to breathe again. There was something about the man which polluted the very air she breathed.

"I'd really like Dan there," Merry said. She squared her shoulders. "In fact, I insist on it."

Bob looked from one to the other and decided to capitulate. "Very well then, although I still don't see why." He huffed. "I'd better let you in on the details, Meredith. Are you staying for this too, Daniel?" he added, nastily.

Daniel put an arm around Merry's shoulders. "I rather think I might. That okay with you Bob?"

"I don't seem to have much choice, do I?" Bob glared.

"None whatsoever," Daniel said cheerfully. "Now, what's she got to do on Thursday?"

Bob huffed some more and then got into his stride. "Right," he began, "you'll need to be at the studio by nine sharp, no later. We'll set up a practice run, show you the mummy's sarcophagus, do a lighting and sound set up, film the head shots and then get going properly. All meals provided, of course and we'll get the press in later that day for interviews. That sound okay, Merry?"

"It sounds fine," Merry said faintly, glad of Daniel's comforting touch. She couldn't imagine anything worse; she wouldn't be able to eat or drink anything and certainly couldn't envisage being in any fit state to face the press.

"So, just how long do you think you'll be able to stay in the case?"

"What do you mean, Bob?" Merry felt Daniel's arm tighten around her shoulders.

"Well, as it makes clear in your information pack, the longer you're able to do your challenge, the more money you'll raise. You have read your pack, I assume?" he sneered.

"Of course she's read it," Daniel answered for her.

Merry nodded, incapable of speech.

"Well then," Bob repeated impatiently, "how long do you think you'll stay in? I have an allocation of filming hours but I can't go over ten for the whole day."

"Ten?" Merry stuttered. "I don't think there'll be any danger of using the whole ten hours. I'll be out well before then."

"Good." Bob gave a sleazy smile. "Pop into wardrobe before you go home tonight and see what they have in mind for you." He leered up at her. "I can just see you in a Cleopatra get up. Be fantastic for the ratings."

Merry left, feeling sick.

***

All too soon, Thursday came. Merry was aware that Daniel had deliberately kept her busy to stop her dwelling on what was to come. But even after fourteen-hour training days, sleep evaded Merry and each night she tossed and turned. She sorely missed Venetia, who was still away, her shooting schedule having overrun. And, as Merry lay awake, staring at the ceiling, she ached for Daniel's comforting arms.

Merry arrived at Fizz TV's main studio by eight fifteen. She'd been awake since three and had only slept fitfully before then. But, early as she was, she was surprised to see Daniel there before her.

Daniel watched Merry as she walked in and a lump came to his throat. She'd worked her butt off that week, he'd made sure of that, but the shadows under her eyes told their own story and her face was thin and tense. He would have done anything to take her place for this challenge. Anything. He loved the way she used humour to deflect any worries, her easy charm and the bravery with which she was facing this.

And he loved her.

He loved Merry. He really did. But he couldn't tell her. Not now. It was very clear she had things on her mind other than him, even if she had any feelings for him at all, which he doubted.

He couldn't resist her completely though. "Merry," he hugged her close. "Merry, I'd do anything to stop this." The words were out before he knew it.

Merry stepped out of his embrace and shook her head. "I've got to do it, Dan."

"Because it's in your contract?"

Merry managed a small smile. "Because I need to prove something to myself."

Bob walked past whistling. He put his hand up in greeting.

"And because I'm not going to let that bastard beat me," she added.

Daniel nodded. He understood. "I'll be right there with you, babe."

Merry reached up and kissed his cheek. "Thank you," she whispered.

"'Bout time you got ready for the lighting rehearsal, Meredith." Bob couldn't keep the smug grin off his face.

"Ready as I'll ever be," Merry replied and stuck a tongue out at his receding back.

Pink-haired Sandy, the tiny and overly enthusiastic floor manager, showed Merry the sarcophagus. "We'll have a close-up of you here and then it'll open," she explained. "If you could do a pose once you're in, that'll be good." She beckoned to Hank, the lighting guy. "Shot here, Hank. That's it Merry, just hold it there for a minute."

To her surprise, Merry found herself admiring the sarcophagus. It towered above even her and was heavily decorated in gold and blue stripes. To her untutored eyes, it looked a near copy of Tutankhamun's. "It's beautiful," she whispered. 'As beautiful as death,' the voice in her head added.

Sandy beamed. "It is, isn't it? Bob did a great job of finding one for us and this one will look great on screen. It's a real eye-catcher. Hank, you got that?" Sandy turned to look up at Merry. "Okay lovie, we'll set up the lighting for the shot of you inside now and then you can go off to costume and make-up and relax a bit."

Merry gave a short, humourless laugh. She sucked in a breath while Sandy struggled to heave open the door. Merry consoled herself with the thought that it only looked difficult to open as Sandy was so little. And feeble. And weak. 'Nothing to do with it being very weighty and solid,' the voice in her head suggested unhelpfully. 'I'm getting as unhinged as that door,' Merry decided, and tried to shake the annoying sound out of her head. She looked for Daniel's reassuring presence and he gave her the thumbs up.

"What d'you say, Merry?" Sandy smiled and then peered at the job-sheet on the clipboard she was clutching. "There we go," she beckoned Merry forward. "Just stand at the entrance for a sec while Hank gets that lighting shot set up." She gestured to Merry to stand just inside the door. "You can see, when you're in it properly, that there's a little seat there. You can perch on that while you do your challenge. Isn't it fun?" Sandy caught the expression on Merry's face. "You're not really claustrophobic are you, though?" Without waiting for a reply, she continued. "No? Good-oh. Must admit to being relieved when it turned out Angie's fear of heights was all faked, although poor old Callum struggled with swimming with those sharks." She shuddered. "Now that I wouldn't fancy. Made a great bit of film though. In you get then. Get a feel for it."

Merry felt her legs begin to shake. Her stomach churned. She forced herself to take one tottering step just inside. She released the breath she hadn't known she'd been holding and relaxed infinitesimally. It actually wasn't *too* bad, at least with the door open. She looked around for Daniel again but couldn't see him and wondered where he'd gone.

To her surprise, Sandy bounced in behind her. There was just about room for both of them but only because Sandy was so tiny. "At the back," she chirped, "there's a hidden door. Any problems and you can let yourself out. See the camouflaged handle? Brilliant, isn't it?" She stared about her with interest. "It's probably how they used to do those disappearing tricks. You know in magic acts. Used to love those as a kid. It's quite plush in here, isn't it?" She ran a finger along the velvet interior. "You know," she grinned at Merry, "I wouldn't mind swapping with you." She sighed. "Could do with a few minutes peace and quiet. It's been raving here this morning. Right, you all sorted then?" She gave Merry a little shove out. "Off you go to costume and make-up then and we'll see you later. Ah, here's Daniel, coming to escort you to the girls. I know Roxie's got something very special for you lined up, so enjoy." She put up a hand. "See you later," and was gone before either of them could respond.

"How are you doing?" Daniel asked.

"There's a door at the back," Merry gabbled.

"I know. I've just had a quick look from the outside. Make you feel any better?"

"A bit. At least I can get out if I really need to. In a hurry." Merry found his warm hand and clung on.

"Come on, babe. Let's get you to Roxie. Maybe she'll take your mind off things. I can't wait to see this costume she's got for you. You said it was going to be fantastic when you had that first fitting."

Throughout the make-up session Daniel stayed, chatting up the girls, sipping coffee and generally getting in the way. But Merry knew what he was really doing. He was trying to take her mind off what was to come. If only it were that simple. She caught his eye and tried out a smile. He winked back.

"That make-up looks great on you, Merry," he said, peering, with interest at the glittery blue shadow and heavy kohl lining her eyes. "It makes your eyes look huge."

Merry pouted. "I think it's the fear that's doing that." She studied her reflection in the dressing room mirror. But it was true, the exaggerated black lines made her features look enormous. She pulled a comic expression. "It's the contrast with the terrified white face that really works."

Jodie, one of the make-up girls giggled. "Oh, I do love you, Merry. You're always such a laugh. Off you go now, we're done with you. Time to get into that costume."

True to Sandy's promise, Roxie had a spectacular costume for Merry to wear. It was in the same vivid tones of gold and blue as the mummy's sarcophagus and vaguely Egyptian. A long skirt made of some fine shimmering material, gathered to fine pleats at her hips and matched a bra top. Two gold serpents encircled her breasts, leaving very little to the imagination. It was all topped off with an outlandishly sequinned turban, sporting yet another snake. If Merry hadn't been so preoccupied by fear, she would have revelled in it.

"Ooh, very Rita Hayworth," Daniel said, camply, as she was ushered out by Roxie, who followed on with a handful of pins. "You should keep that one."

Roxie stepped back to admire her work. She looked Merry up and down with a critical eye. "Mmm. Looking good, girlfriend. Nice to work on a bod with curves and legs, for a change."

"I was just thinking the same thing!" Daniel said and was rewarded by a cackle from the dressmaker.

"You two have fun now, you hear," she said, as she began to retreat to the costume room. "And don't," at this Roxie pointed a stern finger at Merry, "tread on your train. You'll rip it."

Merry looked down at her clothes. If only that were all she had to worry about. "How long now, Dan?" Half-heartedly, she waggled the Egyptian ceremonial crook and flail she'd been given to use as props.

He glanced at his watch. "Five minutes maybe. Less, if they're on time with the schedule."

Merry didn't even have that. As Daniel spoke, a young runner came up to them. "Calling Meredith Denning. Miss Denning, are you ready?"

"It's not too late to back out, Merry." Daniel put a comforting hand on her arm.

She stared into the green eyes she'd come to love, forced a full wattage smile and shook her head. "Let's get the show on the road, dance boy. I'm all dressed up and raring to go." Only the trembling flail in her hand gave her away.

Bob was standing by the sarcophagus when they got there. "Oh Meredith," he cried and rubbed his hands together. "Don't you look a picture?" He did his dead cod impression.

Merry looked away, revolted.

"We'll need some stills of you, if you could just pose in front of the coffin. I mean sarcophagus." Bob snickered and took Merry by the arm. He pulled her none too gently into place.

"I'll be right here," called Daniel. "And don't forget the door at the back," he hissed. "Just push when you're ready and come out." He gave her another thumbs up.

Merry nodded and let herself be photographed. She felt numb.

"Sandy, are the cameras rolling?" Bob yelled and got an affirmative from somewhere in the shadowy studio. "Right, let's get going then. Start the clock. Remember, Meredith, the longer you stay in there, the more money we raise for Jokes for Notes."

He rubbed his hands together again and Merry heard the dry skin rasp. It put her teeth on edge. She forced herself to give a cheery wave and stepped into the case. Turning, she obliged the hovering cameras by giving a thumbs up and then the door swung shut.

Far from the dramatic slam she expected, the door hissed into place and closed neatly, without leaving the tiniest gap. Merry felt panic rise like bile and forced herself to breathe slowly.

It was pitch black. She felt behind her for the little ledge so she could rest her shaking legs and have something to hang onto. Beads of perspiration prickled on her face and she felt sick. At least there was always the secret door she could use if desperate. Or more desperate than she was now. She gulped and tried screwing her eyes shut. It made everything worse, so she opened them to the blackness which was suffocating her.

Outside, Bob was keeping a beady eye on the clock, which was ticking the time and the amount of money raised.

"Twenty minutes now. Don't look so worried Daniel, Meredith will be fine," he simpered and turned to do a piece to camera.

Daniel paced back and forth and tried to imagine how Merry was feeling. He looked up, irritably. The hands on that wretched clock seemed to be moving too slowly. He moved well out of shot and to the back of the sarcophagus. Here, the elaborate paint job gave way to rudimentary woodwork, but the line of the secret door could just about be seen. Daniel prayed Merry wouldn't give in to her pride and stay in too long. He leaned against the case and put a hand up to where he thought Merry might be, willing some of his strength to her.

Merry had lost track of all time. All she was aware of was an oppressive blackness weighing her down. The pressure in her head was becoming unbearable. Her fingernails scratched for the tiny handle she knew was just beside the wooden seat. Just putting her hand on it gave her some comfort. Knowing the release was there, under her control, made it more possible to stay in a while longer. But not too much longer.

An hour had passed and Daniel pleaded with Bob to call an end to it.

"Nonsense, Daniel. Meredith can get out herself, any time she chooses. You reminded me of that. It's been hardly been any time at all. Besides, think of the money we'll raise." Bob gave Daniel a strangely malevolent grin.

Daniel swore under his breath. "If anything happens to her I'll -"

"You'll do nothing, Daniel," Bob said smoothly. "Or we'll have the little matter of renewing your contract to discuss. Understand? And really, you are getting into a state. Whatever can happen to Meredith, in there? If she needs to get out, she can do so, of her own choosing. Do stop being so dramatic."

Daniel contented himself with a black look and resumed pacing. Another five minutes went by.

Merry was suffocating. Her throat closed as the panic took hold. She'd had enough. She turned the handle as Sandy had shown. It didn't give. Merry forced what little breath she could into her lungs and turned again. The handle wouldn't budge. This time, she smacked her hand against it, but only succeeded in hurting herself. The door wouldn't open. Summoning her last strength she thumped the wall and yelled. It was no good. The case was solid, with thick sound-proofed walls. They couldn't hear her from outside. She was trapped.

"Bob, I really think it's time we opened it." It had been another thirty minutes. Merry had been in the sarcophagus for nearly three hours. Daniel was past caring about what threats Bob could carry out. He knew something was wrong. He just knew.

Bob looked at the clock, ratcheting up the money. "Just another two minutes."

"Bob!" Daniel said, warningly. He had threats of his own in mind if the producer didn't comply.

"Oh very well. Ten, nine, eight, seven ... are the cameras rolling? Right, get into position everyone, we're about to open it up!" Bob waited for the signal from Sandy, Hank and the team and then heaved open the door to the case. "Meredith, the fantastic news is you've raised thirteen thousand pounds!" He peered into the gloom. "Meredith? Are you in there?"

Daniel shoved past him and almost tripped over Merry who was curled on the floor. She was very still. And unconscious.

With difficulty, Daniel manoeuvred himself inside so he could scoop her up and carry her to the medic's room. "If anything, *anything* happens to her," he yelled at Bob, "I will tear your miserable body limb from fucking limb. Now get out of my way!"

Once Daniel had laid Merry on the couch in the medical room, the first aid team ushered him out of the way. He was back on the outside again. Back to pacing.

It seemed like hours before Daniel was allowed in. When he was, he wanted to run straight back out again. Merry was strapped into some kind of breathing equipment. She had a mask over her face, but still had a deathly pallor that terrified him. She was sitting up though. And apparently, had been arguing with the medics.

Tom, the doctor in charge, explained. "She really should go to

A & E to get checked out more thoroughly. I've told her but she won't go." He looked at Daniel. "Can't force her." He shrugged at his patient. "I'll leave her with you then, done all I can. Perhaps you could see she gets home?" He nodded to the nurse. "She can take the oxygen mask off now. She won't need it anymore."

"Is she - ?"

"She's fine," Tom pre-empted Daniel's question. "She'll just need a couple of days rest. Make sure she's not left alone, will you?" He looked from Daniel to Merry. "I'll leave you two together, then. You know where I am if I'm needed again." He smiled at the nurse and left.

After the breathing mask had been removed and the room tidied, the nurse, too, disappeared.

"Merry?" To Daniel's annoyance, his voice came out ragged.

Merry eased herself up. "I'm okay. Honestly."

He came to sit on the edge of the couch. He wanted to take her hand but didn't quite have the courage. "Why the hell didn't you come out sooner?"

Merry rubbed her face where the band from the oxygen mask had dug in. "I tried to get out but the door was jammed or something."

"You know it was. Bob locked you in."

"No, I mean the secret door Sandy told me about. She showed me how to get out if or when I needed to."

Daniel was mystified. "Then why didn't you?"

"I tried but the handle wouldn't turn, not how it was meant to. I was stuck. I shouted but I couldn't make anyone hear. I was stuck," Merry repeated. She began to tremble and tears spilled.

It was so unlike the Merry he knew to break down, that at first Daniel didn't know what to do.

"Everything alright in here?" Bob stuck his sweating face round the door. "Ah good, I see you're back in the land of the living, Meredith."

"Get out," Daniel snarled and gathered Merry in his arms.

Bob raised his hands in a placating gesture which was cancelled out by the smug grin on his face. "Only asking, Dan. If Merry needs anything, you only have to say."

"I said get the fuck out." Daniel mouthed the words over Merry's head but they were no less effective.

Bob disappeared.

Merry drew back from Daniel and gazed up at him. "My hero" she said with a little of her old spirit. She sniffed. "It was him, wasn't it?"

"What do you mean?"

"It was Bob who locked both doors."

Dan nodded. He couldn't trust himself to speak.

"He got his own back on me, didn't he?"

"Oh yes, babe. He did that alright. But the worse thing is -"

"What?"

"The bastard's got it all on tape. He kept the cameras rolling the whole time. Even when I was carrying you in here."

"Oh." Merry quivered and laid her head on Daniel's comforting shoulder. "Oh shit."

Step Fourteen.

There was, however, little time to dwell on how much footage Bob would use. She and Daniel had a final to prepare for. He'd camped out in Venetia's sitting room, sleeping on the sofa for a few nights, obeying Tom's command that she should not be alone. They lounged in front of the television, late into the night after rehearsals, mulling over Bob's actions, drinking too much and eating rubbish.

But when Daniel announced they were to learn two new dances, Merry told him he'd gone mad.

"The others are all reprising dances they've done before!" she said in a panic on Monday morning. "We've got just over a week before the final show's recorded. I can't possibly learn two completely new dances in that time."

213

Daniel spread out his hands. "Merry, calm down. You didn't hear me properly. Yes, of course you could learn two new dances but that's not exactly what we're going to do."

Merry pointed her water bottle at him. "Explain yourself then, dance boy," she said sternly.

Daniel grinned. "We do one show dance and one free dance. Right?"

"Right." Merry nodded.

"The show dance has elements of all the other dances we've done before. Some waltz and salsa steps, some story telling from our tango and Paso and we'll put in a couple of show stopping lifts."

"Okay," Merry said cautiously. "That sounds do-able. I think."

"And, for the other, we incorporate some of our quick step into a -" he left an ominous pause.

"A what, Daniel?"

He winked. "A Charleston."

"Oh. My. God." Merry collapsed onto a giant exercise ball. It wobbled like jelly and she slid off it to lie on the floor, spread-eagled. "I can't believe you're going to make me do a Charleston," she said to the ceiling. She sat up. "Me. Great hulking heffalump me!"

Daniel came to crouch beside her, a concerned look on his face, all humour instantly gone. "Meredith Denning, don't ever, *ever* say that about yourself."

"Blimey Dan, this must be serious, you've used my full name."

"I am serious." He came to sit alongside her, the neon green from the exercise ball casting an incongruous glow over his features. "You must stop putting yourself down like this. You've been doing it ever since Evil Bob announced his intention to show the film of you in an extra-long special."

Merry concentrated very hard on the floor of the dance studio. It was sprung and a light beech colour, she noticed. There was a scuff mark by the door where Daniel had skidded when misjudging a lift.

"Merry?"

When she lifted her gaze to his, she had tears in her eyes.

"Oh Merry." Daniel took the bottle of water she was clutching out of her hand and put it on the floor. He hugged her to him, fiercely. "Don't let him get to you like this."

"I'm trying not to." She gulped. She was not the crying sort, she told herself, she really wasn't. But ever since she'd begun this daft, exhilarating TV programme which had completely taken over her life, she'd cried more than she'd allowed herself to do in years. "It's just that, I keep picturing myself in that stupid Egyptian costume, big bum in the air, thighs wobbling all over the place, all five feet ten of unconscious claustrophobic wimp."

Daniel was shocked. He'd never heard her refer to herself in such a derogatory way. "Meredith, you do not have a big bottom, or wobbly thighs. Yes, you're big but you're toned and fit. And you looked sexy as hell in that costume," he added.

"I'm a size sixteen." Merry said it in scandalised tones. "Roxy has to find extra fabric for my dresses. She told me."

Daniel harrumphed. "And – as you've quite correctly pointed out to me, you're nearly six feet tall. How stupid would you look if you were a size ten?"

"Casey's a size six," Merry added, in a small voice.

"Well, agreed, her brain is tiny. Fake boobs though."

Merry looked up at him and giggled. "Really?"

"Of course they are, babe! How could someone as small as Casey naturally be a double D cup? Have you ever seen the girl eat? She's so unhealthy. Starves herself to be the size she thinks she needs to be, undergoes painful surgery to supplement what little she has up top and under all that make-up she's as grey and unappealing as a motorway services' pasty."

Merry took a deep breath. "It's just that, well, I got teased a lot when I was a kid. I was tall even when I was little. If you see what I mean. And Daddy always said if I kept eating like a horse, I'd end up as big as one."

Daniel winced. He might have known the delightful Mr

Denning had a hand in this. What a foul thing to say to your daughter. He bit back his anger and contented himself with saying: "Well, don't ever let me hear you diss yourself again. You're long and lovely, elegant and beautiful. You knock spots off Casey and anyone who says otherwise, is simply jealous."

Merry stared at him, open-mouthed. She'd never heard him sound off so passionately about anything. "Daniel, I do love you." It came out before she had time to think.

He looked at her askance.

"You're such a bloody good friend," she added, hastily.

His expression shifted. "Well, yes, glad to be of service." He cleared his throat and rose, in one lithe movement, from the floor. "Okay then, Merry my *friend*, hadn't we better get on with our rehearsal? I've decided we're fucking well going to win this, so we've got some hard work to do."

Merry held out a hand. Despite all Daniel's compliments, she was nowhere near as supple as he and needed some help getting up, which he offered. As she stood, she looked up into his face, slightly shocked at his swear word. She knew Daniel well enough by now to know he never swore, unless gripped by some extreme emotion.

"Then we'd better get started, hadn't we? Starting positions, Mr Cunningham?" Merry pulled her t-shirt back over her bottom, arched an eyebrow and struck a pose.

"Starting positions Miss Denning," Daniel responded with a slightly forced smile. "And drop those shoulders!"

Step Fifteen.

Once again, the Artemida Hotel played host to a Fizz TV gathering. And once again, the food was lavish and the wine plentiful. Merry hardly noticed though, as she slid onto a chair on the back row of the conference room, which was set up with an enormous screen.

They were there to watch a preview of the special hour-long bloopers programme. It was due to be transmitted shortly before

216

the final went out and was always a hit. It was the sort of show that used to be a favourite of Merry's too, until she became the subject of one. She wasn't looking forward to it one bit and had a horrible feeling Bob had given her the star billing.

Daniel grabbed a couple of glasses of white from a passing tray and slipped in beside her.

Passing one over, he murmured, "It'll be fine."

"You think so? I've got money on Bob making them choose the most excruciatingly embarrassing clips of yours truly," she hissed back.

"Well, we'll just have to wait and see." Daniel squeezed her hand and smiled at Harri and Julia who came to sit immediately in front of them. Harri, along with Suni, were now out of the competition and able to sit back and relax a little. "And the problem is, we can't do anything; it's in our contract."

"Oh yes. That ruddy contract," Harri added, turning round with a boyish grin. "Mind, viewers love this sort of thing. Very popular."

"Oh great," Merry said, mournfully. "That means loads of repeats then." She drank half her wine down in one go.

"Not all bad news then, babe." Daniel winked at her. "Think of the repeat fees."

"Nah. Bob will have thought of a way round that," Harri chipped in.

"Not helping, mate."

"Sorry, Dan. Just trying to lighten the mood, see."

"I think you'd help more by butting out," Julia reproved. "Ssh everyone, look it's about to start."

They turned to watch Bob, who was introducing the programme. He droned on about it going out as part of the celebrations to mark a hundred episodes of *Who Dares Dances*.

It wasn't too bad at the beginning, although Merry had a bad moment when the ill-fated sarcophagus flashed up for a second. There was a contagiously funny montage of various people suffering fits of giggles, including Merry and Daniel. This was followed by an equally hilarious sequence of dancers falling over; Merry featured a lot there too. Then she tensed as scenes showing Callum swimming with sharks was shown. She caught her breath as a diver was shown baiting a shark with fish, in order to swim into shot – and failing as the shark glided away. Merry hadn't thought any footage of the challenges was to be included in the blooper reel. Then there was a close-up of her own face. It loomed enormous and pallid underneath the Egyptian make-up. The shot was out of focus and far too close. Her features took on monstrous proportions. She began to feel queasy, put down her glass of wine and found Daniel's comforting hand. She clutched on. It was followed by snippets of film, all featuring Merry. In them she was seen falling over time and time again, getting her steps mixed up in the group merengue and gurning at her colleagues.

"It's so easy to forget the cameras are there," whispered Daniel, at her side. "Don't worry," he looked around at the audience, "people think it's funny, not humiliating."

"I'm glad you think so," Merry responded. She was close to tears. It was as bad as she'd feared.

The programme dragged on. Merry was given a brief respite, during which a series of scripted moments to camera were shown going horribly wrong and then she was back, firmly as the main attraction. The last segment showed a full shot of Merry during her challenge, the camera lingering on her cleavage, as it threatened to burst out of its snake bra top. It was followed by a supposedly comical sequence of her stuffing her face at any opportunity and finished with a close-up of her behind, enormous and tightly encased in the blue and gold of her Egyptian costume.

There was loud applause at the end, accompanied by catcalls and wolf-whistles. It was the first time most had seen any footage of Merry's challenge and its daring outfit.

Harri gave a long, two fingers in the mouth, whistle. "You go, cariad bach. Star of the show. Where've you been hiding that body?" He got an elbow in the ribs from Julia to shut him up.

Amazingly, his sentiments were echoed by those in the room. Merry got shakily to her feet to be greeted by Scott. He planted an enormous kiss on her cheek. "Knew you were a comedian, darling. Didn't realise how funny you were!"

He was followed by the others, who were all congratulating Merry on her comic turn and gorgeous body.

Merry blinked at them, confused. To her the intentions of the film were clear; to humiliate and link her gluttony to her generous size. And, as she glanced over and caught Bob's eye, she was certain that had been his intention.

As he saw her glare, Bob coloured unbecomingly and disappeared from the room.

"As well you might, Bob the Bastard. It's back-fired on you, hasn't it?" She licked her finger and painted a one in the air, then turned to Daniel and gave him a resounding kiss on the lips, much to his surprise. "A point to me, I think."

Daniel, relieved that Merry had recovered her usual joie de vivre, slipped an arm round her shoulders. "You did great, babe," he said, as he kissed the top of her head. "Just great." And then left her to be feted by her many admirers.

Step Sixteen.

If Bob's motive had been to demoralise Merry before the final, or to turn the voting public against her, he failed on both counts. She and Daniel went into the final as the hot favourites.

There was one other couple who had made it; their arch rivals Angie and Scott. Merry had never been so nervous. She ran to the loo every five minutes and fidgeted until it drove Daniel mad. And it wasn't just the thought of dancing two very tricky routines in front of record audiences (or so Bob said), it was who was sitting in the studio audience.

Thirty minutes before doors were officially opened, Daniel had grabbed Merry's hand and taken the opportunity for a last minute rehearsal on the dance floor where they filmed the show. It was rare that dancers got a chance to practice on the actual floor and it was good to measure out their steps in the limited space available.

Merry and Daniel ran through their routines once or twice and when they'd finished their show dance, they stood, catching their breath. They were startled by the sound of clapping which came from behind them.

Whirling round they saw three figures emerging from the glare of the studio lights, only one of which they could see clearly.

"Meredith," said Bob, with a smirk, "let me reintroduce you to someone. I believe you used to know one another a long time ago?"

A woman, about Merry's age, stepped forward. She was small and thin, with a smoker's prematurely lined face.

"Meredith Denning," she said. "Well, well. Long time, no see."

Merry frowned, trying to place the woman. "I'm sorry, I—"

"No, of course you won't remember me but I remember you so very well. We share an alma mater, Merry."

A memory surfaced painfully. There was something horribly familiar about those cold blue eyes. Merry gasped. "Carly?"

"Bingo." Carly smiled, revealing large yellow teeth. "Perhaps I made a bigger impression on you than I thought?" she added unpleasantly. "When I found out that Uncle Bob had got me tickets for the final, I couldn't resist coming to say hello to an old school friend."

"Your uncle?" Merry looked from Bob to Carly, as realisation dawned. "So that's how you found out about my claustrophobia?"

Bob sniggered. "Carly is brilliant at coming up with these ideas. She's one of my assistants in the production offices. It made a fantastic piece of television, Meredith."

"At my expense!"

"Oh, come now. You knew what you were letting yourself in for, when you signed the contract." Bob began to laugh. "I don't think I've ever seen anything so funny."

Merry sensed Daniel stiffen beside her and put a restraining hand on his arm.

220

Carly linked arms with her uncle. "I must say, I enjoyed seeing it too. You have a gift for making a fool of yourself, Merry." The woman simpered. "But then you always did."

Merry felt the anger build inside and was just about to let rip when the third person emerged from the gloom at the edge of the dance floor.

It was Hillary MacDonald, her old tutor.

"Oh," Merry squeaked, nonplussed. "What are you doing here?"

Hillary had the grace to look embarrassed. "Bob here, very kindly got in touch and offered me a ticket. I was filming nearby anyway, so I thought I'd come along."

"Not really your thing, Hil," Merry said with desperation.

"No, not really but I've heard good things about you Merry. Wanted to see how an ex … erm … student was getting on."

"Well, I'm fine. As you can see." Merry was stunned. All her previous worlds seemed to be colliding, bursting into the safe little bubble she and Daniel had created. She'd loved her time with him on *Who Dares Dances,* and wanted it to continue just for a while longer. She knew that when the final was over, she'd have no reason to see Daniel again. And the thought was killing her. She simply couldn't cope with this intrusion now. Then she caught the look in Bob's eye and the sheer evil enjoyment in Carly's and somehow knew her discomfort was just what they'd planned. Fury at having been manipulated again surged through her. She'd rarely felt as angry about anything.

Daniel knew Merry was about to erupt at any moment. He needed to get her away now. He cleared his throat. "It's time to get into make-up, Merry. Come on." He dragged her away, feeling the rage vibrate through her.

It was a lie; they'd both been to costume and make-up hours before but, if they had any chance of concentrating on the final, he needed to give Merry time to calm down. He followed her as she slammed into her dressing room.

"I can't believe she's here. I can't believe Bob is her uncle! Why the hell did she do it?" She whirled round on Daniel and he knew she wasn't just talking about the fund-raising stunt. "What has she got against me? I've never ever done anything to her. She just took against me from the start. What makes people want to do such snide, conniving, evil things?" She thumped the wall so hard it left a dent and then sat abruptly, on the verge of tears yet again.

Daniel perched on the edge of the dressing table bench, his blond hair haloed by the bright lights surrounding its mirror. It made him look like an angel.

Merry looked up, her face in abject misery. "Why Daniel? What have I ever done to warrant such," she searched for the right word, "*mean* behaviour?"

Daniel longed to take her in his arms, to comfort her, to kiss away her worries and frowns. But he didn't move.

"Why?" She repeated.

He shook his head; he couldn't fathom it either. "I don't know," he said at last. "Maybe some people have a gene that makes them want to get at others." He shrugged. "Bob will do anything for higher audience figures, I know that much from experience. As for Carly, who knows, Merry? Maybe it's simply because they can. They can bully and stir without risking any come back to themselves. Apparently it's the argument behind cyber bullying."

Merry deflated a little. "This is different though. Carly actually met me at school and decided to get at me even before she got to know me. I can't remember that I did anything to her to deserve this," she added miserably. "And then, to get Hillary invited! Why the hell is he here?"

"Perhaps he didn't take your affair as lightly as you did?" ventured Daniel, not wanting to think about Merry and this handsome academic. Someone so resolutely from the same world as Meredith, a world so unlike his.

Merry snorted. "Doubt it. In my college it was considered a rite of passage to bag a prof. I struck lucky with Hillary. He treated it exactly the same way I did; as an enjoyable interlude. We both had other things to go onto."

She stood and tried to ease the tension out of her shoulders. Daniel could see new resolution in her eyes, replacing the anger. "I assume Bob and his Santa's Little Helper thought if Handsome Hillary turned up just before the final, it might put me off," she grinned at her partner. "They don't know me very well, do they? It's simply made me even more determined to win. I'll be buggered if I let them beat me."

She went to Daniel and put her hands into his. "Besides, I can't let my bestie down, can I?" She leaned against him, feeling his heart beat erratically against her cheek. If only she could tell him how she really felt about him. Her feelings for Hillary limped off into the distance compared with how much she loved Daniel. She sighed. But she was sure he was still in love with Julia and what's more, if she had to put up with the thought of Hillary being in the audience, it must be ten times worse for Daniel having Harri and his new wife watching too. Handsome Hillary was just someone from her past. Julia was the love of Daniel's life. That was infinitely worse.

Daniel misinterpreted the sigh. He stroked her hair. "It'll be alright, Merry. We're going to wow them. Just think of holding that trophy up. It's the best revenge."

Merry raised her head and stared into Daniel's glittering green eyes. "Agreed," she said. "It's the very best sort of revenge."

***

And it had been. The final passed in a blur for Merry, but she loved every second. When it was announced with due ceremony, that she and Daniel had won, she backed off a little and let him raise the trophy. As she watched him hold it triumphantly in the air, she'd never loved him more.

Daniel gathered Merry to him. He'd worked so hard for this moment and for so many years. As he kissed Merry's full, eminently kissable mouth, he thought he'd never stop being grateful to her for making this happen. It was her popularity that had got the public's votes pouring in.

"We did it," he shouted over the hubbub surrounding them. "We won!"

Merry turned to him, her eyes shining. "You did it Daniel, my love. *You* did it."

Step Seventeen.
The after show party bordered on a riot. Never before had *Who Dares Dances* been so successful, in terms of votes, audience figures or raising cash for charities.

"They say it's over seven million viewers this series," yelled Suni across the crowded hotel room, to Merry and Daniel, who were standing at the bar. "And everyone wanted to get in here. There are bouncers six deep at the door!"

It was true. The short series, shoehorned into Fizz TV's schedule as a PR exercise to counteract rumour and speculation of vote rigging and racism, had exceeded all expectations. In every way.

"My goodness, this is a crush, darling."

Hearing the familiar voice, Merry turned. "Venetia, you came!"

"Of course, I came. I sat with your parents and that very nice man off the History Channel who used to tutor you at Oxford. The one with the rather rugged Scottish good looks." Venetia sniffed and looked about her. "I have to say, this isn't the most genteel of affairs I've ever been to."

Merry smiled at her. "It's so lovely to see you," she said, as she hugged her aunt. "Go and sit down over there." She nodded to where her parents had managed to find a table in a corner and were deep in conversation with Hillary. "I'll bring the drinks over. Champagne?"

Venetia raised an eyebrow. "I rarely drink anything else." She moved away, majestically creating a clear path before her, like an icebreaker.

Daniel watched as Venetia made her way through the scrum. He saw Merry's tutor, head to head with her parents. The loss he felt, twinned with a sharp longing, was made all the worse following the ecstasy of winning.

Merry waggled a bottle of champagne at him and said, "I'll just take this over and say hello and then I'll be back." She gave him one of her broad smiles. Warm and seductive.

He flashbacked to the one, wonderful night they'd shared. The memory gave him courage. "When you come back, Merry, can we talk?" It was completely the wrong time to do this, but he had to.

She looked up at him, sensing that he wanted to discuss something important. She nodded. "Of course." Reaching up, she kissed his cheek. "Be right back."

Daniel turned back to the bar and nursed his drink. He was half hopeful, half despairing. If he didn't take this chance to tell Merry how he felt, he'd be lost forever. Their paths would separate, and there would be no reason for them to ever meet again.

"What a great night," said Carly at his elbow. She grinned unattractively.

Daniel nodded.

"You two were fantastic this evening. I thought you deserved to win. You were always my favourite professional dancer, Daniel."

"Really?" he replied drily. "Thank you."

Carly sighed. "I'd love to have a go but I'm not a celeb, so there's no chance, is there?"

Daniel drank deeply. "Nope."

"Although," Carly looked up at him coyly, "Uncle Bob's got an idea for a new twist for the next series. To have ordinary people appearing in it. You know, with good back stories."

Daniel turned to her and laughed without humour. "No one would ever say you're ordinary, Carly."

She preened, missing his sarcasm. "Really? You think so? Thanks." She sipped her wine and looked over to where Merry now sat, squashed between Venetia and Hillary.

"Now there's an interesting man," Carly said. "He was telling me earlier that he'd never really fallen out of love with Merry. You know he's left his wife, don't you?"

That got Daniel's full attention. "No. No, I didn't." He too turned to look at Merry and Hillary. They looked very cosy. He began to feel slightly sick.

"That's the sort of girl Merry is," Carly whined on. "She makes you love her and then spits you out. I've never known her to be serious about anything. Or anybody. Likes living in the fast lane, does our Meredith."

Daniel thought back to when he first knew Merry. He remembered her saying something similar herself. He watched as another man, tall and distinguished and with trendy specs, approach her. Merry looked surprised and then followed him out of the room, her promise to return to Daniel apparently forgotten. "No," he replied, half to himself. "She doesn't seem to get serious about anything."

It was useless, he decided. Merry had never, ever given him any indication that she felt anything other than friendship for him. After all, only a few hours ago, hadn't she called him her 'bestie'? He was, it seemed, doomed to be the girl's best friend – and not one she wanted to talk to any time soon. Not only had her ex-lover left his wife for her, she also had this other stranger apparently besotted. He'd give her ten minutes, well, maybe fifteen.

And then he changed his mind. Enough. He'd had enough of falling for girls who were destined not to love him back. He was tired of his best-friend role. He was sick of not being loved back.

Glancing at his watch, he muttered a cursory 'bye' to Carly and began to make his way from the party. He was stopped by a tiny woman dressed in expensive designer velvet.

"Daniel Cunningham?" She put a hand on his arm and looked up questioningly.

"Yes."

"I have something I need to talk to you about. I've got an interesting proposition I want to put to you. Can we go somewhere

226

quieter?" She gestured around. "Can they spare you, do you think?"

Daniel looked over to the gap where Merry had been sitting. It echoed the empty space she'd left in his heart. "I think they can spare me," he said on a bitter laugh. "I don't think anyone would notice I'd gone."

In this he was wrong. Very wrong. Merry came back into the party, desperate to share her news with him. She forced her way through the crowd, asking if anyone knew where he'd gone. No one seemed to know. When she reached the bar, she ordered another bottle of champagne. This deserved more bubbly. It wasn't every day you got offered a part, no, the *title* role, in a sitcom.

When Basil Hynes had asked her to chat, she hadn't realised who he was or that he was about to change her life.

"I saw the footage of your challenge," he began, after introducing himself as a comedy commissioner of one of the main digital channels. "The one where you had to get into the Egyptian sarcophagus."

Merry repressed a shudder. The special, which focused on the challenges, had gone out the previous week. Merry had avoided watching it. She tuned back into what Basil was saying.

"That," he continued, "along with the way you tackled the dancing, got me thinking. I like your enthusiasm, your gung-ho attitude to things. I think we may have a part that's perfect for you. And indeed, that you're perfect for."

He went on to explain that the channel had been trying to cast the lead in a brand new sitcom. "We know there's a market that's been created by the *Miranda* show on the BBC. We think young women want their own brand of comedy. Our show will be a little like *The Liver Birds*."

When Merry looked blank, he laughed. "You're far too young to remember but it was a classic comedy about girls sharing a flat. That's what our show is about, albeit an updated version. Our lead, Charlotte, is a posh girl, a bit hopeless. A bit like a female version of the sort of characters Jack Whitehall plays.

Merry tried not to feel affronted that this Basil Hynes thought her perfect for the role of a posh, hopeless girl. This was the most exciting thing that had happened to her in ages.

"No more stand up," she said gleefully.

"Actually, that's the other thing we liked about you. Charlotte is a struggling stand-up comedian. I happened to catch one of your shows in Oxford just after Christmas. I thought you were very funny," he put in gallantly.

"You were a minority of one," Merry said. "But you're clearly a man of supreme wit and intellect," she added hastily, in case the bitterness was too obvious.

Basil laughed. "I think it's going to fun working together, Meredith." He reached into his suit pocket. "Here's my card. Give me a ring when all this hullabaloo is over and we'll talk. Give my love to Venetia, by the way."

"Oh, you know Venetia?"

Basil put up his hand as he left. "Everyone knows Venetia."

Merry beamed at his departing back. "Oh, I can't wait to tell her the news," she said to no one in particular. "And I've got to find Daniel to tell him as well."

And now, here she was back at the bar, clutching a rapidly warming bottle of fizz and could see neither person she most wanted to talk to in the whole wide world.

"Looking for Dan?" Like a particularly nasty and persistent smell, Carly materialised beside her.

"Yes," Merry said, too happy to feel anything else.

"Think he's got a better offer." Carly nodded her head in the direction of the hotel foyer. "He's just left with Marisa d'Havilland."

"The theatre producer?" Merry whirled round to face Carly. "What can she want with Daniel?"

Carly looked smug. "Rumour is she wants him to head up a new dance show she's putting on in the West End. And you know what they say, no one ever says no to Marisa."

Some of the happiness trickled out of Merry. She leaned back against the bar for support. "No, I suppose not," she said faintly.

"And it would be a fantastic break for Dan. He's worked very hard for it too. Imagine, a lead in the West End. Marisa must like him a *lot* to offer him that." Carly gave Merry a malicious grin.

Merry knew exactly what Carly was inferring. Marisa d'Havilland was well known for her cougar-like tendencies. But she wasn't going to give Carly the satisfaction of knowing she'd scored a bullseye to Merry's heart, shattering it.

"Well, well," she began. "There's Daniel getting the West End and I'm heading for a telly-land sitcom. A starring role, no less. And where are you going to be, in a year's time, Carly? Oh yes, stuck in your loathsome excuse for an uncle's production office." She waggled the champagne bottle at the girl, who was staring up at her, slack jawed. "Do have fun with your tedious nine to five, won't you," Merry added, in a passable imitation of Venetia. "The rest of us will be getting a life. Not to mention fame – oh and fortune! Ta ta." With that she swept off, using her entire five feet ten inches to full effect. She headed back to her parents, and Hillary, chin up and desperately holding back the tears.

Step Eighteen.

"Now Meredith, this will not do. Merry? Are you even listening?"

Merry and Venetia were relaxing in the sitting room of the Maida Vale apartment. Merry spent most evenings curled up on the leather sofa, glassily watching the television, claiming to be exhausted from filming the sitcom all day.

She tore her gaze from the television. "Sorry? What did you say?"

Venetia raised her eyes to the ceiling. "For three months you've been like this. Three months! You won *Who Dares Dances*, your parents are happy and you have this fantastic job with Basil, which I had nothing to do with, just so as you know, and I've never seen you look more miserable." Venetia slid onto the sofa next to her niece. "What is it, darling? You should be cock-a-hoop and positively jumping for joy."

The television programme Merry had been staring at ended, and a trailer for the new series of *Who Dares Dances* began.

Venetia watched as the advert built hysterically, and finished by showing a brief sequence from Merry and Daniel's winning show dance. "You were so good, you know," she said admiringly. "Daniel's decision to put you in an Egyptian costume as a reference to that stupid prank was a master-stroke. By the way, I heard on the grapevine, the delightful Mr Dandry is being investigated by the police; the vice squad, no less. Something rather unpleasant has been found on his home computer, I understand. Did you know? A more gratifying end, I cannot imagine," Venetia added, with relish and complete lack of sympathy. "You haven't seen much of him lately though, have you?"

"Who, Bob?" said Merry, deliberately misunderstanding.

"Don't pull that face, Meredith. I know you too well. We've been living together for how long?"

"About six months."

"Is that all? It seems like longer," Venetia said, with feeling.

Merry poked her in the ribs.

"That's better, at least I got a reaction. Now, come on, tell me all about it. Tell me why it went so hideously wrong with the divine Daniel."

Merry sighed, waited until Venetia refreshed their glasses and then explained. It took the best part of a bottle of Venetia's Merlot before she'd finished. When she had, her aunt looked aghast.

"Is that all that's wrong with you? I thought at least someone had been murdered. I rather hoped it was Bob's nasty niece."

Sulkily, Merry pulled at her fringe, dyed a brighter shade of red for her new role. "Don't be so dramatic, Venetia. Daniel clearly doesn't have any feelings for me. He's still hooked on Julia bloody Cooper and is probably now Marisa d'Havilland's toy-boy."

"Defeatist talk," Venetia said, stoutly.

Merry sat up, thoroughly riled now. "So, Dame Venetia Denning, explain to me just why he hasn't been in touch since the wrap party. Nothing. Nada. Zilch. Not even a phone call." Her bottom lip quivered. "I've never ever run after a man and I'm not about to start doing so now. If he wanted me, he would've come after me. And he didn't," she added on a wail. "He doesn't want me, Venetia."

"Oh hush, now. What nonsense." Venetia put an arm round Merry. "Anyone with half a brain can see the boy is besotted. Let me think for a moment." She tapped her nose. "Do you know? What we need is A Plan!"

Merry gave a faint groan and let her head sink down onto the sofa. The feel of the leather was far more comforting than her aunt in full sway. "As I seem to remember, it was one of your plans which got me into this mess in the first place."

"Ungrateful child!" her aunt said. "You'll be the toast of the small screen before long. That script is marvellous and so suited to you."

"I don't know about that," Merry said and drained her glass. "I was miserable before, when I didn't have any money and no career to speak of. Now I've got plenty of money and I'm still miserable. I thought money was supposed to bring you happiness."

"Nonsense, Meredith." Venetia reached for the bottle of wine and emptied the dregs into their glasses, admiring the sparkling crystal as she did so. "Money doesn't make you happier. It just makes the misery more comfortable."

Merry managed a laugh. "Oh Venetia. What would I have done without you? Now, tell me, have you, by any chance, got A Plan? I can tell from your expression that you might."

"Well, I've rarely come up with a duff one, as you young people say, but I have to admit to lacking in imagination for this conundrum." Venetia sipped wine and glanced at her niece's disconsolate expression. "I rather think we shall have to resort to the direct approach." A smug look came on her face. "This is what we'll do."

A week later, Venetia had bagged two best house seats for Daniel's new show. Not an easy task, as the previews had gone down a storm and the critics had been unanimous: it was a hit.

Merry settled into her third row aisle seat in the dress circle with mixed feelings. She longed to see Daniel again and desperately wanted to see him dance again. She was even looking forward to the after show party, to which Venetia had also wangled tickets. But she was terrified about what she had to say to him. Venetia had rehearsed it with her but Merry still didn't feel confident. But, as Venetia said frequently, 'nothing ventured, nothing gained.'

As the theatre lights went down and the audience quietened, Merry felt the familiar thrill of anticipation run through her. She loved this moment, when the audience began to hush and settle for the show to start. But, this time, it was more than that. She desperately wanted to love this, so that she could tell Daniel. She so wanted it to be *good*.

And it was. In fact it was far better than good; it was spectacular. It was a sort of update on the old film, *The Red Shoes* but with a male dancer as its star. Daniel played the dancer who couldn't stop, until, in a twist on the original to create a feel good happy ending, he was saved from his obsession by the love of another dancer. Merry tried not to feel jealous at the sight of her ex-partner dancing with a spectacularly beautiful and wraith-like girl. And failed. Irrationally, she hated Daniel's co-star on first sight. How dare she dance with him? Why, her hands had been all over him!

Over interval drinks (Venetia insisted on champagne and Merry was glad of some Dutch courage) they could overhear nothing but praise from the crush in the bar. The audience loved it. Merry even heard one woman say it was the third time she'd been.

With the finale music ringing in their ears, they made their way backstage to the after show drinks party. Venetia soon got into conversation with an acquaintance and Merry was left alone, nursing a warm glass of cheap white wine and wishing she was anywhere else. It was cramped and even more crowded than in the bar at the interval, and hot and airless too. Feeling the usual panic begin to engulf her, Merry looked for an escape and, spying a door in between two stage flats, she slipped through into what must be some sort of storage room. In a corner was a rack of gigantic red ballet shoes and leaning against a wall were enormous musical notes, all from the show. And, perched on the corner of a table, swinging one long leg and sipping wine, was Daniel.

He looked up in surprise. "Merry! What are you doing here?" He put down his glass and got up. They stood awkwardly, staring at one another but not moving closer.

Merry thought he looked tired and wasn't surprised. She knew Marisa worked her team hard; it was one of the reasons why her shows were so excellent.

"Have you been to see it tonight?"

Merry could tell Daniel was trying not to look hopeful. "Yes. Oh, it was wonderful," she gabbled. "Marvellous. I thought you were great, Daniel. Extraordinary."

Daniel nodded. "Thank you."

Merry finished her drink in one swallow and covered her nervousness by looking for somewhere to jettison her empty glass. Putting it on the table to join Daniel's, she resisted the temptation to throw her arms around him and resumed her spot a couple of paces away.

Daniel sat again and stared down at the floor. He concentrated very hard on a piece of torn lino; it was extremely fascinating. He pushed at it with his toe. Every part of him yearned to rush into Merry's arms but her three month silence had only confirmed he was nothing to her. Less than nothing. He knew he was being childish but couldn't stop himself.

Merry's eyes took in Daniel's every tensely held muscle. Maybe it was simple exhaustion after the show? But it didn't seem likely to be that. This wasn't the Daniel she used to know. His absence from her life had left her aching for him but now she was here, suddenly confronted by him, her resolve to sort things out began to waver. "I'm so glad you've got what you always wanted," she rushed on, no longer sure what to say. Any plan, hatched up by Venetia, disintegrated. Her aunt had wanted them to casually bump into one another. In Merry's head it had all been simple. Faced by

Daniel in this mood, her optimism fled.

"And what was that, Merry?" He sounded sulky. This again, was so unlike Daniel.

"A show of your own." She made an empty gesture. "The West End."

Daniel snorted and gave a sour grin. "Yes, I suppose I have."

Behind them, someone popped a champagne cork to drunken cheers. But the frigid silence between Merry and Daniel overwhelmed the party noise.

After a long and horrible pause, Daniel looked up at her. "And you, Merry, have you finally got what you wanted?"

"Yes. Yes, I have." She watched as Daniel's face crumpled a little. "I mean," She went on, "I've got rid of my debts, my parents are happy with me, everyone's pretty sure my TV show is going to be a huge hit -" she tailed off.

"So, life's good?"

"Mostly." Merry took a deep breath. It was now or never. "I've found though, that there's something missing. Something fairly major."

Daniel returned to scuffing the lino. "What's that then?"

"You."

Daniel's foot stilled. His shoulders went rigid and then he relaxed. A little.

"I haven't got you, Daniel." She sensed a more welcome warmth in him so took a step nearer. It was proving easier to say it now. "Look at me, Daniel."

"I can't."

She went to him. Gently, she held his face and forced him to meet her eyes. "Why can't you look at me?" she said, with a smile in her voice.

"Because you mean too much to me, to want anything other than the real thing, Merry."

Merry was shocked at his tortured expression. She dropped her hands. "What do you mean?"

He may as well say it, he thought. He had nothing else to lose. "Merry, I love you too much to be another of your light-hearted flings. It's got to be all or nothing."

"Oh," breathed Merry. "You love me!" Her eyes shone. Then she frowned. "What do you mean, 'fling'? Oh Daniel. Is that what you think I'm like?"

Her woebegone expression nearly unmanned him. "No. I mean yes. Well, you told me you never took anything seriously."

Merry smiled slowly, understanding him now. "Ah yes. I never took anything seriously until -"

"Until what?"

"Until I met you. And you stole my heart right from under my nose."

"That's a terrible image, Meredith." He felt himself beginning to hope, to believe.

Merry wrinkled her nose and giggled. She stepped between his legs, so that she was as close as she could be to him. She feathered her fingers through his hair and tugged gently. "I love you Daniel."

"Seriously?"

"I've never been more so."

"And what about your Hillary MacDonald?"

Merry shrugged. "Last thing I heard, he was touring the Italian Lakes in search of Shelley." She gave her mile-wide smile. "He's history, Dan. Of the ancient variety." She arched an eyebrow, the flirty gesture belying a tremor in her heart. "And, um, what about your Julia?"

"Julia?" Daniel gave a rueful grin. "That was over the moment I saw you in those ripped jeans, when you sashayed up to me at the first meet. I've been a fool, Merry. I've been in love with you from the start, I think. It just took me a while to realise it."

Merry giggled, relief making her giddy. "You'd better be over her, dance boy because I have no intention of letting you go now."

Daniel hooked his legs around her calves, bringing her even nearer, if that were possible. He clasped his hands around her waist, relishing the familiar feel of her body against his. "Just as well then."

Merry lowered her lips to his and kissed him thoroughly. "Just as well what?" she whispered.

"That you're never going to get away from me again, either." He kissed her back. "I love you so much, Merry. So very much."

"Seriously?" Merry grinned.

"I've never been more so."

Venetia, passing the open doorway and seeing the lovers reunited, quietly closed the door to give them privacy. Leaning against it, she raised her glass and toasted them – and herself. And then, with the satisfied smile of a job well done, she turned back to the party.